The Phoenix of Persia

THE PHOENIX of PERSIA

Jhangir Kerawala

Publisher
UNICORN BOOKS

F-2/16, Ansari Road, Daryaganj, New Delhi-110002
☎ 011-23275434, 23262683, 23250704 • *Fax:* 011-23257790
E-mail: info@unicornbooks.in • *Website:* www.unicornbooks.in

Branch : Mumbai
23-25, Zaoba Wadi, Thakurdwar, Mumbai-401002
☎ 022-22010941, 022-22053387
E-mail: rapidex@bom5.vsnl.net.in

Showroom : Delhi
- 10-B, Netaji Subhash Marg, Daryaganj
  New Delhi-110002
- 6686, Khari Baoli, Delhi-110006

ISBN : 978-81-7806-347-8
The Phoenix of Persia

Edition: 2014

Printed at : *Param offsetters, Okhla, New Delhi-110020*

In memory of

My Mother, the epitome of love and peace
And
My Father, the pillar of strength and a fountain of joy.

Foreword

To my knowledge, Jhangir Kerawala is perhaps the first Zoroastrian who has penned a novel set in any part of Zoroastrian history that stretches over nearly 4,000 years from around 1700 BC, to date. He is perhaps the only person anywhere who has done so.

That no other novelist has done so till now is surprising. Why? At a time when humanity still worshipped the elements and earthly or supernatural deities, Zarathustra (Zoroaster) was the first prophet to propound the religious faith of an omnipotent, unseen and untouchable Supreme Creator, whom he called Ahura Mazda. His monotheistic religion gradually spread from a corner of east Iran to the north and east across Central Asia as far as today's Xian in NE China, returning some 1,200 years later to Iran when its conquerors from Mesopotamia (the Achameneans) and successive empires embraced and then spread it westwards through Asia Minor upto the borders of Greece and southwards across the Arabian peninsula, Libya, Egypt and Ethopia. Geographically, this is a vast stretch of the world and its millions, with differing cultures and ethnicities, chose to practice that faith. Such a wide canvas offers a rich and colorful background to weave interesting novels. Yet, except for Mr. Kerawala, none has done so from any perspective, much less a Zoroastrian one.

His novel is set in the much later historical period, when the glory days of Zoroastrians were overtaken by the rise of militant Islam. Those years eventually led to some groups of Zoroastrians to exode to other lands. But the one that went to India, enriched that country and the world by evolving into the unique, enterprising, philanthropic and highly respected "Parsi Zoroastrian" community. Mr. Kerawala's strongly etched characters, living in Sanzan in north Iran's ancient Parthia province, project the steely resolve of Zoroastrians in the conquered Persian Sassanian empire to preserve their faith and its values at any cost, even if that meant leaving their beloved homelands to do so.

Despite a Hadith of Prophet Mohammed's successor Caliph Omar that as Zoroastrians were the "people of the Book" like Christians and Jews, they should only be humiliated while paying the Jiziah tax and made to feel the might of Islam, but not be forced to convert or be killed, some Arab army commanders and governors were carried away by zeal in their new-found faith. Yet, renowned western historians like Mary Boyce have not found reliable evidence for the Zoroastrian conviction of massive killings and conversions in the defeated Sassanian Empire. They reckon that humiliations and harassments heaped on Zoroastrians in the first 100 years of Arab conquest, only served to strengthen Zoroastrians' resolve to preserve their faith and just about five percent of Zoroastrians in the empire converted in those years. Mr. Kerawala paints a vivid picture of what was heaped upon them, and yet, their refusal to succumb or leave their homeland, exemplified their resolve.

But when did that take place? As Zoroastrians are notorious for not keeping authentic oral or written records of their long history, there are 2 dates, some 200 years apart, for the exodus to western India. The 716 AD date is based on a 1,600 AD narrative poem, Quissa-i-Sanjan, written by a priest based on oral Parsi traditions at that time. But later day Parsi historians like Hodivala and the renowned Mary Boyce authoritatively place it at 936 AD. Understandably, Mr. Kerawala takes a legitimate "novelist's privilege" to link the exodus to the 716 AD date as it fits and sustains his riveting fictional portrayal of the Zoroastrian travails after the Arab invasion. Since many Zoroastrians still believe in that date, it still provides a meaningful finale to the first novel set in any period of Zoroastrian history.

Adi Davar

Researcher, Writer & Speaker

on Zoroastrianism and its history

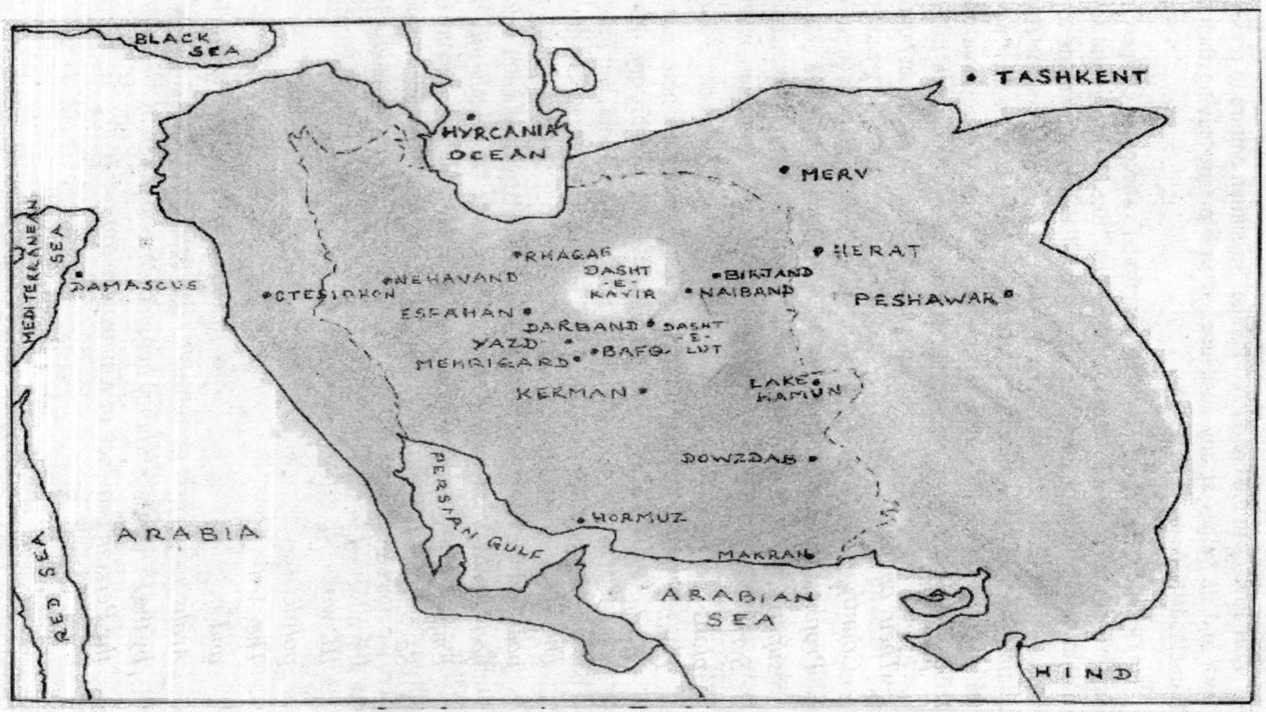

PERSIAN EMPIRE – SASSANID PERIOD

From early seventh century, the Arab juggernaut had begun. Their ambition was to make Islam the religion of the world. Country after country they vanquished, and the religion of Prophet Mohammad was imposed on the conquered. Even the super powers of that period felt threatened. After over-running Syria, Armenia and Egypt in a short span of time, they made plans for faraway places like Spain, Rome and even China and Hind.

But their greatest lust was reserved for the richest kingdom on earth...the great Persian Empire.

The Persian Empire had grown in strength and stature during the past few centuries, conquering all that stood in their way. They had benefitted from a chain of great dynasties, each adding to the Empire's control of land and wealth. The presiding dynasty, the Sassanid Empire, had already ruled over their extensive territory for over four hundred years. But their present king, Yazdegard III, was an inexperienced young man and faced hostile internal politics.

The Arabs recognised the weakness, grabbed the opportunity, and invaded Persia. To get to the heartland of the empire, the Arabs had to first go through territories captured and controlled by the Persians. And they began their campaign in Mesopotamia, the Persian province of Khvararan, today's Iraq.

1

"*Ya, Ahura Mazda!* What evil has befallen my beautiful, beautiful Persia?" implored my grandfather, as he cast his eyes skywards. "*I wish I had never come back.*"

His eyes were moist as his one hand reached out to the sky in exasperation, oblivion to anyone watching. It was a heart-wrenching sight for me, and it would remain etched in my mind for the rest of my life. There he was this giant of a man who had suddenly come into our lives just a week ago, a man who could inspire an entire empire with just his presence, a man with legendary strength and valour. And he was unashamedly shedding tears in front of his grandson.

He saw the troubled look on my face and put a heavy hand, a very, very heavy hand, on my shoulder and pulled me toward him. I just about managed to reach his hipbone. I was seven years old and my grandfather was seven feet tall, and almost as broad. His long, unruly grey hair gave him an unusual 'halo' effect around his head, just as his ill-maintained curly grey beard and moustache tried to shoot out in every direction they could. Such startling features, along with his amputated right hand and the ferocious black eyes under the bushy eye-brows generally produced weak-knees and pure dread to a sudden onlooker.

"Sweet, little Jamshid," he said with a crestfallen voice. "I'm sorry. I'm sorry that I was not with you all for so long a time. What…what has become of you all? How you have suffered…"

The great Zahl, *sorry?* Unthinkable!

We had walked out of our little village, Mehrigard, and climbed up the barren hill overlooking it, about a mile away. This was always my favourite hiding place. We saw the twenty odd shacks down below and their occupants busy with their menial jobs. The ill-clad men were all dressed in honey coloured robes, as made compulsory by our conquerors, the Arabs. They considered us, the Zoroastrians of Persia, as untouchables. So we had to be distinguished by this dress-code.

The men tried looking busy with their occupations, but their movements were listless with no enthusiasm in what they were doing. The colour of defeat, visible in more places than their robes, had drenched them in its pale and sickly shadow. The womenfolk were not in sight; either busy in their kitchens, or not permitted to step outdoors. It was dangerous for them to be seen outdoors, especially as we were expecting unwelcome visitors any minute. And the children, not too many, but all my friends, did what they knew to do best. Play and enjoy themselves, unconcerned with the situation.

I lived in this village with my parents, Peshotan and Dughdova, my older brother, Farehdun and sister Mahafrid. Being the youngest I enjoyed the special privileges of being pampered, and bullied.

"You know when I left our country, there was…"

"*Grandfather, they are coming*. Quick, please get back into the cave."

Grandfather didn't budge an inch.

"Let them come. *I've never run away from anybody before.*"

"Please, you heard what father said. For the sake of the village, you mustn't be seen."

"Bah!!" he spat out vehemently. "It's better they finish us off, once and for all. It's better than living like this...like cowardly thieves, scared of our own shadows."

But he moved back and entered the large cavern reluctantly. I carefully peeped over the edge and saw the four horsemen slowly swagger into the village. They were almost a mile away from me but the clear and quiet mountain air carried their chatter, *and their insolent sniggers*. They were the Ummayad's tax collectors and they came on the first of every month. *Jizyah,* they called it. A tax for being *dhimmis*, people of the Book, non-Islamics. *Jizyah* was also paid by the Christians, Jews and the Sabians.

"Come out, Ajams," the leader of the group called out, as they reached the outskirts of our village. "We're not here to hurt you…so long as you pay up, *respectfully!*"

A burst of laughter from his friends.

I saw my father step out of our small home and await them. It was his duty to face these rogues every month, as he was the head of the small community of Zoroastrians residing in the village. Actually, it was not even a village. It was just an abandoned cluster of shacks in the middle of a range of inhospitable mountains. But we now called it home. We no longer could live in cities as the persecutions there were more severe, and we, the Mahraspandan family, were a marked lot. We were amongst the top five noble families of Persia, directly related to the Kings and owning vast stretches of land. Added to that, the fact that this was the great Zahl's family, we would have been the first to be butchered. Hence, my father took the extreme step years ago of settling down on a remote piece of land in the huge province of Yazd, away from the eyes of our present rulers. They knew that some Zoroastrians had settled here, but as long as we kept to ourselves, and as long as we paid for that privilege, they let us alone. A few other Zoroastrian families, who preferred not to be dictated by the Islamic way of life, had joined us and together we lived as simple peasants.

The tax-collector remained seated on his horse. "Well don't just stand there, *Ajam*. Walk towards us, *head down.*" 'Ajam', meaning dumb, was the term they used when they were in a good mood. Otherwise, we, the Zaroastrians of Persia were called *'najis'*, meaning impure, by our Arab rulers.

My father did as he was told. This happened every time. Their intention was to humiliate us. It was part of the monthly Jizyah collecting ritual.

A small pouch was offered to the tax-collector.

"What, again gold?" He turned towards his friends and dutifully received another burst of guffaws. "Where do you keep getting this gold from? Do you have a secret mine around here?"

"You know we can offer you nothing else of value," my father explained with his head down, still holding up the pouch in his hands. "We have no crops to give, no land to share. We have no…"

"Enough!" Snapped the leader as he snatched the pouch. "Always you have excuses, always complaining." With that he slapped the back of my father's head, insultingly. This was also part of the ritual. "You should be thankful we let you live. As victors we should have annihilated the lot of you. *Zarthoshties?* Hah!! *Pigs!!* That's what you are. Not fit to live alongside us."

With that he whirled his horse round and galloped away with his friends.

As I stood there, helpless and fuming, I heard a deep growl beside me. My grandfather had quietly left the cave and witnessed the entire scene. The next few minutes he just stood there, controlling a fury never witnessed by me before. As his face and eyes reddened to a shade that scared me, his unique beard quivered, his body trembled and he clasped the fist of his left hand in a tight squeeze.

"He…he…slapped my son," he said through his clenched mouth. "He…he…"

And then, before I could stop him he roared out his frustration in a voice that was louder than the loudest thunder I had heard. As his booming voice bounced off every nearby mountain and shook every tree to its roots, I feared the worst. Our game was surely up and the tax-collectors would return and discover my grandfather. Far away on another mountain range, almost out of sight of the village, I saw the group of four Arabs stop. As they tried controlling their spooked horses they looked back towards our village. Then deciding it was the cry of some wild animal, they hurried on their way.

But my grandfather suffered a massive attack as he suddenly clutched hard at his heart and sank down to his knees, and finally, fell unconscious on the rocks. The humiliation witnessed was unimaginable to this proud warrior.

There he laid, my grandfather…the great Zahl, the greatest warrior of all time, the hero of Persia, the saviour of its religion, Zoroastrianism. But he no longer looked the victorious, noble warrior I had heard so much about. Today his crumpled face and broken spirit portrayed but a shadow of that fame.

For this was the year 675 C.E., in Persia, the land of ancient heroes Cyrus the Great and Darius the Great, the land that boasted of the first monotheist religion, Zoroastrianism, and the land that had been considered as the largest empire till date…the land seized and ruled, first by the Caliphs and now by the Ummayads of Arabia.

It was like dusk had set in on our land...and there never again will be another dawn.

❑

When Zahl opened his eyes again the entire family was around him. Two days of good care and medication had helped revive him. It was a strange sight to see this unusual human being lying in bed. Almost a foot of his feet stretched out of the bed, his heavy body covered its full breath and the grotesque stump of his right hand looked like a cut branch of an oak tree.

He silently searched each face around him, and as though not impressed, shut his eyes again.

"Father, are you feeling better?" asked my father, Peshotan.

No reply.

My mother, Dughdhova, gently pressed another piece of medicated cloth on Zahl's forehead. "Let him rest some more. Tomorrow he'll feel better."

Peshotan moved away from the group, his face etched with worry and uncertainty. He sat at the dining table and sadly cupped his head in his hands. I had never seen my father as a cheerful person, maybe because there was little to cheer about at that period of time, but I had not seen him so distressed either. He generally shouldered his problems with dignity and little show of emotions.

"Why doesn't he talk, father?" I asked, a little shaken up from the entire episode. Immediately after Zahl's fall on the mountain top I had charged down to our village and got help. We had no medicine-men amongst us, but the total experience available helped.

"He doesn't want to."

Such short answers demanded more questions for a seven year old.

"Why do we hide him? He is your father, so why can't he live like a normal person?"

Peshotan turned to me with an impatient look but immediately the expression changed to a mild smile. I had always been an enigma to him. I asked a hundred questions to a minute, he would say, but would remember just two answers an hour.

"It's a long story son. The invaders think he is dead: but if they find out he is still alive and living with us, they would not only kill him instantly, but also heap untold vengeance on all the villagers here for sheltering him."

"Why?" I didn't give him the time to take another breath.

"Because he was the main challenge to their ambition of defeating and occupying the Persian Empire. The news that he was killed in battle helped them gain the impetus to fulfil that ambition. If he were not wounded so critically in the Battle of Qadisiyya, the raiding Arabs would have been defeated at Mesopotamia itself. They wouldn't have passed even Khvarvaran, the country to our immediate west that we ruled, let alone invade Persia itself. If only he had not been so grievously wounded."

These were a jumble of words for me, so it took some time to digest them. Reprieved, my father returned to Zahl's bedside.

Two minutes later I followed him. The women folk had resumed their duties and just the three of us, Zahl, Peshotan and I were left.

"Battle of Qadisiyya?" I asked. "What happened there?"

❑❑❑

2

Battle of Qadissiya! Zahl heard the name as he lay with his eyes shut and cringed inwardly. What would not he give to re-live that day and undo the critical mistake he had made?

"One chance, *God, just one more chance*," he pleaded silently, "and I'll bring back the glory of ancient Persia."

But the Arabs did it, he conceded, and without a second chance. They brought the great Persian Empire to its knees. For many centuries no one paid attention to the nomad tribes of Arabia. They were good warriors, but never united. They occupied all their time squabbling amongst themselves, waging little wars and ruling small kingdoms.

And then came the Prophet. He introduced to them a new religion, a new way of life. This religion brought them together. United, they were suddenly a force to reckon with. And he, Zahl, did not pay proper heed to it.

'There is only one God', their Prophet said, 'and I am his Prophet'. Many religions before him had proclaimed 'there is only one God'. *But there were many prophets!* Each appearing at different periods of time, and each preaching the religion as shown to Him by God.

'There can be no other religion,' their Prophet said, 'so make it your duty to convert the whole world. And if anyone resists, kill him!'

So it became their sacred duty to wage holy wars all over the world, and they began their quest by first invading parts of the Roman Empire, and then the Persian Empire, an empire at that period of time greater than any other.

At heart Zahl knew the real reason they lost, and it had nothing to do with the Islam religion. When the Persian King Khusro II took over the reins in 590 C.E. he set his aims far too high…to rule the world, like his glorious predecessors a thousand years ago. He successfully waged wars in different directions, defeating the Huns and then capturing parts of the Roman Empire, Egypt and Palestine. But a further campaign against the Roman Empire proved disastrous. Thereafter he sustained several defeats through the 620s. In frustration he started penalizing his generals and commanders. Discontentment raised its ugly head, and there was little co-ordination left in the ranks. The dilemma culminated in total chaos when Khusro died in 628 C.E. He didn't name a proper successor. His surviving family squabbled amongst themselves, took turns in ruling the Empire, and in a short period of four years ten monarchs changed hands, until finally young King Yazdgard III took over the reins in 632. He tried his best to bring back unity and stability but the Arabs didn't give him the chance. In less than four years of his rule Qadisiyya happened.

When Zahl faced the enemy on the fields at Khvarvaran, he was still confident. He was just thirty one years old and already the world was at his feet. His courage and strength were legendary and automatically became the first target for all enemies of Persia. His commander, Rustom Farrokhzad, was with him and he knew that between the two of them, they could take on anyone.

And they had their most important ally riding with them, their mascot… the sacred burning embers of part of the Royal Fire, *Adur Gushnasp*. This was part of one of the three Great Fires, believed to have been ignited by Ahura Mazda. The holy fire, snuggled within a protected urn, was always present whenever they went to war.

As usual Zahl and Rustom led the charge, confident of a quick victory. His first mistake*...never underestimate your enemy.*

Zahl carried no sword, no spear. He had his huge mace with him. This weapon with the gold bull-head at one end was his singular identity, recognizable everywhere. Many a man had fallen victim to this heavy weapon, his brains splattered around him. As Zahl would set out to battle he swung this heavy weapon with one hand as though he was holding a flimsy stick, much like Asfandyar from the period of King Vishtaspa. In his left hand he held his shield with the engraving of a boar, the emblem of an aggressive and courageous warrior.

The battle in the beginning certainly favoured the Persians. And just when it became predictable, the Arabs got re-enforcements. As surge after surge of the invading marauders poured into the battle-field, screaming their battle cry of *'Allah O Akhbar'*, the tide shifted. The Persians dug in their heels and determinedly repelled the onslaught.

And then on the fourth day of the battle the most unexpected thing happened. A divine intervention for the Arabs. There blew a sand storm not witnessed by the Persians before. As suddenly as it appeared, its ferocity was equally surprising. The Arabs understood these sudden storms and knew how to handle them. Their large, flowing robes provided them the protection they needed against the swirling sand. But the Persians were caught on the wrong foot. Soon their soldiers were a scattered lot; more occupied fighting off the blistering storm than the attacking Arabs.

First Zahl saw Rustom go down in the thick mist of flying sand. A small group of the enemy was cutting him down. As he tried to reach Rustom he heard a warning call.

"Look out Sire!'

But he reacted too late. A spear pierced his own back, reeling him momentarily. In a moment a bunch of Arabs were on top of him. He tried shaking them off with his mace, bludgeoning a couple of them to the ground, but their leader managed to bring his sword down heavily on Zahl's left shoulder. His shield went flying and the blow brought him to his knees.

He once again staggered to his feet and knocked down the leader. Same moment he felt another sword bury into his stomach. He remembered seeing the glee on his assailant's face. It was a handsome face but for a purple birthmark on his forehead. As his eye lids got heavier and the world spun like a top, Zahl felt the assailant try to price the mace out of his right hand. He held on to it doggedly and, at the same time, once again tried to get back to his feet.

Next instant he saw his right hand fall off to the ground, still clutching the mace. The assailant had severed his hand from his body. Blood gushed out from his exposed arm as though it was sprouting out from a hose. In a daze he remembered seeing the handsome young Arab struggling to lift his heavy mace, still bound to his severed right hand. Zahl saw him raise it above his head and wave it from side to side in jubilation, blood from the severed hand splattering all over the field. A roar of a victorious cry came from the Arabs nearby.

Farther away he saw the barbarians dislodge the Royal Fire Adur Gushnasp from its moorings, spill the embers to the ground and triumphantly stamp it to extinction. Thankfully, they had carried just a part of the original fire, thought Zahl as his mind and heart burned with humiliation.

The last thing Zahl remembered was the purple patch on his assailant's forehead. And then he lost consciousness.

In those few seconds a battle was lost, a country vanquished, and an Empire routed.

But worst of all, a great religion was almost annihilated.

When Zahl opened his eyes again it was in a quiet shack on a mountain-side. He heard the merry chirping of some birds and the crisp gurgle of a flowing spring. He saw bright sunlight in a room and was sure he was no longer earth-bound. Then he felt the sharp pain and the burning sensation in his stomach and his arm, and he knew God was not so merciful to him. He tried getting up and groaned aloud.

Where was his right hand? He remembered and let out a roar of anger.

"Ah, you've finally come back to us." An elderly soldier that Zahl didn't recognize came to his side. "You've been sitting on the fence to the other side for the past two weeks, sometimes almost gone, sometimes struggling hard."

"Who…who are you? And where am I?"

"I'm but a foot soldier in your army, Sire. My name is Pourus. And you're far away from any civilization."

Zahl blinked hard and looked out of the window but couldn't recognize any part of the wilderness outside. He suddenly remembered, "And the battle?"

"Lost! We've been routed as never before. Thousands killed, and the rest shackled and taken away, probably to be sold as slaves in the African markets. They have over-run Ctesiphon, the capital city, and have proclaimed themselves as the official rulers of Khvarvaran."

A cold shiver ran up Zahal's spine. *Lost? And to an unfancied opponent?* He couldn't believe it. Whatever happened to his invincible army? What happened to his commander, Rustom Furrokhzad?

"Nobody's left, Sire." Pourus read his master's mind. "The river is running red as the enemy mercilessly butchered the injured and threw the dismembered bodies into it."

"And the Royal Fire?"

Pourus just shook his head and stared at his toes.

Zahl groaned again at the thought of facing the world as a loser, *and an invalid*. "Wh…why did you save me? It would have been better, more honourable, to have died with the rest. Why didn't they finish me off?"

"They obviously thought you were already dead. As the storm was waning off I found you. I put you on a horse and miraculously escaped that hell. Two days back I met another of our soldiers. He said after the storm blew away, when they couldn't find your body, they assumed somebody had thrown you too into the river, with the rest."

"And my…mace?"

"They carried it away as a trophy."

❑❑❑

3

If my father found me a pest and didn't want to answer my questions, there was another source I could tap. I found my mother, Dughdova, in the kitchen, incredibly busy, as usual. Everyone knew she had loads of patience and could hear your grievances for hours. I failed to understand why her calm face, gentle eyes and tender mannerism failed to evoke similar tendencies with the rest of the family. Father was a loner and preferred to be left alone. Farehdun, my big brother, was a grouch and would snarl at any attempt to friendliness. And Mahafrid, my elder sister...well the least said about her the better.

"Why does grandfather look so sad, mother? Isn't he happy being with us after so many years?"

"Oh, no, Jamshid, not now please," she said hurriedly. "I'm busy so run along and play with your friends."

She saw my hurt face and immediately got down on one knee to get to my eye level. She searched my face while thinking of a suitable answer.

She was so happy when Zahl had suddenly walked into our lives. She fussed over him as if he was her father and they were meeting after forty long years. All these years she had only heard of her extraordinary father-in-law, felt the admiration in the eyes of her friends and often dreamt of what it would be like to have him around. Minutes after she saw him for the first time in ragged clothes and hungry eyes she had set about to prepare a special feast for him. And even while the meal was being cooked she had started sewing a fresh robe for him. He had refused the compulsory honey colour for the robe, so she managed a different colour for him. She had flushed so happily when he later appreciated the food and the robe.

"He is happy to be with us," she finally answered. "Only, he wishes he was with us under different circumstances. He's sad we're living like refugees... in our own motherland. He's sad we're going through such hardships. He's sad there's nothing he can do about it."

"If he's as strong as everyone says, why can't he fight?"

"Okay, enough! Off you go now, and play with your friends." With that she smacked my bottom and guided me out of the kitchen. I was sure she had more patience than that.

My family shared all our household duties with each of us consigned to specific responsibilities. Mother spent the mornings in the kitchen and the evenings keeping the house neat and clean. Mahafrid was to assist her in every way. Similarly, father spent the first part of the day working on the small patch of land we maintained, growing whatever vegetables we could. Later in the day he would spend time attending to the upkeep of the house. Farehdun was to help him all day. Mahafrid was in charge of the linen and clothing. My job was to stay out of everyone's way, all day.

Outside none of my friends was around so I went around collecting them.

"What'll we play?" asked Shehriar, my best friend. He was a year older than me and always took my side whenever there was any altercation with my friends. Besides us, there were only two more same-aged friends, both brothers, Cyrus and Darius. Sometimes some of the 'seniors' joined us, too. There was my brother, Farehdun, but he was too studious to indulge in games for any length. There was Ardeshir, but he was now an adult, twice our size and played rough and we preferred he didn't join us. And then there were Rustom and Eruch. But they, too, generally were on their own. They were much older, almost adults, though younger to Ardeshir. The two were inseparable from childhood, finding their friendship sufficient for themselves. Even when work was assigned, the two handled it together.

That left just the four of us youngsters to play regularly and again we got together, glad to be on our own.

"How about 'Arabs and Persians'?" suggested brilliant Cyrus. That was the only game we knew, and played every day. In this game the Persians hid and the Arabs had to find them. The problem was...

"So who'll be the Arabs this time?"

After much haggling Shehriar and me, always a team, had to contend being the Arabs this time. Our turn was expected after a reign of ten consecutive times of being Persians. As we sulked the other two hid themselves within the village.

"Should we look for them, or quietly go home?" Shehriar whispered. We looked for them and in less than two minutes found them. They were again using our hiding place.

Next it was our turn to hide. Shehriar urged me to hide in the back alley, but I was not in the mood to get caught so soon. I took off on my own towards the mountains. After fifteen minutes of climbing I rested. Now they can search till kingdom come and never find me. I always found a special thrill of being by myself. It gave me a feeling of bravado and grown-up, so I occasionally hid far away from the village.

I remembered the first time I did it when I was four. I was totally out of sight of all and was scouting about aimlessly when I heard some strange sounds. I peeked behind the rocks and was amazed to see Ardeshir, the rowdy young man of our village. He was always in trouble with the Arab authorities. He claimed to have got back against them, many a time, in the town he often visited, and because of that, was a constant threat to the security of the village. But that day he was not tackling any gruff Arab. He was with a girl and both seemed to be busy in each other's arms.

A new game I thought. So I quietly walked up to them and asked, "Can I play too?"

It was as though a lightening bolt had hit them. They both shook violently and jumped up in one motion. He grabbed his dagger, she screamed, pulling down her gown, and I got terrified, all in a matter of two seconds. Before I could get away Ardeshir landed a heavy kick on my backside and added a few wallops on my head. Tears rolling down my cheek, I had scampered back to the village. I never understood that young man. If he didn't want me to play, he should simply say so. From that day I maintained a safe distance from him because if I accidentally strayed close to him he would let fly another smack at the back of my head with his long reach and mimic in my tiny voice, 'Can I play, too?'. Long ago he had nicknamed me 'nosy midget', which was bad enough, but what I hated was that he always maintained I would never grow taller and remain short all my life. He didn't spare Mahafrid, my sister, either. "Mummy's sorry shadow", he would tease her till she cried. But as I said earlier, he was much bigger than me, and there was nothing I could do about his ways

But today I had selected another hillside. I had never been here before and was curious to explore its caves while the 'Arabs' searched for me. After nosing about for a few minutes I stood at the rim of a ledge admiring the view below.

"Beautiful, isn't it?" Somebody said behind me.

I froze to the ground as though I had taken roots there, even as my heart found my mouth a good place to jump to. I had not heard anyone coming after me. I turned around slowly dreading that I had tripped onto Ardeshir again.

It was an old man and he was looking at me and smiling. Thin and haggard, but holding a kind face he sat down on a rock nearby and went on searching my face with a mischievous smile. His white beard hung down to his stomach where a blue sash encircled it. But his eyes were so sad, as though the entire burden of the world were on his shoulders.

"Who…who are you?" I ventured, shakily. He certainly was not from our village.

"A friend," he said gently and gestured me to sit beside him. Somehow I wasn't afraid, so I sat down close to him. "What do you think, Jamshid, is this world good?"

He knew my name! I became alarmed and slid a yard away.

"How do you…"

"I know the names of everyone in the village, and some more. So don't be alarmed and answer my question."

In spite of his leisurely calmness and weathered body I noticed his movements were not that of an old person but quite brisk and spirited. And his eyes kept changing from looking sad one minute and alive and dancing the next; they actually twinkled like stars and set my heart racing. My nerves again calmed down and I concentrated on the question he had put up.

"No, I don't think the world's bad. But there are some bad people in it."

"So what does one do with the bad people? Kill them?"

"No. Teach them to be good."

"But who'll teach them? God has almost given up."

That kind of stumped me. "He has?"

"Well, almost. He's given everything He could to keep the whole world happy. But people want more. And when they don't get it, they kill the beautiful things God created. Is that fair?"

Why is he asking me all these questions? I'm the acknowledged questioner of this region.

"My country is good," I tried salvaging the honour of our world.

"Is it? It was good, but today I see only bloodshed, persecution and hatred. All of you in that village are Zarthoshties, so why are you in this hell-hole instead of following your faith with pride?"

"You should know. The Arabs won't allow us to pray in fire temples. They burnt them all down. We had to come here so that we could live like Zarthoshties." I had listened carefully when father would tell us stories of our immediate history.

"But that is the point. Are you really living like Zarthoshties? I can see you living like hunted beasts...like frightened children."

"So what would you have us do?" I asked heating up to the topic. "Give in like some other Zarthoshties and change our religion, just to live in a beautiful city?"

"Of course, not! You are far better off than them. What I'm saying is that if they don't allow you to be Zarthoshties here, then go some place else where they will."

Sounded simple enough, but…

"*But this is our country!* Where else can we go?"

"This *was* your country," he reminded me coolly, "but you've been vanquished. And now this is *their* country…unless you can win it back. The question really is do you think the country comes first, or religion?"

I couldn't answer that. I thought a number of things came first…your country, your religion, your family, your friends and a few other things.

"So I repeat," he continued, "should you continue living in a place where you are not welcome? Or leave it and start afresh in a place where you're not hated...where you are welcome…where your religion will not be a burden to you. Else, you'll soon start hating your own faith."

"But where can we go?"

"Anywhere, where they allow you to be a Zarthoshty, to build fire temples and pray. Anywhere, where you can once again be proud of your faith."

He was beginning to make sense. But what was the point of telling me this. I was no decision-maker. I wasn't even a decent 'decision-abider'. But nevertheless, I liked his argument.

"Will you come with us, too?"

"But I'm always with you. So remember, if an opportunity ever arises, get away from this country and start afresh elsewhere."

The topic was not my forte so I stood up as if I was ready to go.

"Yes you should be getting back now," he said, the smile and the sad eyes never leaving his face.

I took a few steps towards my home and stopped. "Er…I don't know your name…"

"But you do," he said, his eyes twinkling for the first time. "Don't worry, you'll remember it whenever you're in trouble."

"Where do you stay?" I was getting my rhythm back.

"In these mountains. I've lived here for ages."

With that he waved me goodbye and I left him there, still sitting on that rock.

When I reached home and casually mentioned the old man to my parents, I created a minor panic. "*An old man in the mountains?*" My father cried unbelievingly. Soon the news spread and a small group of neighbours collected and a meeting conducted.

"Could be a spy," opined the ever-sceptic Minocher, our neighbour. "Maybe the Arabs suspect we are harbouring Zahl."

"No, I don't think..." I tried to wedge in my view-point, but nobody was listening to me.

Soon a small posse was organised and headed for the spot I pointed out from the village.

"Nothing!" Said my father from between his teeth, when they returned. "Not even a dead rat." Then he turned angrily at me. "Is this one of your idea of jokes? There was no old man in the mountains, was there?"

I tried my best to show my truthfulness, but nobody believed me. A sharp clip on my head and I turned to face Ardeshir. He knew how to take advantage of a situation. "Never believe him," he preached. "Always makes up stories." He turned to me with a wise look. "Don't you know the number one tenet of a good Zarthoshty? *Never tell a lie.*"

Another clip on my head.

❑❑❑

4

Sayyid Abul Yaser was a disgruntled Arab Governor. He held charge of the large and rich district of Pars, yet he was not happy. He strongly believed that he should have been the Ummayad's man to rule over all Persia. He deserved that in the least, he fumed as he paced his room. He had given his entire life to this campaign, and he had brought much glory to their rising empire, so it was time for them to recognize it and give him the deserved promotion. Thirty years he had been the Governor of this province, now headquartered at Shiraz, and yet no indications of further glory. He was now seventy years old, still a terror to his men and enemies, still capable of riding his horse all day, if need be, and still possessing the strength of a young man.

Here he was, the most eligible Governor for Persia, but all he did was push paper and assign duties to his junior staff.

He remembered how he started his career in the army as an ordinary soldier under the command of Sayyid Bin Waqqer. He was then but a handsome young man, and thanks to the purple patch on his forehead that many considered sacred, his group's lucky charm. But when at the Battle of Qadisiyya he did the near impossible, kill the great Zahl and capture his mighty mace, he became the undisputed hero of the Arab world. He remembered that day, almost forty years ago, as though it was just yesterday.

He had felt so powerful that day. At his feet lay the Persian legend, splayed with blood, cut open like a goat in a meat-shop. And for that feat he received many decorations and many out-of-turn promotions.

Yaser turned his head to a corner of his room and smiled. Yes, the great mace was still there, now adorned with the Arab battle flag. He lifted it again, as he did almost everyday, and felt the surge of exultation. Ah, it felt so great owning this piece of trophy. Its intrinsic value with the large golden bull-head was high, he knew. But he will never try to value it. It was priceless to him, and his family, and will remain with them for time immemorial.

His glorious days had not ended at Qadisiyya. He next led in the Battle of Nehavand, *the battle that crushed the Persian Empire*. He did well there, too, and knew he was destined to go all the way up. But that didn't happen. A few years after their eventual victory he was assigned to govern the prestigious province of Pars. A very high honour, no doubt.

There he discharged his duties with zeal and vigour…maybe over zealously. He was told that these Zoroastrians needed to be taught a lesson, a lesson from which they will never be able to rise again. So he had ordered the burning down of every fire-temple, in that region. He had ordered the killing of every Zoroastrian priest and destruction of all their libraries and their sacred text, the *Avesta*. He had ordered the conversion of every Zoroastrian to the Islam religion. He had given a blank order to kill anyone refusing to convert. His final tally was the burning of 347 fire-temples, murder of 2400 priests, and the killing of 37,000 Zoroastrians who refused to convert. He boasted of burning down 73 libraries in Pars alone, along with countless copies of the *Avesta* and other scriptures.

His zeal to conquer, the people and their spirit, was so high that his hunger progressed from cruel to sadistic. A few cities in his districts were to bear witness to sights unimagined. In those cities that housed thousands of Zoroastrians, many refused to bend down to Islamic norms. He hanged them all on poles lined up on both sides of their streets, *and allowed the bodies to rot for weeks.* Yes, he did get many conversions after that.

And the legendary treasures of the Persian Empire? Had not he systematically extracted them from every corner of the province? Pars was the province where Persepolis and Passargade were located. Persepolis had been the Persian's capital city for the past nine hundred years, ever since the times of Cyrus the Great. The whole world knew of the treasures to be found there. Once it was the ultimate city in the world for its riches. But Alexander had taken care of that boast. He had ransacked it, plundered it, raped it and eventually decimated it. When the Arabs invaded it they thought it was in ruins. But in the nine hundred years since its destruction the future kings had tried to revive it to its former glory. And they, the Arabs, found great joy in once again bringing it down to its knees. And what wealth they found there. Yaser had personally supervised the transport of that incalculable wealth to Arabia. Shiploads of gold, long caravans of precious stones, tons of ancient ornaments, all dutifully sent back to the safety of his homeland.

That is everything, except the mace. That was his personal trophy.

So what more did the Caliphs, and now the Ummayads, expect of him? Why was he still languishing in this province, like a caged bird? He wanted to fly out to other great nations and add to his tally. He was hungry to do more. He was famished from lack of challenges.

And it was not that the invaders were doing particularly well in other districts of Persia either. They had allowed King Yazdegerd III to be murdered. They had allowed his son to escape to China. And they had now resorted to in-fighting, and hence there was incompetence in the administration. If the Caliphs and the Ummayads sitting at Medina had shown more faith in him and put him in complete charge of Persia, things would have been different.

Besides conquering the hero of the enemies, Yaser's next biggest pride was fathering two sons. After settling down as Governor of Pars, he had married an Arab beauty, he had the choice of a king, and he was blessed with two healthy boys. Both took after their father and joined the army. The elder son's name was Mohammad. From a young age he was so fascinated by the prophet's teachings that Yaser had no objections when his son took up cleric as his profession. Yaser wasn't over-ecstatic about it but he could see there could be no other future for the lad. Very soon Mohammad's total commitment was recognised and he steadily climbed the echelons of his chosen career, in Arabia.

The younger son, Jamal, was Yaser's pride as he took up military as his career and followed his father's footsteps. Yaser could have started him off as an officer but Jamal preferred to go through the ranks and earn his place. He was stationed in Persia, and had climbed his way to become the Commander of Esfahan. Yaser was immensely proud of both the sons.

But today he couldn't think beyond his current status. He was destined for greater things, so why allow him to rot here? He desperately needed another challenge in life…a worthy challenge, and be a hero again. He couldn't sign off from his long and illustrious career simply as the governor of a district. In sheer frustration he clenched both his fists and brought them heavily on the table he was standing next to.

What he wouldn't give to get a chance to be a hero once again...but alas, there was only one Zahl, and he was long dead.

There came to his ears the sounds of an argument.

"A special messenger from the Ummayad, Sire." An annoyed guard rushed in, followed by an envoy immediately behind him. "He refused to pass on the message to me."

"It is meant only for you, Sire. And it is an oral message." The messenger explained, waiting for the guard to withdraw. What could be this, Yaser wondered. Nothing in writing? And this was no ordinary messenger. He was obviously a high-ranking emissary. Are they calling him back from active duty? Is this the end of the road for him?

Yaser nodded and the guard withdrew reluctantly from the room.

"You are hereby informed," the messenger began as Yaser awaited dry-mouthed, "that the Persian commander Zahl, has escaped from his prison and is believed to have made his way back to his country. He…"

"Wait, wait, wait…what are you talking about? Which Zahl are you referring to?"

"The great Zahl Mahraspandan, the champion of Persia."

"But he's dead! I myself have seen him die at the Battle of Qadisiyya! That mace you see behind you was his. So what nonsense is this about him escaping a prison?"

"He did not die, Sire. We had managed to capture him later and imprison in a secret location. He has recently escaped from this prison and the Ummayad wants all Governors to be aware of this. They now want him desperately, before he can arouse a rebellion."

Allah be praised! Is it true what he was hearing? Is it possible that the ghost of that giant has arisen? Has God heard his prayers and offered him the chance he wanted?

"Whoever captures him can expect a big promotion," the emissary concluded his short message.

That's it! It was the challenge he was waiting for. "Where in Persia do you expect him to hide?"

"We do not know hence all the governors are informed. But the Mahraspandan family hailed from the province of Pars."

I know that, and have already done the needful, remembered Yaser with a sly smile. Zahl will not be meeting any of his relatives there.

"One last thing," the emissary continued, "this news has to be kept a secret. If word of his re-appearance leaks out, that itself could initiate a rebel."

Yaser couldn't agree with him more. The entire complexion of their occupation of this land could change. The Zarthoshties, too, may see this as the ray of hope they were praying for.

The emissary bowed and left quietly. Yaser sat back, unable to control his feelings. He felt exulted and rejuvenated as though fresh blood and oxygen had been pumped into his system. *Zahl was his man!* He won't allow anyone else to get him. He got the better of him once, he'll beat him again. He must work fast before someone else got to him first…but where should he start? And how? if he's not to share this information with anyone? He'll have to rely upon his trusted spies. They were very good in their profession. He had spread them all over the country, even into territories not under his supervision.

He rubbed his hands as he got down to inform them of the top-secret mission. He won't tell them everything, but just instruct them to keep their eyes and ears open.

❑❑❑

5

Zahl heard the fidgeting movements and whispers of Peshotan and Jamshid in the room as he lay recouping in bed. Disturbing? No! After so many years of isolation they were the most pleasant sounds he could pray for. Sounds he could not dream of ever hearing again. But he still refused to open his eyes and acknowledge them. Maybe, if he had opened his eyes he would find out that it was all a dream and that he was still in the dark and lonely prison. Let me savour it a little longer.

In any case what difference would it make even if he opened his eyes, as he was sort of a prisoner here, too, he reminded himself. His family wouldn't allow him to roam around in the mountains. 'In case some Arab rode in', they said. Even within the hamlet he couldn't be seen, 'for some time at least, stay within the house', they argued. They can't expect him to remain imprisoned in this house. He had had enough of that. Moreover they need to show a little more courage. They seem to have totally given in to the dictates of the Arabs. Where is the pride of their fearless ancestors? Where has their anger disappeared to? Why have they so meekly given in with not a semblance of a fight-back? From what he's seen in the past week, he was disgustingly disappointed. This was not what their ancestors had fought for. This is Persia, land of noble kings and warriors. *And today they are afraid to say the word, 'Persia'?*

Worse, far, far worse, even their good religion has been compromised. *That is sacrilegious, unthinkable and unpardonable!*

How did it all start? He once again tried to remember and restructure his own and his country's recent past.

Before the defeat at Qadissya, Zahl remembered, was the humility of the

Empire's first loss to the Arabs at the Battle of Dhu Qar. It was a small victory for the Arabs, but it gave them the sweet taste of victory.

His family, the Mahraspandans, were of the elite class. Being close cousins to generations of kings, this noble family was known to breed warriors of the highest calibre. For generations they were recognized as the principal protectors of Persia, and keepers of its faith, Zoroastrianism. For countless generations their ancestors were either commanders or generals of their fighting forces, or high priests promoting their faith and building their fire-temples.

And I let them all down.

With a moan Zahl turned in his bed. Peshotan was immediately by his side thinking his father was in pain. But Zahl was hardly aware of his physical condition. His mind once again raced back to his childhood.

He was exceptionally tall right through his youth. He was taught the use of all the existing weapons and the only games he played revolved round battle scenes and war strategies. Because of his height he was a clumsy horse-rider, but his great love for his horses, all of them imported from Arabia, made him long to be a cavalry officer.

At the age of 16, Zahl had joined the army. Already one of the tallest and strongest, he was automatically nurtured to be an officer. By 20 he was commanding a cavalry division and by the age of 25 he was a national hero. Always at the head of an attacking division, the strikingly aggressive young man soon became a cult-figure as he led the Persians from victory to victory, in different parts of the world. By 636 C.E., the year of the Battle of Qadissya, he was the champion commander of the Persian army.

"Has he regained consciousness?" Dughdhova entered the room with a bowl of milk.

"No," said Peshotan. "But I think he's pretending. He seems to have recovered."

How dare he?

"He must eat something, or he'll get weaker."

Weak? The great Zahl? What's wrong with them? Don't they know me? My son thinks I'm *pretending*, and now my daughter-in-law thinks I'll get *weak*?

With an impatient utterance Zahl sat up on his bed. Immediately his head swooned and he toppled back on to his pillow.

"He was pretending, and he is weak," confirmed Peshotan.

Zahl's anger simmered to a boiling point. Obviously, I haven't beaten him enough during his growing days. *But I was never at home during those days.* Conquests abroad had taken all my time. Peshotan was brought up by his mother, and hence the cool temper and the non-violent ways. That was the way his wife Sheherzade was, humble, peace-loving and the soothing balm for the entire hot-headed Mahraspandan family. When people wondered how he chose her, he knew it was those very qualities that drew him to her.

But where is she?

'Left without a farewell', they said. Soon after the Arabs invaded her country in 642, six years after Qadisiyya, she left for her heavenly abode. Thirty three years ago? *And he never knew of it?* He remembered why. *He* has returned home after almost forty years. He had left soon after Peshotan's birth. And circumstances compelled him to stay away.

God, what have I done to my family?

But could Sheherzade have survived the persecutions of the invading army? Thankfully she never suffered such indignations. Thankfully, she never had to bow her head to these animals. Thankfully she never witnessed the systematic degradation of her people and of her religion.

But someone must pay for such atrocities!

"You said he returned after forty years," Zahl heard his grandson's voice. Nice and sturdy young fellow, he thought. Maybe a little overweight, but he would have loved to train him to be a warrior. "So why didn't he come back earlier? Why didn't he come to your help when you needed him?"

But he spoke too much. And he asked too many questions.

"Because he was caught and imprisoned," explained Peshotan patiently. "But I've already told you about it so…"

"But why didn't he try to escape from his prison all these years? You said once he was the strongest man in all Persia."

❑

Escape? How could he? Not that he never tried, but the odds were hopelessly against him.

"But you haven't recovered fully yet," Pourus had protested. "Your wounds are too grievous for you to walk around so soon again."

"I'm okay," I muttered, not caring for Pourous's motherly concerns. "And I must return to Persia before the Arabs attack it. I must be back with my king."

"Remember," Pourus gently reminded. "You are not your old self any longer. You have but one hand."

"It will be sufficient for me to take my revenge on those marauders."

With Pourus he set off for the long ride. But it took them an eternity to reach the foothills of Zagros Mountains, the last natural bastion before the Persian mainland.

"God!" exclaimed Zahl. "They're everywhere. This must be the umpteenth division of their army that we have come across." They had trekked for almost 3 months and were now atop a steep slope of a mountain in the countryside of Khvarvaran. And spread below them were thousands of Arab soldiers, whiling their time.

"They seem to be preparing for an attack," opined Pourus, sinking deeper into the grounds and keeping a watchful eye for sentries. "It's good we came, and that too, in time."

"Tomorrow we begin our journey across the Zagroes mountain range," said Zahl feeling the foreboding vibes the great mountains emitted. "It will be tougher than anything we have ever come across till now. *But beyond it, is home.*"

The Arabs had already encountered a few smaller Persian armies guarding small provinces before reaching the Zagros, and had overpowered them easily enough. But there were too many of these skirmishes and they were getting impatient.

Zahl and Pourus came across a soldier from one such fighting force a little later. He kept staring at Zahl for a long time in disbelief but hesitated confirming his doubts.

"Why aren't you attacking them?" asked Zahl sternly.

"We have been, constantly," the frightened man replied. "But they outnumber us completely, so all we can do is delay their advance into Persia. But now we dare not do that either as the consequences have been catastrophic."

"What do you mean?"

"The Arab commander, Khaled ibn al-Wahid was getting tired and frustrated that their advance to the heartland of Persia was being constantly delayed because of the resistance we put up. So at the subsequent battle of Ullais he ordered all the prisoners of war to be decapitated and dismembered, so as to demoralize our main army waiting for them at the eastern side of the Zagros. He ordered the body parts to be thrown into the river and, as there was a dam downstream, he threw open those gates and allowed the bodies to be swept over the cascading waters. The river is now re-named, The River of Blood."

Zahl grunted, Pourus paled and the soldier quietly took his leave.

"The more I hear of such stories the more my blood boils!" Zahl fumed. "Come on, we must make haste and return to our land. The sooner we get back, the better I'll feel."

Another mistake of Zahl...he should have known that patience is the vital virtue for every victor.

Two days later he and Pourus were surprised by a small Arab patrol, far away from their main army. The two put up a valiant fight but Pourus was killed and Zahl captured. When he was produced before the chieftain, Khaled ibn al-Wahid couldn't believe what he saw as he instantly recognised the legend.

"What should I do with him, this once mighty warrior?" Khaled asked his group of counsellors. "We thought the great Zahl was dead, and the threat was behind us. Now he, an invalid, stands in front of us, just when we are about to strike Persia itself."

"Obviously, we should kill him, and maybe throw his body over the Zagros. That will definitely demoralize our enemy further and speed up our triumph."

"Maybe it will, maybe it won't," doubted Khaled. "Maybe it will bring back the unity amongst the Persians. Don't forget, we have got thus far thanks to their internal problems. If word got out that Zahl was not killed and was caught trying to get back to his country's aid, maybe that will unite the Princes and Commanders of their King Yazdegard."

"You're right," agreed the eldest counsellor. "What we must do immediately is get him out of sight. Take him away to the loneliest location and imprison him with a very heavy guard."

What a price Zahl paid for his haste. His impatience threw him once again at the mercy of his enemies. Now he faced an eternity in prison.

So that's what they did. They escorted him back to Khvarvaran, built a special prison for him on a remote mountain and chained him to his cell. A small contingent of guards was kept permanently to guard their single prisoner. They treated him with respect, but never slackened their vigil.

"But I don't want just respect," seethed Zahl. "I want to fight again."

In the beginning an escape was not impossible. In the first year itself he had managed to flee from his captors twice. There were times they had to remove his chains and he took advantage of those lapses. Not only did he manage to break out of his prison, but had escaped the mountains, too. Both times they caught up with him, and each time tightened their security a step further. Then for the next ten years he didn't get a single chance.

When the commandant of the guards changed hands, he took advantage of a weak leader. First he befriended him and was duly rewarded with relaxed vigilance. This time when he escaped he managed to go far. In two weeks time he had travelled a good hundred miles away from the prison. He was certain he was safe as he entered a village. But his gigantic size betrayed him. The news of a giant stranger in the village travelled fast. They caught with him days after he left the village.

This time they took no more chances. His chains remained on him twenty-four hours, and absolutely no respites. He remained thus for the next *twenty-five years.*

❑❑❑

6

Zahl shrugged involuntarily as a cold shiver ran up his spine at the thought of those days of imprisonment and loneliness.

"He stirred again," he heard his son say. "Dughdhova, give him a spoonful of milk."

WHAT!! They want to spoon-feed me?

He threw aside the sheet covering him and sat up bolt upright. Another bout of giddiness, but he shut his eyes tight this time, took a deep breath and held his position.

Zahl grabbed the large bowl of milk and in a few huge gulps, drained it down his throat. When younger he was known to eat a full-grown goat at one go. Milk was consumed in gallons.

I loved to hear tales of his huge appetite when he was young. My favourite one was about the wager he once had with a local chieftain.

"I challenge you to eat a full ass," the chieftain defied the young Zahl. The challenge was accepted without much ado. The chieftain arranged the date and when Zahl came, he was offered forty plateful of fancy *kababs* made from one full ass. The astonished chieftain's eyes almost popped out as Zahl dutifully consumed plate after plate of the delicacy. Just when the chieftain thought he had lost his bet he saw Zahl pushing aside the last plate, without eating the *kababs*.

"Give up?" the chieftain asked gleefully.

"Yes," said Zahl sorrowfully. "If I eat anymore of your delicious *kababs*, I won't be able to eat the ass."

They say the chieftain cried all night.

With awe I saw Zahl put down the large bowl of milk and look around for more. Just then in walked Mahafrid, my sister. This I must watch, I thought in anticipation. Mahafrid was thirteen years old and someone I just couldn't get along with. She had to be the most reserved and meek person ever born. She talked little, laughed even less and never played a game in her life. Sometimes I wondered why she even existed. She had two friends but hardly spent time with them. Her permanent place was next to her mother. And the thing I detested most of her was her habit to cry at almost anything. Anyone bigger than her would frighten her to no lengths and if anyone as much as raised his voice, Mahafrid was sure to cry and cringe. Simply a glare from my father was sure to result in hours of despair and desolation. That is why I wanted to watch her as my bad-tempered grandfather sat on his bed scowling at everyone around him.

She skirted the bed and to my amazement walked right up to him. She whisked out a bunch of wild flowers from behind her and offered it to Zahl. Zahl looked on as though he was just offered something that would blow him apart.

"What's that?" He asked gruffly. I expected Mahafrid to immediately turn around and run out of the room in tears. But she stood there unflinchingly and looked directly into the eyes of her grandfather.

"Flowers. I picked them for you."

I couldn't believe what I was seeing. This was the first time I had seen her talk to anyone but the family she grew up with and her two friends.

I thought Zahl was about to explode as he looked towards his son for help. Flowers and he were two totally different species, and he had never even noticed them before. But now he was trapped and needed help. None came. So he leaned forward and gently took the small bunch in his hand.

"Uh huh," he mumbled and wanted to pat Mahafrid on her head. But he had only one hand and that was holding the flowers. So he leaned forward and planted a light kiss on her forehead.

When Mahafrid had returned to her mother's side, we all looked on stunned. A miracle had taken place in front of our eyes. My grandfather was human after all, and there was still hope for my timid sister.

Zahl, still holding the flowers in his hand, looked about uncomfortably, as though he was a criminal caught in the act, and the flowers were his weapon. He wiped his mouth on his sleeve and got off the bed. "Well, what are you all gaping at? There is to be a *Sedra -Pushun* ceremony in the family, so stop wasting time and get about your work."

❑

The *Sedra-Pushun* is an initiation ceremony into the religion, and the person to be ordained was me. For the past one year my parents spent all their spare time, and unfortunately there was plenty of that, in coaching me for this ceremony. There were prayers to be learnt by heart, there were rituals to perfect and there was some history to know too.

"You must know *every* word of the '*kushti'* prayers", my father, the high priest of this village, reminded me. "I will be performing the ceremony, so God help you if you are not perfect."

Seldom has my father used such strong language so I gathered this must be important to him. But right now my mind was preoccupied with a more delicate matter, so I repeated my earlier question that remained unanswered. "Why didn't Grandfather try to escape from his prison?"

I saw Zahl cringe and look the other way.

"But he did, else how would he be with us today?" reminded my father quickly, noticing the discomfort of his father. "He couldn't be successful in his earlier attempts, but finally he did escape and did manage to shake off his pursuers."

"How did he escape?"

"You'll learn of it after the spanking you deserve from me." With that father lunged for my ear. I may not be that quick in my head, but I was unbeatable on my feet. Before he could reach where I was idling, I was out of his reach and out of the house.

❑

It was not easy, remembered Zahl, escaping that hell.

One has no idea what it could be like being chained to a wall for twenty-five years. In that dark cell he prayed, ate, drank, defecated and urinated, one activity at a time. And did nothing, absolutely *nothing* else. The guards were warned against talking to him ever since his last attempt at escape. It was like an imprisonment for them, too, shunted out from their families and friends with nothing to do but keep a constant vigil over one man. Couldn't be more boring and unchallenging.

And for Zahl, there was no sunshine, no light, just the dark and cold cell...*and the ubiquitous chain.* How he had learnt to hate that heavy chain. It didn't allow him to get far; it didn't allow him to free his mind to anything else, except learn the true meaning of *bondage.* He had cut his wrists to ribbons trying to break free; he had repeatedly banged his head at the point where the chain was bound to the wall. But nothing worked. He had even tried in a mad frenzy to suck the chain, chewed at its links, but to no avail. It was like a determined ally, refusing to let go of him…except it was no ally.

The winters in those mountains were the severest he ever experienced. There were no warm clothes and no hot meals. The cell that saw no sunshine became so frigidly cold that every winter he felt this would be his last. By now he was so feeble he wondered at the wisdom in imprisoning him any further. He was no longer any threat to anyone. All must have forgotten of him by now. Why not simply throw him over the cliff and bury him amongst the rocks? They could save an enormous amount time, energy and expenses by not maintaining this prison any longer. And these poor guards could be relieved of their ghastly duty.

A year of such frustrating conditions and Zahl felt he was losing his mental balance. He started speaking to himself, went on to cursing and abusing no one in particular and finally resorted to bouts of screaming and shouting. Soon the guards realised they had a mental patient at hand and began treating him as such. In spite of being ordered not to talk to him, they teased and mocked him from behind the locked door, till he would charge straight towards them, crashing into the stout door and even onto the four walls he hated so much, uncaring of the injuries he regularly suffered.

It was not just the prison and its guards that depraved his mind and body, but his very soul was in danger of being conquered. Regularly his tormented mind had to fight off evil spirits that threatened to take possession of his soul…the only thing that was still his. *But he won't let that happen!* As nightmares merged into realities, as darkness refused to lift its heavy veil from his mind he experienced the most devastating time of his life. He clung on to his soul with every ounce of his remaining mental strength, fighting off every kind of evil spirits.

Just when all thought it was now a matter of days before this poor soul would meet its maker, Zahl remembered something...something that had been drubbed into his mind since he was a child, and yet he had almost forgotten due to his pre-occupation with continuous wars.

His religion, and its daily prayers.

Being born in a priestly family he had gone through the special *Nozud* ceremony as a young lad. This gave him the privilege to perform and conduct certain religious ceremonies for others. He was faithful to its tenets for over five years, but once he chose military as his career, he stopped being actively engaged in his religion. First few years after the ceremony he went through his daily prayers with zeal, but slowly with the burden of battles, those recitals petered out to the bare basics. Slowly that, too, came down to an occasional mental remembrance of his *Ahura Mazda.*

Now, when he desperately needed solace and comfort, he once again turned towards *Ahura Mazda* for guidance. He remembered very few of his prayers, but he made the start. He somewhat remembered the short *Ahunawar* and *Ashem Vohu* prayers, and he started by mumbling these continuously. The comfort he received from such moments made him pray more than once a day. He started with them first thing every morning, and then repeated whenever he felt like. His final call of devotion was reserved for just before he slept. In a month's time, he felt a different man…more in control of himself, less easy for others to arouse his temper. His nightmares left him and he was more confident of retaining his soul.

The guards saw the change and didn't like it as it meant an extension of their stay in those unforgiving mountains. They tried their best to antagonise him with new methods so as to reverse this positive trend. They even tried physical violence and psychological tactics to humiliate him, but to no avail. Their prisoner simply shut his eyes and concentrated on his prayers. Soon they gave up and allowed their prisoner to be on his own.

He never made a great show of those daily prayers, sometimes praying in whispers and sometimes only in his mind. He tried remembering other important prayers, mumbling snippets as they came to his mind. Soon these snippets merged and he was reciting almost complete prayers.

The renewed and unbending faith in his religion encouraged him to continue surviving the hard conditions prevailing. Earlier into his imprisonment he still wore both the symbols of his faith, the *Sedra* and the *Kushti*. The *Sedra* was a white vest worn inside, against his skin, and the *Kushti* was the sacred thread tied three times round his waist. Both were made with precise religious significance and all those initiated into the Zoroastrian religion were expected to wear them at all times. His *Sedra* had long ago torn to shreds and was finally discarded. But his stout *Kushti* stood by him through the years. He took great care of it now, washing it only occasionally and using it tenderly during his daily prayers.

Another thing his captors allowed him to keep was the Zoroastrian symbol of the Guardian of the Spirit, his *Asho Farohar*. It was made of some heavy metal, he couldn't figure out which, and of no value to his captors. It carried the shape of large open wings, with the head of King Lehrasp on it. It was the symbol popularised by Darius the Great who had the emblem immortalised by having it carved on the walls of his capital, Persepolis, a thousand years ago. For Zahl, his *Asho Farohar* was his ultimate companion.

After his mental recovery it was easier for Zahl to pass the years of imprisonment that followed.

And then there came the providential intervention. A mighty earthquake shook the earth for hundreds of miles around. The mountain, on which the prison stood, rumbled and rocked. Suddenly one entire side of the mountain started sliding down, *along with the prison*. As the guards panicked and tried escaping the wrath of God, half the prison tumbled over the edge and crashed a thousand feet below. The other half, where Zahl's cell stood, simply collapsed in a huge heap.

When the tremors stopped and the dust cleared one could see just a pile of rocks where the prison stood. There seemed to be no survivors, until the sound of a chain was heard. And from the debris, unbelievably, walked out a giant of a man…his eyes shining, his body soaking in the warm sunshine, and his one hand and both legs free of any shackles.

He was already a very weak man, and the fall and tumble of the prison had battered him down further. But to Zahl this was a beautiful day and he never felt lighter and stronger.

Picking his way out of the devastated valley, he reached a small village a day later. It was flattened by the earthquake, too, and there was nobody around. The people must have fled into the mountains, waiting for a suitable time to return. But he found there what he wanted most…food, lots of it, and warm clothing. He ate heartily and stocked up well enough to last him a month. He clothed himself to ward off the toughest winter and immediately set off eastwards, towards another mountain range…*The Zagros*.

When he reached the western slopes of the Zagros, he took a breather of a few days. This was the place he was last captured, twenty five years ago, but now there was no one around to challenge him.

Where were they all?

It took him months to get to the other side of those treacherous mountains. They were bitter winter months but he did cross over. And once over, he saw the miles and miles of flat plateau below him and he breathed an incredibly deep sigh of relief.

Finally, I'm home!

His joy was short-lived as he slowly witnessed the devastations caused by the invaders. There was not a semblance left of the glorious, prosperous Persia he knew. The land lay unattended to, the people looked miserable and there seemed to be no sight of the wealth the country once boasted of.

He made his way southwards toward Pars district, where he was sure of re-uniting with his family. After weeks of travelling and witnessing the destruction the invaders had committed, he reached home. There his heart sank.

His home was destroyed and his entire family was missing. Through some discreet inquiries he found out about the Governor's orders to kill all from the Mahrespandan family, and he also learnt of how the orders were carried out.

"But the son had escaped," an old inhabitant informed him in a hushed voice. "He is believed to have gone to Yazd." The old man kept staring at him in disbelief. Then he shook his head as though saying, 'No, it couldn't be him, who I thought it was'.

Zahl returned to the mountains and travelled back northwards towards Yazd. Can he dare to hope to once again see his son, *anyone from his family*? He failed to locate him in the city of Yazd but from a Zoroastrian family living at its outskirts he found out about the village in the mountains, and the small group of Zoroastrians living there.

It was an impossibly happy moment for him when he finally saw Peshotan standing by his home. He looked the spitting image of his own father and he needed no introduction.

❑

The room had emptied and Zahl preferred it that way. Stay in bed, they had told him. But that was not for him. He swung his legs out and tried standing up. No problems, he noticed gratefully. They fussed over him too much. If they only knew the extent of suffering he had experienced at the prison. This was almost childish.

But why did he suffer a heart attack? He was sure his heart could withstand any strain. Probably, it was the cumulative effect of hearing about the series of atrocities the invaders had committed during his absence and the systemic effect of the degradation brought about by the enemies of his beloved country and religion. He did get that uneasy feeling in his chest this past one week but he didn't pay heed to it, or tell anyone about it. Witnessing the abuse on his son proved to be the final blow.

"So where do I go from here?" he asked himself. Certainly this was not his way of life, he fretted, as he shuffled around the room. And he had to take into account the fact that his presence here was a risk for his family and the rest in the village. He must leave this place and seek his chances for a fight-back against the enemy.

"Grandfather is walking around!" The alarm was set off by his grandson and almost instantly the entire family was around him insisting upon his going back to sleep. That boy needed to be kept on a leash. More importantly, he needed to be gagged.

"I need some fresh air," Zahl said brushing aside all protests and stepping out into the muddy walkway. Once out in the open he relaxed. He took a deep breath and smiled faintly. "Ahh, that smells good. That's still free, along with the sunshine and the wind. Nobody can conquer them…unlike…my people." He shook his head remorsefully. "How they have given in…"

"Father, please don't go far." Peshotan joined him, a worried line creasing his forehead.

"Stop worrying about me," Zahl snapped. "Come show me the houses of your neighbours. I don't seem to recognise anyone."

"You've been away for too long. Besides they're not from our city. Most are from Yazd and some from other regions joined us later."

A couple of houses down the road a man was repairing a small piece of furniture on his veranda, and a young man just lazing around.

"Minocher," Peshotan called out. "Have you met my father?"

Minocher looked up from what he was doing and gave a nervous smile. A quick wave and he returned to what he was doing.

Peshotan introduced the young man next. "This is Minocher's son, Rustom."

Rustom gave a broad smile and bent low in greetings, too overawed to speak.

"Why is he standing around doing nothing?" Zahl wanted to know.

"Because there is nothing to do around here."

"There is always something to do. He could be sharpening his sword or dagger. He could be practising with his spear."

Peshotan just shook his head and walked on.

Outside the next house a man was milking a goat.

"Phiruz, this is my…" Peshotan started saying, but the man had already turned around and hurriedly returned indoors. "Uhm…sorry about that, father. I…I just don't understand…"

"They're scared, son. *Just plain scared.* No wonder we lost the empire and the will to fight back. *Bah!* This is worse than I expected."

"You have no right to talk that way, father. You have no idea what these people have gone through. And it was not just for a year or two; we have all gone through sheer hell for the past thirty years or so."

"So have I, son…so have I. *But I have not lost my spirit."*

Zahl had seen enough, and he didn't like what he saw. In some eyes he saw the replay of abject defeat; in some voices he heard the echoes of the haunted; and in some postures he felt the disgrace and shame of surrender.

"No use walking further. Let's return." So saying Zahl abruptly turned around. "Next week is little Jamshid's *Sedra-Pushun* ceremony. What are the arrangements?"

Peshotan looked taken aback. "Arrangements? What kind of arrangements are you expecting? A music band, invitation cards?" he asked hotly. Peshotan wanted to love his father, but he was not making it easy for him.

Zahl sensed Peshotan's irritation and didn't answer. He didn't much care for sarcasm. It was not his way of fighting. If you disagree with a person, *say it!*

Both stood in front of their house trying to look the other way. A cold war threatened to chill their moods.

"We'll do it in our house, and I've invited everyone at the village." Peshotan offered the truce.

Zahl made no show of hearing him. He intently studied the barren mountains surrounding them. Once, Zahl imagined sadly, they were regularly trekked by Persian families, by Persian heroes and by proud Zoroastrians. Today it was but...

"And naturally I'll be performing the ceremony," Peshotan added, trying to put an end to the silence.

"House?" Zahl asked quietly. "A *Sedra-Pushun* ceremony used to take place in a Fire Temple. *Never in a house!"*

"*I know that*. Look father, you're being totally unreasonable. *Where in God's name will I find a Fire-temple in this wilderness?"* Peshotan was by now at his wits end. Hasn't his father heard of 'compromise'? Can't he understand that in today's context, this was the most he can do.

"And the sacred fire? Or is that going to be forsaken, too?"

Fire was the most sacred element to a Zoroastrian and the very centre-piece of every Fire-temple. A Sacred Fire from a consecrated Fire Temple was even more holy. But a fire from the original fire lighted thousands of years ago by Lord Zarthushtra himself, was the absolute ultimate.

"There will be a scared fire, and of the highest order," said Peshotan, vehemently. He saw Zahl's puzzled look and ordered, "Come, follow me."

Behind the rows of houses were a few cowsheds. Besides a small herd of cows, they also housed a couple of horses, a few mules and some poultry. It considerably took care of the community's fooding needs. At the front of one of the sheds worked an ironsmith. A burly fellow with an angry frown. A furnace was blazing nearby. He held a flat piece of red-hot iron with tongs in one hand and was using a large hammer to forge it into shape. It was easy to see he was shaping a sword. Each time he brought down the hammer it was with vengeance and anger as though the metal had cheated him.

The moment the man realised he was not alone he squared up, ready to attack.

"It's okay, Noshirwan. This is my father."

The man smiled broadly and said, "I've heard of you all my life. I would have loved to fight alongside you. It's an honour to meet you today."

That's more like it, thought Zahl. Here was a man after his own heart. So there still lived real men in this country.

"Come in, father," said Peshotan, beckoning him to the crude stable-cum-forge.

They entered the shed as Noshirwan returned to his duty of hammering down the metal sheet. Zahl looked around expectantly, but was disappointed. "I can see only iron scraps, and a cow."

"Come behind this secret partition." Peshotan pushed and slid aside two layers of wooden frameworks.

When Zahl turned round the edge of the partition, he almost stopped breathing. There in the middle of the clearing he saw what he dreaded he may never see again. Sitting on a small tripod was a silver Urn.

And in that Urn burned the most beautiful fire he had ever seen.

Speechless, tears rolled down Zahl's face. *All was not lost, after all!* There has been some resistance, some show of self-respect. We have not given in blindly. A quiet whisper of the prayers '*AhuNozud*' and '*Ashem Vohu*' and he knelt down in reverence.

He got up and turned towards his son to ask a question, but Peshotan had already anticipated what was going to come next.

"The fire is from the *Atash-Behram* in Yazd. Part of the holy fire that was first ignited by Lord Zarthushtra."

❑

When out in the sunlight again Zahl was quiet for some time.

"I know it's a small *Urn*," explained Peshotan nervously, "but we couldn't carry off the main vessel..."

"A small *Urn*?" Zahl cut off Peshotan. "It's the sacred fire, son. That is more important. And what you've achieved is the biggest thing I've seen in many a year. Son, I'm proud of you, and the others in this village. But how did you manage it? We're miles away from Yazd."

"You may not know it but many other priests have done it too, during these past few decades of occupation. Before the invaders could vandalise our fire temples some of the priests have taken the initiative and did what we have done here. Some have even managed to carry away the original large vessel into the mountains of Khorasan, Kerman, Yazd, Kuhishtan and other places. Many are hiding the *Urns* in caves and some in underground cellars."

"I like your hiding place, but the smoke could be a give-away."

"That is why we have a forge there. The smoke from the furnace camouflages the smoke from the holy fire."

"And during the *Sedra-Pushun* ceremony?"

"We'll carry the *Urn* to our house."

❑❑❑

7

Manashni; Gavashni; Khunashni;

Good thoughts; Good words; Good deeds;

The very cornerstone of Zarathushtra's teachings. And the tenets all Zoroastrians live by. Basic, yet so difficult to practise; Concise, yet it touches every aspect of one's life; Simple, yet so powerful.

That was what I was going to learn about today on my initiation…my *Sedra-Pushun*. It will be a short ceremony but what I'll be invested with, will be within me till my last breath. I was not unduly troubled with that prospect, but time and circumstances ensured there was no other option for me.

That was one of the busiest mornings I had ever gone through in all of my seven years. Everyone was in a hurry. Orders were shouted out, the house was full of neighbours scurrying around to complete jobs assigned to them. Clearing of furniture from our main room was followed by the thorough cleaning of the house. Flower garlands were hung at every doorway and paintings of our family ancestors. The largest garland was reserved for the painting of our prophet, Zarthushtra. Fruits and sweet dishes were arranged in large silver dishes and all us youngsters' attention was instantly diverted to that table.

By nine in the morning all was as it should be. The preparations for my *Sedra-Pushun* were complete. A few minutes later my father stepped out of his room in immaculately clean white robes, mandatory with our priests. Next my mother and my siblings came forward. My sister for the first time was giggling. She had warned me of what was to come next. I didn't believe her when she had earlier announced that I would have to sip a bull's urine, called *'Nirang'*. It was part of the ritual, she said. I was petrified at the prospect and had resolved not to swallow the liquid. What she didn't explain was that this urine was from a very special bull, an albino. The urine was then purified through a series of unique prayers over a period of many weeks. Miraculously this urine never putrefied and could be stored for years. We obviously had a steady stock at hand for the entire community.

"Father, we're beginning the ceremony," my father called out to his. When my grandfather stepped out of his room we all took in a quick breath. He looked so distinguished and dignified in his spotlessly clean white robes. He had combed back his hair and his beard was immaculately trimmed. On his head he had tied a white cloth, as was required in our religion.

Meanwhile two men brought in the *Urn* with the holy fire and placed it on a carpet in the middle of the room. A box of sandalwood was placed by it along with a plate of incense powder and flowers.

My father started the preliminary prayers as I sat in front of him. At a certain point a small glass was passed on to me and I saw my sister cover her face as she chuckled quietly.

"Take only a sip," my father ordered. I hesitated at the prospect of sipping the *Nirang*. I saw my grandfather glowering at me and I quickly took a very small sip and involuntarily made a face.

Next I was given *Nahan*, or ablution, by my father. Purified, I was made to sit in one place as the rest of the family, and the neighbours gathered around me. My grandfather was seated right up front, looking sombre and proud as ever. He gave me an acknowledgement nod, and I never felt more happy and important in my life.

The ceremony began with the chanting of our most sacred prayer, the *AhuNozud.* I chanted along with my father, making sure I didn't lag behind or make a mistake. My father had made me practise reciting the words for months in advance.

I could see my mother was the most excited person in the room as she beamed radiantly to no one in particular. Uncharacteristically, she insisted upon prompting me from aside by framing the prayer words with her mouth for me and nodding her head empathetically as I repeated them. It was quite unnecessary really as I had learnt my prayers well under father's strict disciplining methods. I have my red ears to prove it.

Soon I was donned with the *'Sedra'* a white sacred vest that I was never to be without again, except for my bath. White, as it was the mark of purity. The *'Sedra'* also had a tiny pocket at the end of the neckline that symbolised a 'pocket of virtues'. It is where I will symbolically store all my good deeds for God to see when my time comes. Next my father tied the *'Kushti'*, a sacred girdle made of a white lamb's wool, thrice around my waist. Now I was symbolically protected against all evil. A few minutes later I was officially a Zarthoshty.

Hugs and kisses were followed by gifts. I made a mental note of all the gifts I had bequeathed, lest one of my siblings should manoeuvre it out of my sight. They were both capable of it. Just when I thought it was all over, a large figure stood over me. I had forgotten my grandfather in all the excitement. Good, I was sure of something special from him.

He knelt down before me, (I still reached only his shoulders), and gathered me in his left arm. Comforting, but scary as he increased the pressure. After planting a big kiss on my forehead, he stood up. And I started breathing freely again. He removed the necklace with the *Asho Farohar* from around his neck and proudly placed it around mine.

"Never ever be without it. It will protect you."

The significance the emblem *Asho Farohar* carried? I was told that when our Prophet Zarathustra trod on this earth he introduced to the world the first monolithic religion. One of the concepts he explained was about the making of a being. Every living being had three parts to it; the Body, the Soul and the Farvashi or Farohar. The Farohar, the guardian spirit of a being, was the element of God in you to help one to choose between good and evil... in modern terms, one's conscience. Upon death the body turns to dust, the soul is held answerable for ones deeds and the Farvashi returns within God, untouched, pure and sinless.

I humbly accepted it, and when I was alone again I checked it out. It was very old and rugged and the chain was so large the emblem reached my stomach. It was crude and the figure of the spread out wings with a man's head was definitely the work of an amateur. Worse, the whole thing was made up of some cheap metal, *that was not even silver*! What will my friends say when they see it? One thing I was sure of, nobody will want to pinch it from me.

Just then I heard an uproar in the main room, above the feisty sounds of our guests.

"Three men are coming down the mountains," someone shouted. "It's those tax collectors, I think."

"But they were here just a week ago," I heard my father say. "*Quick! Carry the Urn into the kitchen.*"

Two men hurriedly carried it to the kitchen and set it next to our cooking fire. "Even if they come here, they'll think it is part of the regular kitchen fire."

“Oh no,” my father suddenly cried out. “*Father,* you too must hide in the kitchen. No time for you to hide anywhere else.”

“*Me, hide? Again!* Son, you are expecting too much of me!”

“Please father, you must understand. This has nothing to do with you or your dignity. This is for the entire village. You know well what could happen if they recognise you.”

With a great ‘Hrmph…’ grandfather strode off to the kitchen as though he was being sent to the prison again.

A few minutes later the cocky tax-collectors rode in. It was not difficult for them to zero in to our house directly.

“Salaam, *Ajams*! Salaam to you all.” The leader called out jovially as they got off their horses. “Celebrations? Good, good. See we allow you your moments of joy, too. But who appreciates such leniency?”

My father, who had quickly changed his white priestly robes to the mandatory honey-coloured one, tried smiling as he welcomed them. “But we do, Sir, we certainly appreciate your leniency. Please come in and join us.”

“Sedra-Pushun!” The leader said spitting on the pathway. *How did they know?* We always suspected spies in Yazd. “You know it is prohibited! That’s the problem with you *Ajams*. We allow you to exist in peace, and what do you do in return? Perform illegal ceremonies.”

By now all three had entered our house. The other guests looked extremely uncomfortable and gathered on one side of the room. The leader rubbed his hands as he gleefully noticed the food on the table and the womenfolk in the corner.

“Please help yourselves,” my father offered. “Our food is yours.”

“Of course it is!” The leader said, laughing at his own brand of humour. “So, no need to offer. We’ll take what we like, when we like.”

As his colleagues helped themselves off the table, they looked at the womenfolk with lust.

Manashni! Didn’t they know it was wrong, and demonstrated a sinful mentality?

The leader snooped around to other sections of the house.

“Something smells different here,” he said sniffing aloud and heading for the kitchen. We all held our breath, knowing what was within.

We don’t know what happened inside but in next to no time he was out again. His grin had worn off as he tried to bully my father again.

“So what special token of appreciation for our co-operation will you offer us this time?" An ugly sneer had replaced the grin. "Come on, Ajam, speak up! Or do you want another kick up your backside to get you activated, you chicken-livered pig?"

Gavashni! Whatever happened to kind words? Father was doing his best to co-operate so why use such words?

They had spotted the silverware on display so without further fanfare my father emptied out a few, placed them in a sack and gave it to them. They took fancy to some of the ornamental tableware and without a word put them into the sack, too.

Khunashni! A little consideration for the host, their auspicious occasion and their ceremonial instruments, would have gone a long way as good deeds in our eyes.

The sack and their tummies full they prepared to leave. "And," the leader pushed a finger into my father's chest, "you better teach that cook of yours in the kitchen some manners. Not only did he glare at me, but he is wearing white robes, and you know that's illegal. I'm letting you all off today, knowing it's a big day for you. But don't let it happen again." Then throwing a quick glance towards the kitchen, he followed his friends and rode off.

The big question they left behind, *did they recognize Zahl?*

There was a collective sigh of relief when the sounds of the galloping hooves faded away. But the festive mood was ruined and no one was in the mood to enjoy any longer. A few nibbled at the goodies laid out and went back to their homes, hours before the scheduled time.

When the house was empty again, my mother cried, my father looked sullen and my grandfather, who returned from the kitchen with a leg of roast mutton, glared at the door as though it was responsible for letting the tax-collectors in.

Thus ended one of the most significant and memorable days of my life, my *Sedra-Pushun* ceremony. My mind was full of questions, my tummy empty, and my scrawny neck sported a worthless piece of metal with a strict warning that I was never to remove it.

❑❑❑

8

Our village from that day onwards became very quiet. It had never been a place of gaiety or fun after my Sedra-Pushun ceremony it seemed everyone was waiting for something ominous to happen. Nobody was seen outdoors, not even my friends. Nobody chatted towards evening as they used to. And if by chance anyone had to pass our house, it was with an acutely bent head. It was clear to us; Zahl's presence was not welcome.

Suddenly on the third day after my initiation we got a huge scare.

"The taxman has come back!" The warning was given by our sentry. We constantly maintained this vigil, a lookout on the veranda of our outermost house, so that we get a chance to organise ourselves against such unscheduled calls.

"Quick father," Peshotan cried, hurrying into our house, "into the back alley and the stables. This time you must hide in the hidden passage with the holy *Urn.*"

Before Zahl could comprehend the urgency, he was whisked away through the back door, into the alley and into the stables. A lightening quick adjustment to the partition and Zahl was pushed into the hidden passage.

"So where is your leader, the one you call Peshotan?"

Peshotan heard the chief tax collector and half ran back to his house vide the back-door. "Coming Sire," he shouted back, adjusting his attire and ensuring everything in the house was as it should be. He opened his door and stepped out with a smile. This time the tax collector had come with five armed guards. This could mean trouble. "We weren't expecting you back so early, Sire."

"That tall cook, I want to talk to him." He got to the subject immediately.

"Last two days I was wondering about him. I've never seen him before, so where did he spring from?"

Father had to do some quick thinking. "The tall cook? Ah, I know who you mean. Tehmasp. That's what he told us his name was. Sire, neither was he a cook, nor a fellow villager. He was just a traveller. He had walked in that morning and seeing there was a celebration on, and some free food, he helped himself to some in the kitchen. He left our village an hour after you had gone."

The tax collector skirted Peshotan and walked into our house. I saw him and got nervous. His eyes looked wicked and dangerous. I was sure he would not fall for my father's lie. He walked straight toward me.

"Boy! Why are you looking so tense?" He was suddenly smiling and trying to look as casual as possible. All the while his snake-like eyes studied those present in the room. He stroked my head and asked softly, "Where is the tall man with one hand?"

I was not known for any great feats of bravery so I thought it best to keep my mouth shut. Suddenly he grabbed a bunch of my hair and pulled. I involuntarily let out a yelp and looked helplessly toward my father.

Here was another reason I wanted to get taller fast. My current height was just too convenient for the seniors. My head reached just about the height of their fists. So before I know it I become the recipient of a quick slap on the back of my head, or get my ears twisted and now even my hair pulled.

My mother stepped forward and tried to set me free. "Leave him alone, you bully!" she shouted. One firm push from the tax collector and she went crashing on to the table. Instantly my father and brother rushed forward to grab him.

"Guards!" he bellowed and three of the guards charged in, swords drawn. My father and brother, Farehdun, were pushed back.

"Now tell me youngster," the tax collector turned to me again, his hold on my hair still firm, "where is that tall man?"

Tears had welled up in my eyes when I saw my mother fall earlier, and now as he twisted my hair hard, they spilled over.

"Ha, ha, ha!" tax collector laughed aloud. "Just like an *Ajam* is expected to be. *Cry-boobies!"* He suddenly pulled my hair so strongly I was sure that soon I'll be the youngest bald-headed fellow in the country. He not only pulled the hair, he swung my head as though it were a toy, making me lose my balance. "Tell me, little girl," he again laughed at his own joke, "where is that man?"

"He's gone," I said, trying my best not to let the crack in my voice be noticed. "But he promised before leaving that he'll chase every barbarian out of our country."

I knew I shouldn't have said that. The tax collector loosened his grip on my hair in disbelief as he readied for a violent rebuff.

"Why are you questioning a little boy?" my father came to my rescue. "You are not satisfied with our answers, then search the village!"

I was expecting a heavy slap before being set free, but it never came. The tax collector just let go of me and shouted, "*Out everyone! We'll search every inch of every house in the village.*"

So that's what they did for the next three hours. They didn't indulge in niceties as they barged into every house and checked every inch of it. When they didn't find anything worthwhile in the house they searched the back alley. They entered the stables but the stench of our faithful cows and horses brought them out quickly. Loud snarls and dagger looks from Noshirwan, discouraged them from further investigations.

Search over, they left the village sullenly.

They left, but they left behind a very worried village. We were simply thankful that neither Zahl, nor our holy fire in the cave, were discovered. Yes, we had escaped, but barely.

❑

"*Never do that to me again!*" seethed Zahl as he emerged from the stables. "I don't hide from soldiers."

I could see he was controlling his temper, just about. I dreaded to see the day he would blow up.

"It had to be done." Peshotan replied nervously. "For the sake of the village."

"You've already said that before. But surely there has to be a limit beyond which you will not bow down. Whatever has happened to the noble Persian spirit?"

"It blew away with the winds of Nehavand."

Father seemed to be in a hurry to get away but Zahl stuck to him.

"Nehavand, Nehavand…that's all I hear of since I returned, but I still don't know the whole story. I know we lost that battle. So what? We lost battles before, *but we never became mice*. We always fought back."

Father stopped and looked hard at Zahl. "Okay, you want to hear all of it, you will! Battle of Nehavand wasn't a one-day affair. And it didn't end at Nehavand either. Thirty three years down the line and we're are still battling the effects."

"I'm listening. Why did we lose?"

I had heard much about that battle, but never in systematic details. I wanted to know more so I stuck close to them. We were still in the back alley, and quite on our own.

"They say it was the beginning of the end," started Peshotan. "But really, it was the end. The main battle lasted but a few days. It was what happened after the battle that really defeated us. They never allowed us to recover. Each day pushing our spirits and will to live, a step backward. Each day robbing us of some dignity. Each day reminding us of who we now were and what they expected of us. Each day raiding, raping and plundering our people. Each day converting thousands into their religion. Each day executing thousands who defied. *Each day was an eternity to us*."

Peshotan paused as I saw a lump on his throat bob. He controlled his feelings and continued.

"It was not as though the play unfolded day by day. *It was all well planned*...to break our spirit. Into our cities and villages they poured, shouting, 'Convert, or die!' In the beginning we did resist strongly, hitting back with rebel groups and runaway soldiers. Nobody converted to Islam easily. Then the bloodshed started. Thousands upon thousands executed daily, hangings or plain slaughter…men, women, children…didn't make a difference to them. First a few Zoroastrians took the safe road and converted, but the killings didn't stop. It was not long before the wholesale conversions started, and that was not difficult. All one needed to do to convert to Islam was to pronounce the *Shahada*.

"And yet the persecutions continued. They demeaned us, even the converted ones, degraded us and humiliated us at the slightest opportunity. Many, like us, left the cities and towns and elected to live in remote places like this village. It was once inhabited by Zarthosties, but they were all massacred at one go. A few years later we found it deserted, and made it our home. We, of course, have to constantly appease our conquerors, in the form of taxes and gifts. The system has worked for the last twenty five years, and we don't want to disturb it."

Zahl had remained mute during the disclosure, but he was far from content as he heard his son, uttering guttural sounds now and then.

"But why did we lose at Nehavand?"

"You should know better. King Yazdegird III was almost alone in this fight. He got little support from his princes and the army was mostly stationed in other territories. When the Arabs crossed the Zagros Mountains and threatened to invade Persia, Yazdegird had to depend upon the civil population to help him. We did. We raised an army of almost 150,000 men, but very few amongst us were professional soldiers."

"I heard the Arabs had an army of just 25,000 men. And they defeated such a large army?"

"I told you we had no fighting skills, and knew even less about battle tactics."

"But we had the numbers!" Zahl thundered, thrusting his clenched fist into the air. "And we're known for our courage, so what happened? Why did we still lose?"

Peshotan felt Zahl's accusing eyes on him and made him feel almost guilty for the defeat. Doesn't he remember Peshotan was only seven years old at that period of time? But how will he remember? Zahl was not there. He never was there. He was either fighting in some far out place or, rotting in some prison.

"At one stage I believe the Arabs were on the run." Peshotan decided to forgive Zahl's attitude and continued. "Our army chased them blindly into the mountains, and suddenly, they were surrounded. The Arabs had fooled them into a trap. A bizarre massacre followed, and the Arabs poured into our country. They had only one agenda on their list, convert every Zoroastrian into the Islam religion. And they set about that task immediately."

A thousand years ago, Zahl remembered his history, Alexander the Great had similarly invaded Persia and sacked it thoroughly. *But he did not demand any conversions!* He was a conqueror, and conquering territories was his sole aim. And neither did they, the Persians, convert the people of the countries they had conquered. And there were plenty of those. When the Persian Empire was on its way to become the largest empire, their army had conquered many other nations. But not once had they put the vanquished country's religion in danger. They allowed free religious thoughts and only the ones who wanted to convert to Zoroastrianism, were taken into our religion. And this was the norm through the ages, for centuries.

So why were we then put to such shame?

A shuffling sound came and we turned to see Minocher stepping into the alley. He saw Zahl and turned around again and disappeared.

"What's wrong with that man?" Zahl demanded.

"Minocher? Nothing. Why?"

“Every time he sees me he looks as though he’s swallowed a live frog. I haven’t harmed him, so why does he behave such?”

“Er…I don’t know. Maybe…”

“Maybe he just needs a lesson in good manners.” Zahl started walking briskly towards Minocher.

I thought this was a happy change from the depressing talk of war and persecution. And I didn’t much care for Minocher either.

“Wait father, wait…” Peshotan quickened his pace to block Zahl from going further. “S*top it, father, will you please*?”

Zahl stopped and looked inquiringly at his son. “What?”

“Haven’t we had enough excitement for the day already, without you taking on Minocher? This village has got used to living a life in low profile. We don’t want anything to upset that. Minocher simply thinks your presence will…”

“Will what?”

“Nothing. Let’s just forget about all this.”

But Peshotan had already said too much.

❑❑❑

9

That night I couldn't sleep so I walked out to our shabby porch and sat with my legs dangling out. The half moon was shining to its full potential, covering the village in its gentle light. There were lamps burning in some of the windows of our neighbours, but it was quieter than other nights. The invasion on our privacy by the tax collector and his guards had left us all worried and thinking. It also left us insecure and lonely.

"It's cold out here son." Dughdova, my mother, came and sat beside me. Hers has always been a firm but gentle hand as she brought up her three children. It was a difficult job, under the circumstances. She always made sure we never went to sleep hungry, or sad, and there were many a day when that could have happened. Her quiet authority maintained a sense of security and balance amongst us youngsters. And her arms were the ultimate medicine for any sickness…physical, mental or emotional. But the best part of her that I appreciated most was her talent in treating us children equally. There never was a favourite. She distributed equal doses of slaps and hugs, and never held grudges against a misdemeanour.

"Couldn't sleep, mother." My hand automatically slipped under her arm. Suddenly things didn't look so depressing and lonely. I was vacantly studying the dark mountains around us, fleetingly admiring the silver outline of every rock. But my mind was elsewhere. "Mother, why don't they leave us in peace? We're not bothering anyone in this far-out place."

"Don't worry son, we'll be okay once again. It has been prophesised many, many years ago that our religion will go through three bad phases, each time we'll come out of the dark phase stronger than before, until finally, we'll reign supreme once again."

"Three times? Is this the first bad phase?"

"No. The first difficult period for us was almost a thousand years ago when Alexander invaded our land and destroyed most of our scriptures and cultural places. In time we got over that period and had become very powerful worldwide again. Some believe that we once again came to being destroyed about four hundred years ago, but recovered to rule again. This must be the third time our religion faces devastation. But I'm sure we'll soon come out of this phase, too, and be even stouter Zoroastrians and human beings."

"And if we fall once again? Will we be obliterated forever?"

She smiled with a far out look. "You know what I believe? I believe that our religion is like the Huma bird…indestructible. Just as the Phoenix rises from its own ashes, and then continues its life for another long period, and then goes up in flames only to rise again, and again, and again. So will we."

It sounded good, but honestly I seriously wondered if we'll ever come out of this difficult period at all. If the Arabs despised us as much as they showed then how could we survive their reign? They had already succeeded in breaking us, so it was just a matter of time before we totally give in and cease to exist.

"But this regular dose of humiliation has begun to bother. Makes me wonder if there is anything now for us to live for. Why should we go on with this struggle? Why not simply wake up tomorrow?"

Mother looked at me as though this was the first time she was seeing me. "We will go on waking up every morning because in our hearts there must reside at all times an ally called *hope*...hope that we once again will live with dignity and freedom. The day we lose hope is the day we are doomed...and stop playing with that. You'll break it." With that she smacked my hand that was fiddling with the chain that held the *Asho Farohar* Zahl had given me.

"Why do I have to wear it all the time? It's so heavy and uncomfortable."

"You'll get used to it in time, and as your grandfather said, it will protect you always."

"I have the *Sedra* and *kushti* to protect me now. Isn't that enough? Why do I have to wear another religious symbol?"

I heard a shuffling sound behind me and I knew more than two of the family couldn't sleep. My father ruffled my hair with a smile. He always found my questions amusing.

"Because it is more than just a religious symbol," explained Peshotan patiently. "It is a family heirloom. This *Asho Farohar* was crafted by one of our ancestors, three hundred years ago, and has been passed on from father to son on his *Sedra-Pushun* ceremony, down all those years. I should have received it at my initiation, but alas, Zahl was captured and imprisoned. Now you are the possessor of the most cherished treasure of our family."

Goose pimples ran through my body as I heard my father. I held the talisman tighter in my fist as I felt the lives of all my ancestors run through my fingers. I promised myself there and then that I, too, will protect this treasure while it is with me, and duly pass it on to my son, on his *Sedra-Pushun*.

Later that night I couldn't sleep at all. All sorts of thoughts invaded my dreams. I saw myself in a shiny armour, riding into battle, at the head of a vast army. I saw a noble figure smiling and blessing me. I saw angry and ugly enemies screaming and charging towards me, and I am holding them back single-handed, shouting 'nobody will endanger my religion again'.

And just when I was beginning to enjoy my valour I saw the old man in the mountains float towards me and tell me, 'Leave this country, if you want to save your religion'.

I got up sweating and shaking…and totally confused.

❑

"You had told me this village liked to keep a low profile," Zahl spoke to my father a couple of days after the incident. "But now it seems to be dead. What's got into your neighbours?"

We were tending to the *Urn* at the stables. Once a day we placed small logs around the holy fire. These glowed by the heat of the burning embers, and burnt slowly throughout the day. Sandal wood was offered only twice a day as we had a limited supply.

"They're worried that you may have been recognised by that tax-collector. He would not have come back just for a vagrant." My father had put on his white cap as he attended to his duties.

"*Recognised?* How? They all think I'm dead. That man returned with his guards because he felt there was more juice to be extracted from this bunch of chickens you call neighbours. If instead you would have acted more aggressively, it probably would have been the last time you'd have seen him." Annoyed, Zahl shifted to the doorway and watched Noshirwan, the ironsmith, at his work.

"Last time, you say? Yes! But not because of what you think. Last time, because they will have wiped us out clean, once and for all. *That's* what the neighbours are scared of."

"*Bah!* They seem to be scared of everything. Whatever has happened to the courage we Persians were known for?" For the umpteenth time in just a few days Zahl again reminded us of our weaknesses. He picked up a large hammer in his left hand and helped Noshirwan in shaping a piece of metal. It was difficult balancing the tool and he often missed the target. He saw me smile at his clumsiness and scowled. I quickly returned to my father's side. In his anger Zahl brought the hammer down harder than he should have and the metal piece shattered into fragments. "They should think of hitting back, *instead of scuttling around like rats in a gutter!* Why can't they even try to plan a strategy, anything, to show them we're not dead? This silence only encourages the Arabs to call us *Ajam* and such!"

The argument was taking a dangerous turn and I wished I had not smiled.

"*Because they know what it is to defy these people!*" Now my father was heating up. "Most have suffered personally and submission is all they know today. We were not enjoying living like refugees, but we had little choice if we wanted to maintain our religion. Now they fear the worst. They feel your presence here will bring them trouble, sooner or later. *They don't like you to be here.*"

The hurt on Zahl's face would have melted the heart of Zuhak, the fabled evil king said to be in chains somewhere on Mount Demavend. In an instant Zahl tossed aside the sledge hammer as though it were a small spike.

"Very well, so I shall leave!" With that he turned around and headed for home.

"I didn't mean for you to leave," cried my father hurrying after him. "You know you are welcome to live with us. But we have to be more careful... more..."

"*Cowardly?* Like your friends? *Scared of my own shadow?* Is that how you want me to be?"

"I didn't say that. I just want you..."

"Not another word!" bellowed Zahl. "I will leave this instant, and I will show you all how a Persian warrior lives. I will retreat into the mountains! I will raise an army! *And I will hit back at these savages!"*

With that he stomped off.

"And I'm coming with you," said the burly Noshirwan, tossing aside his tools of trade and picking up two stout swords he had made and hid them in the stables. He turned to Peshotan, "Don't worry, I'll look after him. *God*, I've been *waiting* for a day like this."

Ten minutes later, the two were ready to set off. Noshirwan carried some bare essentials he felt they needed. Zahl stood empty handed, a sword tucked in his belt.

"Please father," Peshotan pleaded, "this is not the right step. You will be caught and punished before they kill you. Let's try and work out another plan. There has to be another…"

But his pleading remained with him as the two men, along with some of us, reached the outer limits of the village. My mother and Noshirwan's wife stood together with tears in their eyes. And between them stood Mahafrid, hollering for all she was worth.

There was no reasoning with these two resolute men. There was no hesitation in their strides as they walked on. From the neighbours' windows peeped a few pairs of nervous eyes. Happy to see the back of the man they feared would invite trouble. Yet for some, there were mixed feelings. It's not easy to let a hero walk away.

"Wait for me!" Ardeshir came jogging, a small sack on his shoulder. "I'll join you, too."

Now they were three.

Suddenly Zahl stopped. He turned to me and hesitated. He wanted to tell me something but couldn't find the words.

"Always remember who we were," he said in a gruff voice. "And never forget your religion, else all will be lost."

Not a large parting speech, but it said all.

We waited till they reached the mountains. Without a backward glance they disappeared behind some rocks. When completely out of sight the rest turned around and started walking back to their homes. I remained there alone; wanting to catch a last sight of my grandfather, from a small gap in the mountain wall that I knew existed. After some time they reached that spot and to my amazement he stopped right there and looked back. Ardeshir must have known of the gap, also, as he pointed towards me. I saw Zahl stare downward for some time before he raised his left hand in a short wave. I waved back. And then they were gone.

Later, we heard many stories of them, but that was the last time I saw my grandfather, the great Zahl…the man who had returned to our lives barely two weeks ago, but who will remain etched in my mind forever.

❑

There was a community discussion going on when I reached home. As usual, my father was in the middle of it. I've never seen him look so distraught and helpless. An old man, the community's elder, came forward and placed a gentle hand on Peshotan's shoulder. "Don't distress yourself so much," he said softly. "It is best this way. If he had remained here, he would have died a slow death. There is no place for a man like him in this country any longer."

Peshotan nodded in quiet submission. He must have known he'll never see his father again. To reunite after so many years, and then separate again within a few days was unfair. There was so much for them to share, but alas, life was never meant to unfold as you would like it to.

"Now we must take care of the other danger in our village," said our neighbour, Minocher, now joining us. "We must remove the Urn."

"Are you calling the holy fire a danger?" My father was no longer in any mood for loose talk.

"It will be a danger to itself, if the Arabs come back looking for Zahl." The man whose voice couldn't be heard when Zahl was around, now let himself be heard louder than before. Minocher quickly took the lead by raising his voice further as others joined the small party. For its safety we must take the *Urn* to the mountains, until we're sure the danger is over. We've been lucky till now no one has discovered the holy fire. But we cannot take things for granted any longer, or this village may get annihilated."

Much to the reluctance of most it was decided to temporarily shift the sacred fire to a cave...the very cave Zahl had hid in barely a week ago. Peshotan was to go daily to the cave and attend to it.

A small party carried away the Urn. Some of us walked behind in a line, maintaining a studious silence, as though a funeral was on. We hid the vessel deep inside the cave, so that no light from it could be seen from the entrance. I did not feel as depressed as the rest as I felt the holy fire was instead bringing light and warmth to a place that has always been cold and lonely. The inside of the cave was now so gaily lighted. I thought the little fire, too, was happy as it's flames danced about joyfully.

But it was painful when it was time to return. It was like we were abandoning our very own child to the wilderness. Peshotan had already felt that way when his father left, now he felt totally hollow and void within. He went straight to his room, locked it from inside, and didn't come out the rest of the day.

We couldn't see the cave or the glow from the village but we knew exactly where it was. So thereafter every morning and night, we would fold our hands and bow towards that particular spot on the mountain.

❑❑❑

10

"A giant with one hand?" Screamed Sayyid Abul Yaser. *"Why wasn't I told about this earlier?"*

The tax collector shivered at the rage unfurled at him. Two days after their second trip to the Zoroastrian village he had casually boasted to a friend in Yazd of the giant he claimed to have bullied. Two days later he was rounded up by the spies of the governor of Pars and brought to Shiraz, their temporary headquarters, a few miles away from the ruins of Persepolis.

"But…we didn't know it was important…"

"*Shut up!* When did this take place?"

"Now about five days ago…but he was not there when we went back two days later. They said he was only a wanderer."

"*Allah be merciful!* How am I to govern this province with oafs like this?" He seriously considered slaughtering this man on the spot for ruining his chances of being a hero again. But he needed him for the time being. "Get the horses ready," he yelled to his commander. "This man will take us straight away to this village he talks about. We will find that man," he turned to the tax collector with a sinister look, "or you'll wish you had never left Arabia."

Yaser and his troops reached the little Zoroastrian village two days later. It was mid-day and no one was out, but the thunder of 50 horses galloping in changed the scenario almost instantly. Curt orders were given and every villager, every man, woman and child were rounded up and made to wait in the sun.

Next the troops ransacked the village. Every piece of furniture was thrown out of the house, every corner of every room closely examined, and they checked for secret basements and niches in the walls. A lot of hidden jewellery and gold was discovered, but they were simply flung away in contempt. When the houses were complete they searched the surrounding area. The back alley was equally scoured. The secret compartment in the stables was not a secret two minutes after they entered the place. They pulled down the partition walls and called Yaser to inspect their discovery.

After a quiet inspection Yaser returned to the villagers. Till now he had not bothered to ask them a single question. Now he paced the road in front of them. Meanwhile, the tax collector today was a mere shadow of himself, skulking in the background; fear writ on his face.

"A secret room," he almost murmured to himself. Suddenly he looked at Peshotan sharply, knowing he was the group's leader. "What could you have hidden there?"

Peshotan gulped softly, trying his best not to show his nervousness. He had never seen this man before but he could guess his identity. Yaser's notoriety had far preceded his appearance. *This was the man responsible for the liquidation of his earlier family in Pars*. This was the man he had escaped from as a boy. This was the man who boasted of defeating Zahl in the battle of Qadisiyah, of killing him and claiming the prized trophy, the celebrated mace, as his own. If the powerful governor of Pars was here, then they were in serious trouble. He quietly prayed that his name, Mahraspandan, be not known to him…or his current family would be wiped out, too.

"It is no secret room, Sire," Peshotan replied nervously. "It is simply a storeroom for the stables. It…"

"*Shut up!* Take me to be a *fool?*" When I saw his eyes I thought I was looking at a snake. How could such a handsome man turn to something so vile in seconds? He carried some kind of a whip for his horse, and he brought this down on my father with vengeance. As my father fell the evil man, in a kind of frenzy, rained down this whip several times on him. His robe in shreds and blood oozing out of several cuts, Peshotan tried standing up but immediately collapsed. As he got back to his knees I could see my mother trying to rush to help him, but some neighbours forcefully held her back. Nobody else moved.

I could bear it no longer. I ran to where my father lay and tried getting him to his feet. A moment later, you guessed it, Yaser had me by my hair.

"A boy with more courage than all of you put together?" he asked, forcing my head towards the ground. My Asho Farohar came out from within my tunic and dangled an inch above the ground.

Yaser let go of my hair and set his attention on my ornament. "Aha! What have we here?" He held it in his palm and yanked. I felt a sharp pain in my neck, but the chain held on. Yaser pulled at it harder, sending me down on all fours. But the chain didn't break. Frustrated, he pulled it from above my neck and examined it.

"*Bah!* Your fancy soul-saver. *Today only I can save your souls, you miserable lot!"* With disgust he flung the Asho Farohar across the road. *"Do you understand that!!"* he bellowed.

Finally, the village elder stepped forward. "If you can tell us what you want, maybe we can help."

A guttural chain of laughter from Yaser. "Help? Ha,ha, ha! *From you?* Ha, ha, ha. Old man, who needs your help? But yes, you'll need some help soon. *A lot of help!"*

Yaser was perspiring freely now as he surveyed the rest of the villagers again. He hadn't had so much fun in a long time. "So who's going to tell me where the tall man with one arm went?"

Total silence followed as everyone tried to avert eye contact with him. As I was the only one staring at him, he stared back. Then he started walking towards me. I braced myself for another hair-pulling session.

"If it is the tall man you are seeking, we already informed the tax-collector that he has gone." The village elder, Eruch's grandfather, was not yet subdued. The rest of Eruch's family was wiped out by the Arabs in a raid earlier at Yazd. His grandfather had escaped the city with Eruch, only a baby then, and found his way to this village. They were amongst the last of the settlers here.

Yaser's colour changed as though he was a chameleon. Red-faced he looked down at the old man as if he would strangle him there and then. But he didn't do any such thing. He just slapped him with force with the back of his hand. The old man stumbled and hit the ground hard. He tried getting up, but I think he broke his hip bone, as he winced and stayed down. Instantly, Eruch was by his side but a couple of soldiers dragged him back. Rustom, his friend, tried restraining him to avoid further trouble.

"So who's going to tell me, where did the giant go?" Yaser once again turned to the villagers, confident he'll get his answer. But now he saw a change in the villagers. They looked angry and didn't seem to be as cowed down as they initially behaved. Good. Some fight-back finally. "No one? Okay, maybe you need some encouragement."

He walked up to the officer of his troops and said something calmly to him. The officer shouted out an order and two of his men picked up Eruch's grandfather and put him on a horse. A long rope materialised from nowhere, a noose was made and placed around the old man's neck. The other end of the rope was tossed over a projection from one of the roofs and fastened to a banister.

"*Last time!* Where did the giant go?"

No answer. Eruch tried shaking off the hands of his friends, screaming, "*Let him go!* Please let him go!"

Yaser nodded his head. A sharp smack on its hind and the horse sprinted off. Eruch's grandfather fell off it, but not to the ground. The rope held him a foot above. There was an anguished sigh as the old man hung in mid-air, swaying quietly in the still mountain air. He twisted and gurgled for a minute, and then all was quiet as he hung there lifeless.

The villagers looked on, stunned. Eruch was wailing aloud as Rustom tried to shield his eyes. It was the most shocking event of my life. But before I could get over it I heard Yaser's confident voice.

"So who's next?"

A chilled gloom passed over all as they could not tear their eyes off the swaying figure on the rope.

"No one yet? Okay, maybe you need time to absorb today's events. I'll come back tomorrow. I better have the right answer then, or *ten* of you will be hanging in the air."

"Sire, back to Shiraz?" asked his commander.

"No! We'll be guests of the governor at Yazd. It's just 30 miles away, so we can return as planned. Meanwhile," he turned to his men and said maliciously, "not a word of the reason for our presence to anyone there. If word leaks out why we are here, I'll have the tongues of all fifty of you, pulled out!"

"And what if these Zarthoshties try to escape during the night?"

"*HA!* Where will they go? But let them try. I will personally catch each and every one of them and what they'll get is something that will make this demonstration today, seem like a picnic."

With that they all rode off. But nobody moved amongst the villagers, even as Eruch wailed on holding his grandfather's feet to his chest.

That was my first sight of death. And I didn't like it. I was numb with fear and couldn't tear my eyes away from the horrific spectacle. I knew that image of the old man's body, silently swinging in mid-air, will remain in my mind like an unwelcome guest, for the rest of my days.

I quickly retrieved my Asho Farohar and silently vowed that I'll never again let anyone remove my grandfather's gift from me, that easily. And I also vowed that I will never give myself to their ways. And if possible, I'll listen to the voice of the old man on the mountain and somehow escape the clutches of these murderers, *even if I have to leave my country.*

❑

After a little while Peshotan carried out a tall stool and with the help of a shaking Eruch, brought down the body of the old man.

"We'll now pray for his soul and then take him up to the mountain to lay his body to rest."

"We don't have time for such niceties," protested Minocher. "Didn't you hear that governor? We need to decide immediately what we should do."

"We need time to think, too. We'll think as we pray and go up the mountain." Peshotan didn't wait for anyone's help as he arranged a small temporary fire and began reciting the rituals prayed for the dead. He ignored the deep cuts he had received from the whip lashing, burning as they must be, and continued with his duties. Slowly and hesitatingly the others assembled around the corpse.

Thirty minutes later, upon completion of the prayers, a party of ten men, including Eruch and Rustom, lifted the old man on a make-shift stretcher and silently made their way to the mountain where the dead were earlier taken. It was an improvised *dokhma,* but it served the purpose.

Zoroastrians do not believe in either burying or burning their dead. They do not wish to pollute either the ground or the fire. They leave the bodies on a high mountain top for nature to take its own course. In minutes the vultures and other big birds clean the body of all flesh, and the strong sun and wind in time dry the remains till nothing is left. A natural and hygienic method of disposing the dead.

"So what do we do now?" Minocher wasted no time as they wound their way back towards their village.

"We shall have to leave this place," said Peshotan through gritted teeth.

"*Leave?*" One of the villagers spoke up. "How can we leave this place after calling it home for such a long time? Why not simply tell them which way Zahl and the others went? They will not be able to catch up with them now, and we can be left in peace so that we can at least follow our religion."

Peshotan stopped abruptly and glared at the man. "*They will never leave us in peace!* Not after today. And how can you call this hide-and-seek game we are constantly playing, a peaceful existence? We hide our most precious gift every time we see those hooligans, *and you call it following your religion?*"

All silently trudged on. Finally our quietest neighbour Phiruz spoke up. "And where do you suggest we go? They're at every corner of our country."

"For everyone's safety, it is best that only a few know where we're going. Phiruz and Minocher, who I know will not stay back, will suffice to know my plans. The rest, who wish to take their chances with us, should go home and start packing. We leave tomorrow morning, before dawn."

As the rest started dispersing, Minocher called out, "Rustom, from today Eruch will be with us, wherever we go. Take him home, and prepare for our departure."

I always wondered about Minocher's motives, his over-careful ways and his uncooperative attitude. But there never was any doubt of his loyalty to my father.

When the three were alone Peshotan divulged his plans.

"I think our best chances will be to go to Quhistan, in the southern section of Khorasan province. I heard that Zoroastrians are much safer there. There are thousands of Zoroastrians in that region who still maintain their religion, and as the governor there is more lenient, some of our fire temples have been left untouched."

"*Khorasan!* How can we get there?" Minocher looked aghast. "The great salt deserts are in between. No way will we, along with our families, be able to cross that vast expanse of arid land. And if we try to skirt the deserts by taking the north road to Rhagae and then turn eastwards, it could take us over a year to reach Quhistan."

"That is the point. We will not have to take the northern route. We will not even have to travel across either Dasht-e-Kavir or Dasht-e-Lut. *There is a route between the two salt deserts that very few people know of.*"

Minocher looked completely bewildered. "Between the deserts? Never heard of it."

"It is hardly being used, but between the deserts there is a narrow strip of small hills and mountains. It will be along this chain of hills that I aim to cross over to Quhistan."

Minocher and Piruz thought Peshotan had lost his mind. A group of fifty, with old people, children and cattle, hiking over parts of salt deserts, mountains, and God knows what? It cannot be done.

"And what about the heat and water? You know that area is just about the hottest and driest in our country. We will die of that heat if we are out in the open. And the thirst? There is no fresh water in that region. How can we carry gallons of water?"

"I believe there are small settlements for about a hundred miles from both ends. They could help us. That means we may have less than three hundred miles only where we'll be on our own. Look, it certainly won't be any picnic, but if we travel by night it'll be cooler, and safer. But believe me folks, that heat will be nothing compared to that of the governor...*if we stay back here.*"

That brought back everyone's thinking process to the right perspective.

"Why not go to Kerman?" asked Minocher. "It is so much nearer, without having to cross salt deserts. And our people are there, too."

Peshotan let out a sigh of impatience. "Because it is the most obvious place. Equally obvious is the western road to Esfahan. If we take either of the routes that governor with his men will be on our backs in a day's time. And if he catches us, it'll be *mass-murder and nothing short of that.* Don't forget, he's the man who boasts of defeating Zahl in battle and capturing his mace. We'll have to out-think that man...or we're in deep trouble. He wants Zahl, or he'll make us pay for it."

"What about the Hyrcania region in the north? I believe our people are living quite freely there and the Arabs fear going there. It would be a much easier journey."

"To go there," Peshotan explained patiently, "we'll have to use either the Esfahan route, or the Yazd route. Both will be thoroughly checked by Yaser. We'll be caught in a matter of a couple of days. The same reasoning applies to our not going south to Hormuz. Zoroastrians are comparatively free there, as well. But these routes will be plugged by Yaser and his men. We'll have to take a course that is totally unexpected and seemingly impossible to them. *That's our only hope.*"

"And you know this route between the deserts, to Khorasan?" asked Piruz, after some thought.

"I know where to start from. We'll have to take it from there in stages. There will be a total of about 500 miles between us and our destination...all rough country. But it is our only hope. At the crack of dawn tomorrow, I'll leave with my family. Whoever wishes to join us is welcome."

Saying that with some finality, Peshotan made his way towards his home.

❑❑❑

11

A heavy heart! Never knew what it meant till now.

When father walked in that night and announced his decision to leave the village, a strange mood set in. First the shock of the move gripped us all into a sort of dumb response. Duties were allotted to us and we went about completing them in silence.

I had felt sadness earlier, particularly when mother scolded me. I had been disappointed earlier, mostly when I was never allowed to leave this valley…neither me nor my siblings had ever seen the world beyond these mountains. But what I felt now was different. I should be glad we're finally leaving this 'prison', and finally making an attempt to live a free life. But instead, there was an unexplained lump in my throat and I suddenly felt the urge to re-visit every inch of the village.

We had decided to take two of our mules; one to carry a full load, and the other to carry half load, and one rider. Mother and Mahafrid, were to select the most essential clothing required for the family, sufficient food and a few utensils. My brother, Farehdun, and I were in charge of one mule each so we set about preparing their light harnesses and their food. Farehdun had the added responsibility of bundling the poultry in a strong net for hanging on one side of the mules.

I could never control the mules and was always wary of their back kicks, but Farehdun helped me out and my share of the duties was completed first. He could actually make the beast listen to him and make them do whatever he wished. Making a mule move forward was itself a task. The only method I knew was a sharp whack on its hind. But with Farehdun there never was the need of a stick. Unbelievably, he could even make them walk backwards.

But what was most astonishing was that he could actually make them bray whenever he gave the order.

Next I saw Farehdun busy making some sort of a light contraption. I couldn't figure out its purpose so I went back to the house to see how the others were progressing.

Father, I saw was busy prying open boards from our kitchen floor. From under them he removed about fifty pouches, each the size of a man's fist.

"These have been our saviour till now," he explained as he noticed me looking on. "These are the gold bags I had brought when I left Pars thirty years ago…family jewels and treasures collected through the centuries. I had more than twice as much when we came here," he added ruefully, "but the monthly jizyah for the village and other expenses has reduced it. It has protected this village for thirty years".

"But…the soldiers didn't find them, earlier today?"'

A half smile played on my father's lips. "How could they? This is no trap door or any temporary arrangement. I knew the importance of this treasure to the village, so right in the beginning when we first came here I had dug this hole under our house and sealed the planks permanently. Every year I break open the floor and remove just enough gold to grease the hands of those tax-collectors, and give them their monthly *jizyah*. And then I seal the floor permanently again. It took time and effort, but it was worth it."

He poured out the contents of one of the pouches on the table and even I, who had little knowledge of their value, took in a deep breath. There were about twenty large gold coins, an assortment from different countries, and some gem stones of vivid colours. Each pouch, I learnt later, contained enough wealth to take good care of a family, for life.

"Naturally, I don't part with a full coin every month to appease the tax collector," he explained when I picked up one of the coins and noticed it covered my entire palm. "I give it to Noshirwan to melt it in his furnace and break it into about twenty smaller pieces. I give away a few of them at a time. This way they don't discover we have gold coins, which would have made them more suspicious."

"How did you manage to rescue this treasure? You were but a boy and alone when you left Pars."

That was a story very few knew about. Peshotan remembered those terrible days at Pars, those terrible nightmares he still had.

"And how did you escape being caught by the Arabs? You've never talked about it." I added.

Peshotan looked at his son disdainfully. I really don't need Mr. Question

Mark around me right now, he thought. How am I going to escape his interrogation? Still, he thought, his son deserved to know more of his family than he does. He had always avoided discussing about those days, but it was time now…before it was too late.

"I was little more than a kid, no older than Farehdun now, when disaster struck us while our family was in Shiraz, the beautiful city in Pars. We lived in a palatial house there and were considered the first citizens of the province. When the Arabs conquered Persia, and the new Governor of Pars settled in, the first order he gave was the elimination of every Mahrespandan in the province. It was the man who often boasted of his victory over Zahl. He proved this victory by displaying the great mace of my father at every function he attended, and at every occasion he could find. He knew Zahl's family still existed and didn't want to risk a future retribution. When the soldiers came in looking for the Mahrespandan family, I was running a chore at the local bazaar for my aunt, where I and my brother stayed."

"You were staying with your aunt?"

"Yes. My mother had already passed away. She couldn't bear to live without father. And as you know father was supposedly killed at Qadissiya. At the bazaar my friends warned me of the raid and the subsequent massacre of my family, including my brother, and all those who bore our name."

"I didn't know you had a brother."

"Well I had. He was younger to me and a studious boy," remembered Peshotan sadly. "That fateful day I lost everyone I loved in that raid."

"Yes, but how did you escape the soldiers? Didn't they catch you at the bazaar?"

"No, they didn't," Peshotan replied impatiently. "And if you let me speak on without disturbing, maybe I'll be able to complete my story before daybreak."

That kept me quiet, for the time being.

"I did manage to escape Pars and the stigma of being a Mahrespandan by pretending to be a deaf and dumb farm-hand. I headed for Yazd as that's where the Zoroastrians were yet safe. I lived with another priestly family there for a few years. They were aware of my true identity and helped me a lot."

"Sorry to disturb, but who were they…this family?"

Peshotan looked up for help but knew he was alone in this narration. "You know Minocher Uncle, next door?"

"Couldn't be him! He's a real grouch."

"No, he isn't. And it was not him, but his father who helped me. And this is the last warning. No more interruptions."

I consented meekly.

"For my safety," Peshotan continued, "they tried to make me change my name to theirs, Athavian. But I declined. I wanted to remain a Mahrespandan." Thank God for that, I thought. Who would want to have the same name as Minocher Uncle.

"After a couple of months of the massacre I sneaked back to Pars to see the damage the soldiers had done to my family and our property. There was no one left, my brother, my uncle and aunt, their children and others, were all wiped out."

"What was your brother's name?" I wanted to know.

Peshotan obliged with the answer without any annoyance. "Bahman."

"I wish he were here with us today."

"Yes. But to get back to the story, I had lost not just my entire family, but our large house had been razed to the ground. There was no one and no place left for me to go to. I returned to Yazd."

"But what about this treasure that you said you brought back?"

"I'm coming to that, I'm coming to that, if only you'd let me," said Peshotan, glaring at me and regretting missing the right sequence of the story. "Before leaving Shiraz, one late evening I bought an ass and went into the nearby mountains, close to Pasargadae. I knew where uncle had hidden the family's wealth just after the Battle of Nehavand, as he had taken both, me and my brother along at the time of hiding it. It was the wisest move on his part, to safeguard our wealth. Though night had fallen I found the site easily enough. I unearthed some of the treasure and loaded it on the ass. I had to leave behind most of the treasure, as there was a lot of it, for a future date, if ever circumstances permitted.

"Now I knew my danger was multiplied as I made my way directly back to Yazd. So I travelled only by night, never using the main road, but staying within a mile of it. It meant extra and more difficult travel, but I could reach Yazd safely."

"Gosh! That must have been frightening."

"Yes," said Peshotan, thankful that his mission was finally acknowledged. He started segregating the different pouches on the table, keeping in mind that he no longer had Noshirwan to melt the gold coins. He may later try to break them with a hammer.

"But this gold isn't the only treasure I rescued."

I opened my eyes wider. More?

"But before coming to that I must say that the most important thing my adopted family in Yazd did for me, was to arrange my *Nozud* ceremony so that I could become a priest. As you know that ceremony requires a group of priests and days of ritual to complete it." I didn't. "You must remember that even at that period of time there was a blank order against ordaining any new priest. So the hardships faced by the performing priests and myself were manifold. But we did it. Now that I was a priest, I could perform most of our ceremonies. I wanted to continue my religious studies and undergo the *Maratab* ceremony and become a full-fledged *Mobed*, but circumstances wouldn't allow that.

"Soon the Arabs decided to burn down the *fire-temples* at Yazd. It was a body-blow to all Zoroastrians living there. There was no point in staying at a place where there was no fire temple and no freedom to pray. So the night before the pillage took place I sneaked into our Atash Behram at Yazd. As you know, the holy fire there originated from the Royal Fire of Adur Burzan-Mihr."

I didn't know, and my blank face must have shown it.

Father took a deep breath and continued with a show of impatience. "This is not the time for educating you of our religion's origins. But suffice it to say that it is believed that In The Beginning, Ahura Mazda had lighted three Great Fires. They were called, Adur Burzen-Mihr, Adur Farnbag and Adur Gushnasp. They were also known as the three Royal Fires."

"And the fire at Yazd was…" I prompted.

"Consecrated centuries ago with the Royal Fire of Adur Burzen-Mihr."

"And our fire…?"

"Is part of the fire at Yazd. That night I transferred part of that fire, or at least the burning embers, into a smaller *Urn.* The same *Urn* we have today. That very night, we, that is myself, the Athavians and a couple of other families, escaped the city."

I was dumb-struck at what I was hearing. *The holy fire in our house originated with one of the Great Fires, ignited by Lord Ahura Mazda himself!*

It took me time to register the gravity of what was said. And this great act was done by my father! And all along I thought he was a meek and mild person.

I was thrilled to the bone. But I still needed some explanations. "Father, we consider all fires as holy. Why couldn't you simply pray at home in Yazd, in front of the kitchen fire?"

"Two reasons. The holy fire at Yazd had to be saved. The fire that remained lighted for centuries could not be allowed to die. And remember, our family were the royal priests at one time, and we had to have a proper praying place, and a genuine consecrated fire…or we'd stop breathing. One of the families who travelled with us was aware of this secluded and uninhabited village, so we came here and settled down, and continued with our sacred religious practices."

"What happened to this village's original inhabitants?"

"We learnt that it used to be populated with Zoroastrian craftsmen and traders. They used to mostly keep to themselves, and once a month, go to the city of Yazd and sell their products. After the Battle of Nehavand this little settlement was not noticed for over two years. But when one day the traders went to Yazd to sell their ware they were questioned and the village was discovered. Very next day the Arabs raided it and the villagers were given the ultimate choice…convert to Islam, or die. Not a soul converted. After all were butchered, the place remained uninhabited till we came."

"Wow! What a story!" I was really impressed. My father never displayed the tons of courage he obviously had…obediently wearing the honey coloured robe required of all Zoroastrians; bowing low to all Arab tax collectors; accepting physical blows without retaliating. But he was a real hero and I now looked at him in different light.

"So that night you carried two precious treasures with you…the gold and the *Urn.*"

"No. I carried one more treasure. That I'll show you tomorrow."

I couldn't believe my ears. My father was a regular treasure collector!

"Wouldn't carrying these treasures tomorrow be dangerous for all during the journey?" I asked, breaking his chain of thought.

Peshotan stopped what he was doing and smiled at me. "My little boy is getting smarter. Yes, it will mean endangering the group, it will mean tremendous responsibility, but it has to be done. We don't know what dangers we'll be facing, but this," he lifted one of the small bags, "is the remedy to all ailments. Now go and see if you can help your mother and sister."

❑

In the other room mother was having difficulty convincing Mahafrid that we could carry only two pairs of clothing per person, one to wear, and the other to wash and keep dry. As Mahafrid fussed over her selection, which I didn't understand as they were all of the same required colour and design, mother went about her duty with a sorrowful determination.

"Don't be so sad, Mother," I tried encouraging her. "Maybe we'll find a better place wherever we're going."

I suddenly remembered the old man on the mountain. He had said that we should move on to a new place if we had to safeguard our religion. That is exactly what we were doing. I reminded mother of the old man and his advice that we'll be better off if we shift to a new place.

Yes, maybe we will, she thought. But this was *her home!* Couldn't Peshotan realise that? Yes, it was but a shabby hovel, but it had everything in it that she ever loved.

Dughdova remembered the day, a little less than thirty years ago, when they had moved in with another four families. Peshotan's adopted family and two other families were already settled in this abandoned village.

Her own family arrived about two years after the first lot. They could no longer bear the oppression in Yazd…and the monthly *jizyah.* There were still many Zoroastrians in Yazd when they left the city, but these were the rich ones who could afford the *jizyah.* She wondered what would happen when their riches slowly drained away. A job within the new government? Yes, they were available, but only for those who converted, and under *their* supervision. The conquerors were mostly uneducated and unprincipled, but the machinery of governance had to go on running. So they used the learned Zoroastrians available…who worked harder, were intelligent and came cheap.

It was not that they led an easy life here in this remote village; it was not that there were no hardships; and it was not that they were living free of any danger either. The height of recreation she could indulge in was the occasional chat with her neighbours. But this was where she met Peshotan as a kid, this was where they fell in love and this was where they were married. And this was where her children were born and raised.

And now she was asked to pack overnight and leave the place forever.

So how could she not be sad? She wanted to ask her little son.

But maybe, she mused, there could be advantages of leaving this place. She always worried a lot about Mahafrid, who was now almost a woman. There was little scope here of finding a suitable boy. There was the womaniser Asfandyar, who she was glad had left with Zahl. The other boys, including Rustom and Eruch, just didn't instil any confidence in her of looking after her daughter.

Maybe, Quhistan had better prospects.

❑❑❑

12

Next morning we saw the first rays of the day's sun gently caress the rows of shabby houses down below. If the sun hoped to give them some colour, some brightness, it failed. The houses still looked dirty and gloomy. We stood at the last ridge of the mountain range before the village will be out of sight forever, for us. There were tears in almost every eye as we bid goodbye to it…this place of non-descript and grubby houses…the place we called home for the last thirty years. The place that used to go by the name of Mehrigard.

Me? No, there were no tears in my eyes. My sadness had evaporated the moment we were on our way. Actually I was now looking forward to this adventure. My family and all of my friends were with me, and we were finally going to see the world…or at least the outside of this village. We would see new places, meet new people and do things we never did before.

I was only sad that my grandfather was not with us. What fun it would have been if he too was travelling with us. First, I was sure nobody would try to bully us on the way. And then the stories we would get to hear from him. We did hear a few, but I was sure he was good enough for another thousand at least.

There were eighteen families with us that bid goodbye to this valley. The rest had decided to stay back and agree to be converted to Islam. Some of them had very old dependants for whom it would be an impossible journey to Quhistan. Others just couldn't take it any more. In total we were now forty eight souls, (actually forty eight and a half as one of our younger women, Behruz, was seven months pregnant), and about an equal number in livestock. Managing food and water for the lot, in a desolate salt desert, would test the best of organisers. We could have carried much more if we could take along wagons and carts. But knowing the terrain we would be travelling, father had strictly instructed all, 'No wheels'!

At one point as we moved passed my favourite hiding place father had stopped the group and along with Farehdun had gone to retrieve the holy fire from the nearby cave. How were we going to carry that, I wondered? That's when I realised the smart contraption Farehdun was making last night. Obviously father had instructed him properly as to what was needed. The contraption was made of a few strips of metal. Its shape was that of a bowl with a metal sheet on top, bottom and one side. The *Urn* was placed inside the bowl on the flat bottom. When the top metal sheet was in place, the fire, or at least the embers, was protected. The fixed side metal protected the mule from direct heat. Some hay and clothing were also squeezed between the beast and the *Urnyu,* so it was quite safe. Once in place, Farehdun became a different person. His mind and body acted as one in performing one single duty…protect the holy fire, and ensure it kept alive under all circumstances.

Peshotan instructed on how to maintain the burning embers with a minimum of wood and other fuel. "We don't need the flames; just maintaining the embers by adding small portions of fuel is enough. We'll bring the fire back to life when we reach Quhistan. It is now everyone's responsibility to safeguard the holy fire against the elements, and the Arabs," he announced, as he adjusted the shade above it. There was a silent acknowledgement of this important responsibility. All understood that under no circumstances was this fire ever to extinguish. In a nutshell, it was what this flight was all about...to keep the flame of our religion burning. Without it we'd be just another tribe, without an identity, without a past.

A little while later, as we moved on to another mountain side Peshotan once again stopped the group.

"Wait for me here," he told the rest. "It will take me a few minutes. Then we can proceed unhindered."

All looked on questioningly, unable to fathom this halt. After seeing the back of our village all were keen to get out of this region at the earliest.

"We don't want to get caught by those Arabs," complained Minocher. "Can't you wait till we pass the crossroad?"

About five miles away from our village was a large crossroad. Directly north of it was the road from Yazd. A road towards west, over a much larger mountainous region, took you to Esfahan. And the South-East road went to Kerman. Till that crossroad we would be using the same route the soldiers from Yazd will be using, and hence it was vital we covered that area fast and got out of their way.

"Not to worry about them. At the earliest they'll reach the crossroad not before noon. By then we should be far away from there. Jamshid, come with me," my father commanded and guided me and one of our mules through a narrow crevice on the side of the mountain. It was little more than a crack and the mule barely squeezed in.

The others quietly waited where they stood, totally baffled at this sudden change of plans by their leader.

Father and I continued going deeper into the crevice, careful of not scraping against the rough stone edges on either side. The mule was getting panicky but father had a firm grip on its lead. Soon we were totally engulfed within the folds of the mountain and the only other thing we could see besides the mountain walls was a thin strip of the sky, high above us. And that, too, at times disappeared out of sight. Ten minutes later a large cave opened up on one of the sides and we walked into it. I was getting anxious but didn't dare question my father.

"Hold on to the mule's tail and follow quietly," he instructed.

The cave was unusually deep within as we wound our way through several sections. Each turn made the cave darker, till it became blacker than a witch's heart. The mule and I were frightened out of minds, but father determinedly plodded on. How he could see through this darkness (though he has seen through much darker days) was beyond me as I held the mule's tail tighter.

When finally we stopped, me by barging into the mule's backside, I stood gaping all around, expecting to see something spectacular. There had to be some meaning to this trek. But it was only the stifling darkness that was visible.

A bright spark and father lighted a small lamp that he had removed from the sack on the mule. It was as though we had walked into the sun itself as the entire cave leapt to blinding brightness. Why couldn't he have lighted it earlier?

Shielding my eyes I quickly scanned the huge cavern we were standing in. *Nothing!* Just the empty sides, each trying to look more scary and sinister in the flickering light. So what were we doing here?

"Give me a hand" called out father as he started unpacking one particular load from the mule.

So that's it, I concluded, he's hiding the gold here.

"If we hide the gold here, how are we going to use it during the journey?' I asked, helping with the heavy sack.

He laughed. "This is not gold. This is something far more valuable than gold. These are the complete sets of our holy scriptures. It is the third treasure I told you about last night."

He saw my gaping stare and explained further. "As you may already know the Arabs have destroyed almost every copy in existence of our scriptures, comprising the Avesta, the Gathas, the 21 Nasks, the Visparad and the Vendidad. A thousand years before them, Alexander the Great had carried out a similar mission and at that time it was thought we had lost all. But like today, a few precious sets were saved at that time, as well. In the coming centuries after Alexander, copies were made, and now even those have been mostly destroyed. Very, very few of them are now in existence. This lot comprises one complete set, and could be the last direct link we have with our prophet, Zarathushtra...besides the holy fire that we carry," he added apologetically.

"I...never saw them in our house..."

"No, I couldn't risk that. I had buried these next to the gold. We'll not be able to carry such load on this journey. Also we would be risking an additional hazard of losing *everything* if the Arabs catch us. So we'll hide them here and come back for them when, and if, we can. I knew of this special place during my explorations of the area, and kept it a secret. Now you know it too. Remember it, and pass on the information to your sons if you are unable to retrieve it during your lifetime. *We must never let our heritage die with us.*"

He shifted some small rocks at one corner of this cavern, dug a hole with his hands where the stones were no larger than pebbles and placed a large piece of an oilskin within it. Then we carefully placed the sacred books, about thirty of them, on the oilskin and wrapped the sides over the books. The pages were of treated lamb skin, all well preserved as the books were individually covered by oilskins. Upon completion of the transfer we once again covered the hole with small loose stones; next we used larger stones, and finally shifted some heavier rocks over the lot. Our hiding place was not air-tight, but considering the absence of humidity deep in the cave, the books were well enough preserved.

"Thirty volumes," I wondered aloud, "and all handwritten. It must have taken a lifetime to write them."

"Longer. These books are over three hundred years old and it took almost three generations of our forefathers to compile and write them. Now, maybe, you'll understand their true value. From today, *you* are the keeper of this treasure."

"Why have you not given this responsibility to Farehdun? Why me?" It was insolent of me to question my father's ways, but it did puzzle me.

"Farehdun has been entrusted with the top-most responsibility. He is the keeper of the holy fire. Nothing must disturb that duty of his. *There is nothing more sacred for us on this planet, than that fire*."

The return journey out of the cave was thankfully easier as father carried the lighted torch.

Our fellow travellers were in a state of panic when we returned. There was tension written on every face and Minocher was definitely angry.

"*What's wrong with you, Peshotan?* Those Arabs will be here any minute and you've risked all our lives! And for what?"

"Sorry, but it was very important," was all that Peshotan would say. His duty was done, and that was all that mattered to him.

We travelled in a single file on the narrow mountain road, little more than a ledge. Mother led the group determinedly, not even looking back to see how the others progressed. Her mind seemed to be on other things and did not show her face to the others. Farehdun walked directly behind her, helping his mule now and then as it carried a full load on its back, including the *Urn*. Mahafrid and I walked with father and our second mule, with the half load on one side and our poultry on the other. An elderly village neighbour took a free ride on it. Almost all had similarly draped their poultry, wrapped in a net, on their mules too. It would have been so much easier if we could have taken a few carts along, but as already mentioned, Peshotan had made it clear that the rocky terrain we'd be using later would make a cart useless. wrap

Behind us came the rest of the group, some with mules and some with horses. The rear was brought up by the village's cattle and other livestock. They were managed by some of the younger men, including Minocher's son, Rustom, and his friend Eruch. Though Eruch still looked totally shaken up after last night's incident, he had no time to grieve for his grandfather. He had to keep his presence of mind with the rest, and that helped.

The young men understood the importance of making haste at this juncture, but their task was not easy. With as little noise as possible they were trying their best to make the tail end of the procession remain with the main body. We knew it was this part of our group that was going to slow down our progress right through our journey. But they were indispensable as we would be heavily dependent upon these creatures for our future food stocks.

Speed was of essence, at least till we reached the cross road, so all concentrated on hurrying on. There was no chit-chat as the silent procession moved on as though they were attending a funeral, and everyone's attention was only on the road ahead. If Peshotan miscalculated the Arab's arrival, then the group will have nothing more to worry about. We would all be surely annihilated.

After five minutes of walking with my father I got impatient with the overpowering silence, though Mahafrid was quite enjoying it, and drifted back in the line to be with my friends. We tried playing a game as we trudged on but somehow no one was in the mood, so I skipped on forward and gave mother some company and comfort.

"Feeling better?" I asked encouragingly.

She put her hand around my shoulders and smiled. "Now that you're here, yes."

It was still pleasant climate and the going was comfortable. After noon, Peshotan knew, the trek and the spirits will take its toll as the sun will beat down on the travellers on foot. The best shelter they could hope for was the light shawl over their head. And when the sun goes down, it could get worse with the chilly mountain breeze taking over. Hopefully all were prepared for both conditions. Luckily rains were a rare commodity in Persia. They had their share of downpours, and the season was not far away, but they were few and far between.

Their progress was good as the tension of getting caught by the Arabs was uppermost in everyone's mind. Two hours later Peshotan breathed a sigh of relief. They were about to pass the last of the mountains and in front of them were the plains, and their immediate target. "There's the crossroad," he called out happily. "Another fifteen minutes and we'll be out of danger."

Just as every one started relaxing a sharp cry from Minocher, alerted all.

"Stop!" he cried with anguish. "Look, the Arabs are already on their way."

❑❑❑

13

Minocher, who was now leading the group, was the first to pass the mountain side they were on. In front of him the ground eased out and slowly levelled to the plains. As soon as he alerted everyone, he hurried back on the road so that the mountain side they were on, shielded him once again. Peshotan ran to his side and slowly peeked past the mountain side. He followed Minocher's trembling finger and confirmed his worst fear. Across another mountain range and on the road to Yazd were the Arabs, galloping towards them. No way was the group going to beat the soldiers to the crossroad. Peshotan fell to his knees in sheer fear and frustration.

"Dear God! *How could they have arrived here so fast?* They shouldn't be here for another three hours at least. Ahura Mazda! Even you cannot help us now," he moaned. What a mistake he had made wasting valuable time hiding his books. Surely his own people would lynch him if they found out the purpose of his delaying their journey.

"They haven't seen us yet," Minocher observed, "thanks to these mountains. But we're trapped."

Suddenly Farehdun came panting to them. *"We do have one hope!"* He exclaimed excitedly. "Just behind us there is a small open space in the mountain side. A minute ago, I went to relieve myself there."

Peshotan took an immediate decision. *"Guide us to it!"* He shouted to his son even as Farehdun streaked to the back of the procession.

The open space was bout two hundred yards behind them. It was a chaotic sight as the young men frantically pushed and prodded the cattle towards it. It was where the mountain sharply curved in and created a large open hall. The entrance was ten feet wide and the open round hall about fifty feet in diameter. If someone from outside the entrance peeked in, this was no hiding place. But if someone just rode by, they could be out of sight.

Five minutes of mayhem and they were all in. Peshotan could ask the people to be silent, but how were they to control the cattle and the poultry? He asked all to be with one creature each and softly stroke its head to calm it down, to somehow keep it quiet. The poultry, he asked God to take care of. Farehdun further controlled the small wisp of smoke that emitted from the holy fire. Finally, there was silence.

We all crouched in a huddle, almost in plain view of the road. "Nobody look up", warned Peshotan softly. Heads down, we waited as our hearts beat faster and louder than their fastest horse.

Two minutes later the Arabs galloped by.

When the coast was clear Peshotan once again took control. "From here on, *no more walking*. We must reach the crossroad on the run and continue running for another mile on the trail I will show."

No more time was wasted as the entire group worked as one team to complete the race from death. Soon we reached the crossroad and Peshotan guided the rest on to the road to Kerman. A short while later he detoured left, right into the plains.

"I thought you said there would be a road," Minocher complained, jogging along with Peshotan. "So where is it?"

"You're running on it."

Minocher looked around puzzled, and then he noticed the difference in the terrain. They were on some sort of a path, almost an ancient roadway, hardly visible or distinguishable to the untrained eye. It was a hazy path with an abundance of vegetation growth scattered over it. There were no distinct sides to it as it merged unevenly with the surrounding plains.

"See those low mountains," Peshotan pointed to a small knoll some three miles in front of us. "That's our next target. Once we reach there, we'll be out of sight from the main road. We can continue the journey later, after dark."

The plan simple, we now started hurrying towards our new destination at half-trot. Not easy for the elderly, but no one complained. Behruz, the pregnant woman was accommodated on a mule. Almost an hour later, breathless and weary from the recent narrow escape, we snaked our way to the small clump of low mountains and sneaked out of sight. The elderly flung themselves to the ground, breathing heavily. It was still morning and the shaded area was on the side toward the road so they simply covered their heads with their shawls and waited for the sun to go on the other side of the mountain. The younger men herded the cattle into a corner and took up positions to contain them within.

I and my friends gathered on a higher rock, excited as ever. We took great care not to be seen by anyone on the road. This was no game and yet so much more thrilling than any we had played till date.

There was so much to look forward to in the coming days.

❑

Sayyid Abul Yaser was breathing heavily as their horses turned right at the crossroad on ones way to Kerman. It was not that he was exhausted. It was sheer excitement.

"Once those stubborn Zoroastrians tell me the route Zahl has taken, we'll set off after him immediately. He will not escape from me and destiny."

The scent of the hunt ahead of him had made him lose all thoughts of sleep last night. In fact, he didn't sleep a wink and was up much before dawn. He ordered his men to be immediately ready for the ride and had left Yazd, much to the bafflement of the presiding governor there. They were out of the town even before the sun could come up.

Now he could barely conceal his eagerness to get into action. He was sixty five years old and, he regretted, heavy from inaction for years. But that won't stop him. This was what he longed for during those lazy and corrupt years.

Shortly they took the last turn to the Zoroastrian village and thundered down the slope.

Strange! No one around? Fifty men on galloping horses should have been enough to wake the dead. He rode to the house of their priest and called out aloud.

"*Ajams, OUT!! Everyone out of your stinking houses!*"

A middle-aged man was the first to step out. He had suffered an injury to his leg recently, and gangrene had set in soon. A few days ago his leg had to be amputed at the knee and hence he was in no condition to journey with the rest. As he painfully limped forward two other couples, with their elderly parents, also ambled out of their homes and stood meekly on the road.

Yaser looked around in utter disbelief. *"Where are the rest?"* he bellowed.

"They've all gone away," said the middle-aged man, afraid of the response to his news.

Yaser couldn't believe his ears. He ordered his men to search every house as he sat fuming on his horse. It was a quick search.

"Nobody, Sir, not even the livestock." his second in command reported in as much disbelief. "These nine are the only ones left."

Yaser still refused to believe what he heard. It was simply impossible. "Gone away?" he muttered, almost to himself. *"Where could they have gone away?"* He pointed to the middle-aged man, "*You? Where did they all go?"*

"They wouldn't tell us, Sir. They left while it was dark. We are the only ones left here."

Perplexed, Yaser scratched his unshaven chin. "Is there another route out of these mountains?" he asked the tax collector who was ordered to remain with the group.

"No Sir, this is the only route. They could have avoided the roads and walked over the mountains, but that is unlikely too. They are burdened with the entire livestock from the village."

No Zahl! And now most of the village has escaped him! He'll be the laughing stock of the country.

Yaser stared at the crippled man furiously. He suddenly charged his horse at him and pushed him out of his way. Then he sprang down and walked menacingly towards the whining man on the ground.

"Tell me why Zahl chose to come to this village?" Yaser suddenly changed his line of interrogation.

Pin-drop silence.

Yaser fumed silently as he still hoped to learn some indication of Zahl's plans. The villagers were of no importance to him. He will find them, sooner or later, and he would punish them severely. But his priority today was only one...*find Zahl!* Why was he here? Why did he leave? *Revenge!!* It had to be that! The man must be looking for him. The thought brought perspiration above his brows. If that was the case, fine. It'll make the challenge more interesting.

He turned around and scanned the mountains around them. There could be a thousand hiding places within those mountains. But he sensed the inevitable. Zahl and the rest had gone away from this valley.

But they'll pay for this treachery.

"Tell me why Zahl was here, or I'll cripple your other leg too.!" He shouted and placed his foot heavily on the man's raw wound.

The man screamed with pain and almost collapsed.

"Tell me!" Said Yaser, and with almost manic excitement pushed his foot harder against the man's knee.

Another pathetic scream from the fallen man.

"Stop it, you cruel man!" A small old woman, one of the elderly couples standing by, came forward. "We don't know where Zahl or the others went. But we know why he was here."

Yaser looked up and smile. He knew the simple rule of interrogation. Eventually they always talked.

"He was here," the old woman continued, "because his son was here."

Yaser's eyes almost bulged out. *Son?* What son? Hadn't he wiped them all out from the face of this world? His eyes narrowed as he asked, "And who was this son?"

The old woman half winced as she realised she had said too much. But it was too late to back out now.

"It was the man you spoke with...our priest and our leader, Peshotan Mahrespandan."

Yaser stood stupefied. *What a mistake he had made.* He had not even asked the people for their names, else how would he have forgotten the name, *'Mahrespandan'*. He was sure he had already eliminated all by that name, even the ones who lived away from Pars. He couldn't take the chance of someone looking for revenge. He had even ordered the killing of their infants, just in case. So how did this one escape me?

He cursed himself for his foolishness. If only he had known of this Peshotan earlier, he could have had Zahl in the palm of his hand. But all was not lost. He will still catch the father and the son. And why should he take the blame. He called for the tax-collector.

"How many years have you been collecting tax from this village?"

The tax collector shivered under the hot sun, knowing what was coming. "Er...about twenty years, Sire."

"*Twenty years? And you did not know the name of their leader?"*

"I...I did not know...of its importance..."

"Twenty lashes for this man," Yaser instructed his commander. *"Here and right now!"*

A whip was brought out and the tax collector tied to a post. Each time the whip swished down, the collector screamed with pain. The commander showed no mercy considering he was whipping his own country man. After the twentieth blow the poor man lay writhing in pain, too afraid to protest or ask for mercy. No one dared to as much as help him up.

"Now it is your turn," said Yaser sneering at the trembling villagers. "Which way did Zahl go?" He asked very softly. There was no need to shout any longer. After the demonstration with the tax collector he had their full attention. Everyone was almost hanging on to his every word.

"The last we saw him was on that ridge," the old woman pointed out the mountain range across them. There was no point in withholding any information. Zahl must be out of harms way by now. "They were headed northwards."

"They? He was not alone?" Yaser walked up to her purposefully.

The old woman shut her eyes in defeat and submission. Another unpardonable mistake by her. Her husband had had enough of this humiliation.

"No, two of our men joined him too," the old woman's husband confirmed.

"Was his son one of them?"

"No."

"Anyone from the Mahrespandan family?"

"No. Both were just neighbours."

So Zahl and two others were headed north. Where precisely, he was convinced these villagers wouldn't know. But where could he have gone? Yaser wondered. The nearest city northwards was Esfahan, but his purpose wouldn't be served in a city. If he wanted revenge, he'll be in the mountains, *near* a city, trying to play havoc with the invaders, goading Yaser to face him.

"Now what will I do with you lot?" He asked with a smile.

"You dare not harm anyone here," the old woman said finding her voice again, and wagging her finger at Yaser. "Zahl will come to know of your wickedness, and he'll come after you."

Yaser was still smiling as he moved towards the old woman. "And why didn't you leave with the rest of the villagers?" he asked menacingly.

Her old husband once again butted in. "We wish to..." the old man gulped hard as the words refused to come out. "We wish to be converted...to Islam." His head slumped to his chest as he spoke.

Yaser laughed aloud, and looked for support from his men. They immediately joined in his mirth dutifully. "You wish to be converted to Islam?" he repeated the old man's words softly. *"You think we need invalids and cowardly people like you in our midst?"* He bellowed in frustration and passed a sign to his commander.

Moments later the nine Zoroastrians were cut down with swords, as though they were cattle. Next a sharp order was rasped out and the soldiers began burning down the entire village.

"Throw the bodies into the fire," yelled Yaser. "You lived by the fire;" he muttered, as his order got carried out. *"Now die by the fire."*

It was not a pleasant sight to witness and the soldiers nervously moved back. Not everyone found the murder of old and disabled people as desirable as most heads hung low with remorse.

"*No pity for the Ajams!"* yelled Yaser, bringing everyone out of their stupor. "We have work to do so pay attention. We shall now have two targets," he lowered his voice as though his words were top secret. His troops pretended to pay attention but their minds were elsewhere as they watched the towering inferno from a distance. "One lot will hunt down Zahl, wherever he is, however long it takes. *I* will lead this group. *And I want him alive!* Only *I* am worthy of his head, and *I* will execute him in a public place. The other lot, commanded by my captain here, will chase those ignorant villagers. They think they can outsmart us? They think they can outrun our horses? We'll teach them a lesson, once and for all. You should be achieving the second target by today itself, as they are burdened with their livestock. Once we finish off those villagers the entire group will concentrate on Zahl."

"Sir," the second-in command asked, "which route shall we take? They could have gone anywhere."

"No, not anywhere. The group will have to use a road to travel. There are only two other roads from this area, besides the Yazd road, and they obviously could not have taken that as we were on it. I will take the north-western road to Esfahan. My gut feeling says Zahl will be in those mountains, raising an army or preparing to fight alone with his two accomplices. In Esfahan my son Jamal rules the roost. If I need reinforcements, I could safely rely on him. If these villagers have taken the same route as Zahl, to Esfahan, then all the better. We will get them in no time. You," he said turning to his commander, "will take the second road, to Kerman. If you find them, do the needful and hurry back to us. If by tomorrow you don't come across them, take it for granted they were destined to die at my hand, and turn back toward us."

This is going to be a far greater hunt than he ever hoped for. *Allah be praised,* for giving me such an opportunity. He, Sayyid Abul Yaser, will get the balance of the Mahrespandan family, not for the Caliphs sitting at Mecca, *but for himself.* People will remember him as the greatest hero of Arabia.

Yaser was smiling once again when they all rode away, as the ill-destined village roared on in flames.

❑❑❑

14

That first night of our flight was like a picnic for me. We had waited till it was completely dark, lest an occasional traveller on the road should spot us. We didn't need any light to show us the way as the part moon and the bright stars were enough to guide us. At times, the landscape looked pretty with silvery effect from the natural glow. At times it looked scary and ominous. We did keep a constant check on our backs too, in case the Arabs found out the route we had taken. Remote as the possibility may be, it did help in making us keep a steady pace.

There was little talk within the group as all tried to gauge the enormity of the task their leader had chosen for them. Is this at all possible? Are we all going to die in this vast wilderness? Once we do reach the salt deserts, how will we carry on? No one had that experience. No one understood the effects of such a cruel environment. But we walked on, mindful of the old and the sick, hopeful of some divine intervention to guide us to safety, and watchful of any stray wild animal that we knew existed in these parts.

What was most startling about the solemn procession that marched on silently was the eerie glow that emitted from the mule that carried the holy fire. As Farehdun dutifully walked alongside, he, too, was covered by that glow. Together they could have spooked off the staunchest Arab.

I have no idea what directed my father as he walked on in the lead, so purposefully. What lay around us were a series of low-lying mountains, and vast open lands in between. In the distance I could see a mountain range, and we were headed directly towards it. Earlier, at noon, I had seen father discuss his strategies with a few village elders. He had not revealed the route or the destination with most, and was now explaining all.

At the conclusion of that meeting, I saw them look more confused and unsure than when we had started off.

"Are you sure?" One of them asked, looking around like we were already lost.

"Is it really possible?" another elder inquired, looking as confident as though he had been assured he could walk on water. He turned to Minocher for his views, but Minocher simply looked the other way.

I didn't like the lack of confidence so early in our quest. Definitely father had something concrete in his plans, else he would not suggest it. All I knew was that we were going to go through an ancient path between the two great salt deserts, and reach the southern part of Khorasan, to a place called Quhistan. But we were hundreds of miles away and there were no towns or landmarks along the way. And certainly there were no sign posts showing us the way to Quhistan. So how was father going to guide us? He had neither made the trip earlier, nor did he have any definite map showing the way.

"How do you know we are headed in the right direction?" I finally had to ask my father, later, as I walked alongside him.

Maybe he felt betrayed with my lack of confidence as I noticed the slightest of a hurt look in his eyes. He turned to me sadly and explained, "Quhistan is a far away place. Very few people will know the entire route. So we'll have to cover the complete journey in stages…one stage at a time. My first target is Bafq. It should take us about three days to reach it. This is a fairly large town before the salt deserts, on another road between Yazd and Kerman. I have a decent idea in which direction that place lies. Once we cross that road and the town, we'll be entirely on our own. Totally away from any civilisation, and at the mercy of nature and God."

Didn't sound too encouraging to me either. No wonder the village elders walked out of that meeting as though they were told this was their last day of existence.

"But we're taking so many twists and turns in this mountainous region, yet you seem to be so decided in your directions."

"Right after the crossroad we're using an ancient trail, almost unused for centuries. I'm simply following that trail."

"What trail? I can't see it."

"It depends on how you look for it. Even in the night, the signs are plainly visible. See those few stones in a line? They have to be a part of the edge of that trail. There are many stones all over the place, but in a line? It's a sure give-away. Then notice the growth of the vegetation in front of you. See the difference between the more even growth beyond the road, and the meagre growth where the path once stood. Another sure sign. And if you focus still farther you may even notice the leftover marks of trees that must have lined the road, once upon a time."

Now that my eyes were trained to these small details, I, also, could spot the winding road that had been invisible to me till then. Too simple to satisfy my non-stop curiosity.

"You said Bafq is a fairly large town. If it's a large town, won't we get caught?"

Peshotan wondered if it would be better getting caught by the Arabs. Explaining his plans to his neighbours was tough enough. But this…?

"We won't enter it. We'll skirt it, keeping a healthy distance between the town and us."

"And then?"

"Why don't you walk with your friends? You'll have more fun with them."

I knew when I was not wanted so I stepped back to my own group and explained the plans to them.

"This has to be the best period of my life," confessed one of my friends after hearing the journey plans straight from the horse's mouth. We were all pumped up; a great adventure lay ahead of us. Already the memories of our village and the bullying Arabs were fading fast. There was no sleep in any of us so we skipped ahead of the rest, and marvelled at our courage in leading the group. I was proudly displaying my new-found prowess of spotting the signs that marked the road. So quickly we seemed to be growing up, from boyhood to young men. Why, if need be we could be on our own against any natural element. Nothing scared us, no one could…

"There are many leopards and wolves in these parts," called out my father. "So be careful."

We did more than that. We swiftly retreated to boyhood and the safety of our elders and made our way to the middle of the caravan. Manhood could come later.

❑

Yaser was up once again before dawn could break. There was too much going on in his mind; too much blood rushing through his veins; too much excitement in his heart. A final showdown with Zahl! How could he sleep?

All night he wondered if his captain had caught up with the villagers and done the needful. When by dawn the captain or his team didn't show up, he smiled. "Obviously, the captain has caught up with them, and done the deed. They will probably get back with our group during the day."

Yaser got everyone up and once again they hit the road while still dark. Zahl already has a big lead; he was not going to allow it to get bigger.

Around noon the captain and his team caught up with them.

"Not on the south road," he reported. "You must have got them by now."

"Wh…? Are you sure?" Yaser stared at him, mouth open. It was as though someone had told him that tomorrow the sun will rise from the West. *How could it be? Where else could they have gone?*

He dismounted and thoughtfully walked towards a tree. The one thing he had done all these years sitting in his camp was to thoroughly get himself acquainted with Persia; its provinces, its topography and its roads. He knew every road that existed in this country. So where did he go wrong?

He was sure they couldn't have used the mountains around that village to escape him. They were too high and impossible for a group with livestock to tackle. They certainly did not take the road to Yazd, or even Esfahan, else he would have got them by now. And now his captain says they have not used the Kerman road either! There are no other…

Oh no!! The ancient road to Bafq! They must have taken the ancient road to Bafq he had read about! There can be no other way they could have taken. He knew it started from about 30 miles south of Yazd, *exactly where the mountain road to that Zoroastrian village branched out from the Yazd-Kerman road.* He remembered how odd it had seemed to him when he came across that reference. What purpose that road served was beyond him, as it seemed to emerge from out of nowhere and continued to Bafq. Maybe, there was a bigger civilisation in that area centuries ago.

"Captain!" He called out, and quickly explained to him the spot from which the ancient Bafq road branched off from the main Yazd to Kerman road. "Get back there, find it as it will be near invisible from centuries of disuse, and get after them. You must reach them before they reach Bafq else we'll have to start our hunt afresh. And if you don't catch up with them, don't come back. You'll be better off anywhere else in the world, but near me."

The softly spoken command was enough for the captain to make haste as he quickly re-grouped his troops and set off towards the Kerman road again.

By the time they reached the spot where the Zoroastrians had disappeared on the road to Kerman, it was dark.

He got off his horse and addressed his group of fifteen men. "No point in trying to locate that ancient road now. Rest your horses and we'll search in the morning."

❑

Zahl shifted his sitting position to be more comfortable. He sat on a large rock overlooking the green valley below. No matter how many valleys you look down from, the view can never be the same. Some differ due to natural beauty, and some differ depending on the extent of affinity you attach to it. His affinity to the valley he had just left behind, a barren and desolate valley, where the remainder of his family now lived, had grown by the day. Though he had spent just a fortnight there, he found it beautiful beyond words.

The valley below him now was greener, the flora and fauna much more visible, the air cooler and crisper…but it lacked something.

They, Zahl, Noshirwan and Ardeshir, were now on the Zard Kooh range of the mountains, just below the last of the great Zagros Mountain range. Close by was the town of Qomsheh, about 60 miles south of Esfahan.

It had taken the three over ten days of speedy trekking from Mehrigard, mostly over barren plains and low brown mountains, to cover the 150 miles. Zahl insisted upon covering as much distance as possible from that village. He told them he didn't want any trouble to befall on those villagers, because of him. But in reality, he was enraged that the villagers were so scared of the Arabs that they had agreed to sacrifice three of their own kind, just for presumed safety. He knew their safety would have been more ensured, had they allowed the three to remain with them.

Along the way they had gathered the loyalty of four more Zarthosties from the little settlements they passed. When the four heard that the great Zahl was alive and leading the team, they dropped whatever they were doing and joined them.

"Now that we have reached the destination you had in mind," asked Ardeshir closing in on Zahl, "When do we attack?"

Zahl, who never communicated well with his men, now found it impossible to have this young lad in his command. He followed no rules, was too frivolous, and just didn't seem to have the qualities to be a good soldier. The four new recruits were all young, and more-or-less held the same attitude

Quite unlike his senior lieutenant, Noshirwan. Now there was a true soldier. Ready to take any order and no questions asked; and always armed and prepared for battle. Even at this moment he was sharpening his sword against a rock.

"I'll tell you when," replied Zahl coldly. If this was going to be the average quality of his recruits, he might as well give himself up and convert to Islam.

He turned his gaze back to the valley and tried reliving the short but happy time he had with his son and his family. Why couldn't he live out the rest of his life with them? Deep down he knew why. He wasn't like them. His spirit was still free. The day that broke, he'll pray for death.

Noshirwan studied his leader and suddenly asked, "Do you really think we can pull this off? I mean the Arabs are getting stronger by the day, and I don't mean only in Persia. They've gone farther east and captured Kabul. On the western front they already are in control of most of North Africa, and last year…"

"Yes, yes I know," Zahl interrupted impatiently. "Last year they have overthrown Constantinople and sacked the city. But if nobody puts up a stand, they will one day rule the world. And nobody wants that."

He switched over back to their current situation. With six men under him he could hardly take on the Arab army. His strategy has to evolve day by day. Presently, his group won't be able to handle anything larger than small Arab units…that too, if, God willing, the youngsters with him have the stomach for it. It was one thing to raise one's sword and curse the enemy with vigour. It was quite another to face the enemy and drive the sword into him. That's where the stumbling block stood, and that's where many failed.

"What about our supplies?" asked Noshirwan from where he stood. "We are almost out of food and some of these lads do not even carry a sword."

"Qomshah is a couple of hours trek from here. Tonight the two of us will go down there and see what we can do about the supplies."

He knew there'll be little of interest for him in that old town. But his ultimate aim was Esfahan. *That's* where he'll do the maximum damage to the enemy. *That's* where the enemy garrison will be located. *That's* where the cream of the Arab society will be. And his group will make them regret the day they decided to conquer Persia. It'll be great once again to be in a fight. A satisfied smile crossed his face at the prospects.

But an instant later he returned to his brooding ways. It would have been better, he thought, if he could play with his grandson, listen to his endless questions and watch him grow to manhood.

Hopefully, they were all safe in the village.

❑❑❑

15

Next morning Yaser's captain spread his thin resources over a stretch of half a mile on the road from Yazd to Kerman.

"We're looking for any signs, however remote it may be, of a change on the ground to our left. Remember, we won't be seeing a road as it disappeared centuries ago. We'll be looking for any leftovers of that road."

Leftovers? He received blank looks.

"You'll move out towards the open land for a short distance. If you don't find any signs, you'll get back on this road, and we'll tackle the next half-mile. We'll go on doing that till we find the remains of that road. Clear?"

He got no reply, so he ordered them to begin the search.

Five hours later and twelve miles down the road the captain himself spotted the ancient road. A minute later they slowly moved up that road, towards Bafq. They had to keep an alert eye for signs of continuation of the road as every now and then it vanished from sight.

❑

"There is Bafq!" Called out Minocher, now leading the group of villagers.

They were on higher grounds and the township was asleep about ten miles below them. The distance was great and it was only thanks to some lighted lamps spread out over some space that they could identify it. But it was enough for many of them, as it was the first sight of a proper township for them. They could also just about distinguish the road going through it, the one parallel to the one from Yazd to Kerman. It was, as expected, deserted.

They had travelled all night, their third, and now though still dark, it was almost dawn. All this time they had kept a constant watch on their tail, in case the Arabs found the route they had taken and were giving them a chase. After the first night Peshotan had maintained a scout on a horseback to keep vigil at their rear. He trailed an hour behind them and was there to warn them if anyone was to follow.

"Okay," said Peshotan excitedly, happy that he had guided them to the first destination correctly, "we now veer off to the right and cross that road another ten miles south. We'll cross it tomorrow night." He pointed out to the open land on the right and further up to a point where he thought it will be good to cross the road.

"And after we cross over?" asked Minocher. Till now he had blindly supported his friend, but was wary of the plans hereon.

"Thereafter we'll be safe from the Arabs, but still have a much greater opponent…nature. Nobody will follow us as there is no civilisation after that road, all the way to Khorassan. The terrain eastwards of Bafq, the route we'll be taking, will be much harsher than the one we are travelling on. Barren of any vegetation, dry of water and coverless from the harsh sun, we'll need to be much tougher, mentally and physically, than ever before. And the only company we'll have are the great salt deserts on either side of us."

An eerie silence followed the revelation. Were we being tossed from the frying pan and into the fire? The idea of converting to Islam and settling down in Bafq ran through many a mind.

"And when we reach the deserts, our route?"

"I already told you. When we reach that spot, the Dasht-E-Kavir will lie northwards and that boundary will be marked by a range of mountains. We'll move directly eastwards along that range, go through the southern tip of Dasht-E-Kavir till we touch a small village, just a few houses I believe, called Darband. From here the mountain range changes course and shoots up in a north easterly direction. We remain on that range heading upwards and pass Lut-E-Kavir directly to our South. The rest of the way Dasht-e-Kavir will remain to our left and Lut-e-Kavir to our right."

Peshotan saw the sceptical look in everyone's eyes and tried infusing enthusiasm in them. "It's not impossible, this journey. People have done it before."

"And after we move north-east?"

"We'll have two choices. We can move on in the same direction till we reach Birjand. Or move more northwards and reach Gonarbad. We can decide on that when we reach the cross-section. From either of the two places, Herat, the capital city of Quhistan, and our ultimate destination, can be reached easily. There we'll be complete safe."

He tried to make it sound simple but I was glad the onus to lead this group was not on me. Whatever he said after Bafq made absolutely no sense to me, or for that matter, to most of the others. We'll surely all die in those mountains he talked about, or in the hungry salt deserts. Suddenly, life didn't look all that bright.

"Looks like our scout is hurrying back." Somebody drew our attention to the rear, from where we had just come.

"Riders coming this way!" Yelled the scout from afar.

❑

An ice-cold glove encircled Peshotan's heart. The Arabs must have found the road, he surmised in a state of panic. *God! We needed just a little more time to beat them.* The rest of the group too looked devastated. A second time to get caught just short of their target.

"How many of them?" Minocher took the lead seeing his friend in a state of despair.

"Over a dozen. They'll be upon us in a short time."

No good! If there were a handful of them maybe they could have stood there ground and challenged them. They will be of no match against a dozen armed guards.

"Then let's hurry with the original plan and go to our right, away from this road," suggested Minocher.

"No," opposed Peshotan, now regaining his senses and spirit. "On the right there is muddy and open ground. They'll see our tracks and easily follow us. We'll move into the rocky area to our left. We can hide behind the rocks and maybe they'll not notice our detour and ride on towards Bafq. It's still dark and there's sufficient cover so we'll be safe. Quick everyone, *move!*"

So once again we scrambled for cover within the rocks and low mountains to our left, pushing and prodding the mules, helping the seniors to move on, and praying…most of all praying, to Ahura Mazda to come to our aid once again. Even as we ran, Farehdun was busy covering the open side of the holy fire, leaving no glow exposed. Rustom and Eruch managed the livestock, now quite adept at it, and my friends and I now understood the reality behind our 'Persians vs. Arabs' games.

We had gone less than half a mile when we heard them. We were out of sight by now, covered by numerous rocks and layers of uneven ground.

The soldiers were not in much of a hurry as they slowly cantered by. We stopped moving, held our collective breaths and heard them go by.

"Good, they've passed us," said Peshotan in a whisper. "They'll probably look for us in Bafq after sunrise. It'll give us sufficient time to stick to our original plan and cross that road. But we'll have to…"

"They've stopped!" hissed Minocher urgently, as he kept a watch on the Arabs from a higher rock. "*Oh no, they're turning back.*"

The soldiers seemed confused as some of them got off their horses and walked back studying the road carefully. "They seem to have discovered the absence of our tracks," observed Minocher, keenly following their every move. "This is not good. They'll surely find us now."

Whoever was guiding them must have been an expert scout to have tracked us down in this darkness. We saw them return to the spot where we had turned left and stop. We saw them search the horizon in all directions but remained rooted where they stood, undecided. A couple of them rode out in the opposite direction for a hundred yards and returned. We could hear their low voices as they now concentrated their attention in our direction. We were surely done for.

Suddenly, we saw Rustom and Eruch make a quiet exit on their horses. They had already covered a hundred yards and were coaxing their horses to move on without any sound.

"*Rustom, get back!*" Minocher hissed through clenched teeth, but his son didn't hear him. He half ran after them but decided otherwise and returned with a hurt look.

"Are they ditching us at a time like this?" Phiruz asked incredulously. "I always was suspicious of those two. They were too close to each other for my comfort and were never around when needed."

We could see the boys treading their way slowly through the rocks, going back the way we had come from our village, half a mile from the ancient road. And then they were out of sight. Minocher looked on disbelievingly, his shoulders hunched and his mouth open as his wife sobbed openly. But this was no time to indulge in personal feelings so he turned his attention back to the more urgent issue at hand.

We saw the Arab soldiers walking steadily toward us, some on foot and some still sitting low on their horses. They were very studiously searching the rocky ground for signs, seemingly uncertain if they should go on with the search, or move on for Bafq. They had spread out, but were moving generally in our direction. We pushed against the rocks we were shielding behind, praying that we could melt into it. But miracles don't happen everyday. We simply held our position, not daring to even breathe.

When they were just twenty yards from us, and all hope was lost, there suddenly erupted a loud commotion. It came from the opposite direction, some distance beyond the ancient road we had travelled on. It sounded like many horses and people were on the run.

"Run!" "Faster!" "Quickly, all of you!" Were some of the shouts we heard, apparently from a number of people. What group was this? Where did they spring up from?

"They were on that side, idiots," shouted the Arab captain angrily. *"After them!"* Next instant the soldiers turned around, charged down the rocky section, over the road, and into the open fields beyond.

Stumped, we looked on in amazement. Who were they who came to our rescue? We saw the Arabs giving full chase in the darkness, heading towards the noise that was fast fading.

"It's the boys!" said Peshotan suddenly. "Rustom and Eruch created that ruckus, to draw the Arabs attention and give us the chance to escape. *Quick,* let's make the most of the opportunity."

Not waiting for reactions he caught his mule's girdle and hurried eastwards, directly toward the second road from Yazd to Kerman. Fast as we could we all tumbled along with him, no longer caring for the din we were making.

"You are heading for the road from this side?" asked Minocher panting alongside his mule. "You wanted to cross-over from the south?"

"We don't have that choice now. It will be getting bright soon and the earlier we cross-over, the better."

The sky had begun to get lighter and the chirps of birds were getting louder as they passed some houses on the outskirts of Bafq. By the time we reached the road, about a mile north of the main town, the countryside was awash with light.

"We are in open sight of anyone that comes on that road," panted Minocher, looking behind for signs of his son. "Let's stop this madness and return to the rocks behind."

"*No!* It's now or never."

Peshotan was the first on the road with his mule. It was still deserted, and no one in sight at either end. Like a mini flood we all poured over it and rushed to the other side.

"*Same speed everyone!"* Peshotan commanded. "We won't be safe till we cover at least a few more miles."

Behruz and her young husband hesitated. "I don't think Behruz can manage to move on any further," her husband complained. "She felt some pain a little while earlier."

Peshotan looked stumped. He didn't want to be responsible for a miscarriage.

"I'll take care of her," my mother stepped forward. "Let her ride our mule and I'll make sure she doesn't suffer from jerks."

Without waiting for a protest she helped Behruz on our mule, arranged her legs at a certain angle and guided the mule at a decent pace.

The group moved on as one for another mile when Minocher pulled over.

"Now is not the time to stop," pleaded Peshotan, his voice coming out in short gasps. "We must cover another two miles at least."

"You all go on. I'll wait here for Rustom and Eruch."

"They'll join us as soon as they've given the soldiers the slip."

"How will they find us, Peshotan? They won't know where we crossed over and which direction we continued. I'll wait here behind this rock and keep an eye on the road. When I see them, I'll draw their attention."

"I'll wait with you." It was Minocher's wife, not in the best of health. She was still sobbing as she nuzzled next to her husband.

"No you won't. It is better you remain with the rest. I'll join you all soon with the boys."

Peshotan could see Minocher was determined so he didn't waste further time. "We'll be headed for that large gap in the mountains," he pointed out another cluster of brown hills on the horizon. "We'll wait for you once we reach there."

As we moved on we felt that finally our flight was successful. We had beaten the Arabs, and now they won't follow us knowing we'll be reaching the salt desert soon…and nobody goes there, unless they want to die.

There was no sense of cheer amongst us even as we came close to completing this mission. We were now leaving behind all semblances of civilisation and our homes. Two of our youngsters were not with us, and the large opening within the mountains ahead of us, reminded us of nothing but the open jaws of death.

We waited within those mountains all day. It was hot that morning and we tried finding solace in the shadows. One of the men had taken position on a higher ridge to keep an eye for Minocher's return. The sun went down but yet no sign of Minocher. But thankfully no sign of the Arabs either. Either they were still chasing Rustom and Eruch, or had caught them.

Around midnight Minocher quietly walked in. He went up to his wife and took her in his arms. He didn't need to explain further as tears rolled down their eyes.

When he felt Peshotan's hand on his shoulder he looked up pitifully. "They caught…them," he said shakily. "When I saw them bringing the boys in I moved closer to the town. They were…bound tightly and thrown across the horsebacks. A little later…they hanged the boys…at the town's square."

It was a pitiful sight for all, in that silvery light the moon provided, watching a grown man break down and weep like a little boy. A sight not easy to erase, but locked in our minds, to be opened whenever we had to relate that terrible journey we undertook.

Eruch's grandfather at Mehrigard, and now Eruch and Rustom. I wondered if suddenly a shield had been shattered and now I was completely exposed to every heartbreak in life. The death of the old man was a shock, but now death of two young friends completely paralysed my mind and body.

A little later, when Minocher and his wife had somewhat regained their composure, Peshotan arranged for a special prayer, the *Pydust* prayers. The complete prayers could not be performed as the bodies of the boys were not present, as required by the customs. But the supporting prayers were chanted in full earnestness. It was one of the most sombre experience for us as we all sat around the glowing *Urn,* in the wilderness of those desolate mountains, and father recited one of our most sacred prayers in a soft, low tone.

I think I grew up by a few years that night.

❑❑❑

16

Next morning we continued our journey eastwards. There was less tension in our minds, less apprehension of being chased and caught. But the atmosphere was full of gloom. Nobody could forget the sacrifice of the two brave boys. Minocher and his wife kept to themselves, and knowing their emotions could dispirit the rest, they maintained a dignified silence.

The women-folk made it their responsibility to take care of Behruz and fussed over her well-being. Her ration was special as they made sure her supply of dry fruits never ran dry. They also took care of her two-year old daughter, Tehmina, making sure the child never bothered her mother. This duty everyone enjoyed as Tehmina was the group's life. Playful and pretty, she brought joy to whichever family had adopted her for the day.

Two days of blind travel in the mountains and we stumbled on to a house. Two brothers were living there and were as aghast to see us as we were seeing them. They were staunch Zoroastrians, too, refusing to give in and preferring to live a reclusive life. Once every few months the two would sneak into Bafq, collect sufficient supplies and return. For a living they farmed on flat grounds around them. As the heat here was very high, very few crops could be farmed. Worse, it was in areas less than twenty square feet, and sometimes little more than a crack in the mountain side, but it sufficed as they had entire mountain ranges at their disposal. They stocked these crops and bartered them for essential commodities at Bafq.

No women? We inquired. They looked embarrassed and explained. "Bringing up a family here is not our ambition. We wouldn't want our children to grow up in these conditions. Our closest neighbour, five miles down south, did go to Bafq and find himself a Zoroastrian bride who was ready to settle down here. But that's rare."

The brothers had sacrificed a normal life for their religion.

"And water?" asked Peshotan, voicing his prime fear.

"Wells. We have two wells here and enough water for an army."

"Not salt water?" we asked, fearing the deserts will be influencing the surrounding areas.

"No. They are underground drinking water."

We replenished our almost exhausted water bags and rekindled our sagging spirits with the reassuring stories the farmer told us. He told us of other farmers along the way, up to the start of the salt desert. He pointed out the general direction we should continue with, in order to reach Darband, our next destination.

❑

After a couple of relatively easy raids at the town of Qomshah, Zahl and his men settled down to more serious business. His younger recruits seemed uneasy and eager for action.

"The first raid you handled only between you and Noshirwan," Ardeshir started his argument one afternoon as the seven lazed on the slopes of Zard Kooh. That raid had fetched them some food and a sword. "The second raid you took a couple of us along and we returned with so much more food and supplies. And ever since it has been a week and we have not done a thing. I think, and so do my other friends, that we're wasting our time here. Let's hit those Arabs so hard they'll never forget us."

Zahl glared at him so hard the man mumbled something and returned to his young friends. Ardeshir, Zahl thought, was a real upstart. If this had been the army, he would have got the young man executed. And the other new recruits who had joined them along the way, he had no confidence in them. They were all very young, like Ardeshir, unseasoned and full of false bravado. Not the kind to depend on in times of crises. Still, they were young and could improve…if providence spares them their lives during the first few encounters.

But Ardeshir was right this time. It was time for him to move.

"After dark we'll go down towards the road to Qomshah," he announced unhappily. He would have preferred to wait a little longer, be better prepared, and then attack. He knew once they start, there would be no turning back, or any respite thereafter. "We'll attack unarmed travellers to start with."

Noshirwan immediately set about preparing the five young men for the attack, demonstrating the skills needed to make it short and effective.

The first raid was on an Arab family returning from a wedding. The pickings were good and they faced no resistance. The family was allowed to continue their journey without further harassment. The younger recruits were overjoyed by the encounter and were jubilant enough to boast of their bravado.

An hour later, three horsemen arrived. They were soldiers from a local garrison. Zahl was apprehensive of attacking them. His troops were just not prepared well enough to take them on. But the numbers favoured them, and the recruits had to start sometime.

Zahl led the attack, bringing down one of the soldiers with a single blow. The rest of his group cornered and disarmed the other two.

"What do we do with them?" asked Ardeshir, jubilantly.

"What would they have done with you?" Zahl asked nonchalantly.

A sudden silence fell on the young recruits. They waited for someone else to answer the question.

"They would have butchered us," said Noshirwan, and unhesitatingly drove his sword into one of the unarmed soldier.

A louder hush from the younger recruits as the soldier dropped dead without a sound. They had never seen this happen before…a Zoroastrian killing an Arab soldier. Their mind-set till now was that of young boys enjoying a prank. A cold-blooded killing of one of their oppressors was beyond their imagination. They now had an inkling as to what the future could be like.

"What about this other soldier, and the one lying there?" Zahl goaded them. "Who will kill them?"

They all took an involuntary step backwards. The standing soldier looked on pleadingly at them even as he stared disbelievingly at his slain mate.

"Why not just let them go. They are…" One of the youngsters started saying.

"They are your enemies!" Thundered Zahl, towering above them, his fiery eyes demanding some action. "They will kill you if they get a chance."

Still no one stepped forward.

Zahl looked disgusted. "If you want to remain with this group you lot better learn to act like men. What did you think when you…"

Suddenly Ardeshir stepped forward and in one motion sliced off the soldier's head. As it toppled over and rolled towards the young group, there was a scramble to get out of the way.

Zahl shook his head in despair. He cursed the young lot aloud and walked up to them. He surveyed their reaction for a moment and then thrust his sword into the hands of the man who was shivering the most.

"*You,* take my sword and kill the third soldier."

The lad almost looked like he would burst into tears.

"*Do it!*" shouted Zahl. "Or leave us."

Instructions clear cut, the young man hesitatingly moved towards the fallen soldier. He raised the sword as he intently studied the soldier.

"I think he's already dead," he said, relief showing on his face. With a weak smile he walked back to Zahl to return his sword.

Controlling all his emotions, Zahl clutched the petrified young man by the back of his neck, bodily lifted him off the ground and walked back to where the soldier had fallen.

"*He isn't dead!* Now finish the job!"

Gulping a few times, the young man once again raised the sword, shut his eyes and brought it down with some force. The sword clattered loudly on a rock as he missed the target.

"I'll...I'll...Kill you for that!!" Bellowed Zahl as he charged towards the hapless lad.

The commotion got the soldier moving. The moment he opened his eyes he gauged the situation. Before anyone could re-act, he removed a knife from his belt and pushed it into the side of the terrified young man standing near him.

Noshirwan was the first to reach the soldier and he brought his sword down heavily on him, killing him instantly. A moment later the injured young man saw the blood gushing out of his sides and fell unconscious.

❑

Later that night when the young man opened his eyes he saw they were back in their hideout. He felt his side and let out a yell. He was bandaged, but the pain was excruciating. His cry of pain brought the others around him.

"You were lucky," said Zahl unsympathetically. "You don't deserve to be alive." He spat on the ground and moved away.

"There's appreciation for you," said one of the young man's friend, staring angrily at Zahl's back. "You almost give your life for him and he..."

"Shut up!" Noshirwan confronted him. "This man endangered the lives of all when he didn't carry out orders. Let this be a lesson to you all. Either you do exactly what you're told, *or we don't need you.* What we have set out to achieve is an extremely difficult and dangerous task, and we can succeed only if we obey orders...*completely.*"

When Noshirwan returned to Zahl he found him pacing the ground in deep thought.

"Well, we have started the ball rolling. By morning their bodies will be found and they'll be hunting for us."

"We have enough arms for all now; we can fight them, even with this lot."

"No, not enough men. We shall have to play a hit-and-run game. I don't like it myself, but we'll be no match to even a small patrol of ten men. Tonight we'll move away from this area, set ourselves up at another mountain far away, and plan a similar attack after a few days. Till we have more men, we'll content ourselves to be just a thorn in their sides."

"And the injured boy?"

"We'll carry him."

"What about you?" asked Noshirwan, concernedly. "The marriage party we raided had seen you and they will surely report your presence."

"Nobody yet knows of me. But when they put two and two together, I'll be glad. Let them know who they are up against."

❑

Meanwhile our journey towards the town of Darband continued. It was a continuous trek in the mountains with no proper route or path to maintain. After each range we redirected our course towards east, our general line of direction.

"Can we rest for a few days," said Minocher one evening, a week after the Bafq tragedy. His wife had taken ill these last few days, and Minocher was anything but well. The lean man had lost weight and the will to move on.

"Yes, I think we all can take a day off." Peshotan was not keen on any delays to their overall plans. But he owed Minocher and his family and he could see the bereaved couple's health deteriorating.

The break worked wonders for most as we all basically relaxed and the womenfolk caught up with their chores. There was some chatter amongst the youngsters, but games were forgotten. I wondered if ever we'll be young enough to play games again.

Another few days of trekking and Minocher's wife died. There was little anyone could have done for her as her melancholy over the loss of her son was incurable.

Another *Pydust,* another milestone left behind. I wondered how many such tragic milestones will finally mark our complete route. In the days that followed the briskness in our steps was missing. The sense of adventure and excitement that was with us at the start of this journey had slowly evaporated. A cloud of gloom had overshadowed the brightness of hope, even in the hearts of us youngsters.

I wondered what my father was thinking. He had always been a quiet man, but now I hardly heard his voice. Have doubts appeared in his mind about our endeavour? Gone was his confidant self; gone was his re-assuring smile. Hopefully the immense faith he had in our religion did not also diminish.

I was beginning to wonder as to the purpose of this journey. If we are all going to get killed anyway, why go through this ordeal?

"Father, they were killing us at Mehrigard, we are also dying during the journey, and they will probably kill us when we reach Quhistan. So why do we keep going?"

"The same reason why we get up from our beds every morning," he answered philosophically. "*Hope!* As long as we have that, there is every reason to go on striving, fighting for what you think is right."

"Hope of what?"

"Of living freely, of saving our religion, so that one day we'll be able to follow our faith once again, without discrimination, without fear. Isn't that a good reason to continue our journey and look forward to that day...whenever that may be...wherever it may be?"

I thought of it but was left with some doubt. There seemed to be too much unhappiness in our group to look forward to any meaningful happiness.

I wondered why my mother no longer hugged and cuddled me as she so often did earlier. Did she no longer love me? Had our arduous journey so far already affected her? And she sobbed so often these days; something I had never seen her do before. I always thought she was the epitome of courage and resolution.

I wondered where my grandfather was. If only he were with us, there would be no slouching shoulders and there would be no doubts in our minds. Did he remember us? Did he think of me?

And suddenly, one afternoon, as we crested yet another mountain range, we came face-to-face with one of the most feared places on the face of this planet…the vast salt desert, Dasht-e-Kavir.

It looked as inviting as hell, as reassuring as a devil's smile and as menacing as Satan in a bad mood.

❑❑❑

The Muslims continued on their victorious path as they completed the annexure of the entire Arabian Peninsula and North Africa. Their destructive and uncompromising ways continued as they sacked Constantinople, and even razed to the ground the great library at Alexandria.

Things slowed down with the advent of the first Islamic civil war in 656 E.C. Even so, their march eastward continued and they soon overran Kabul. Now their access to China and Hind was within their grasp.

Though Persia by now was in complete control of Arabia, there were pockets of resistance...some direct, as in the region north of the Albruz Mountains where they waged war on all Arabic settlements in the area. And there were indirect resistances too, when the locals stubbornly continued to follow their faith, as in Khorassan in the east and Hormuz in the south.

17

If one was to paint a picture illustrating the rest of our journey, it would look like a surreal painting. The landscape would look like something out of another planet…unimaginable; the people like zombies…apathetic.

The sight that presented itself to us was that of a frozen sea, immense and barren. An uncovered mound would occasionally peep out like a lone sentinel and patches of water of melted salt broke the monotony.

"How did it come about here?" I finally asked my father, unable to form a theory.

"Legend has it that centuries ago there was a great flood. The seas had even reached the Albruz Mountain range in the north, and years later, as the sea drained back to its origins, sea water remained in the low-lying areas. As this water evaporated in time, salt residues remained. The central part of Persia, basically this section, is a low-lying area compared to the rest of the country, and hence, this, strange desert."

Wisdom passed on, my father returned to his duties. Burdened by this knowledge, I too went over to my friends and off-loaded whatever I understood of the lesson.

We had not wasted any time on getting on with our journey after we first sighted Dasht-e-Kavir. As earlier indicated by Peshotan, we walked through the southern-most section of the desert, careful not to entice the sleeping giant to roll out its tongue and consume us. We were terrified of the consequence if we strayed too close to the monster, and it showed on our faces. It was almost as if everyone had mentally decided that we were going to die in this vast expanse of wasteland, so the sooner the better. Kuhishtan and Khorasan were just unrealistic dreams, millions of miles away. The salt desert was the reality we had to face first.

"Jamshid," my father called out, "you are to help Farehdun tend to the Urn."

A light breeze had drifted towards us on this fifth evening of our discreet affair with Dasht-e-Kavir. It came from the north, where the desert lay, and normal Persian experience had taught my father that such winds generally intensified towards late evenings.

I walked up to my brother but he showed no delight in my presence. "Don't touch anything till I say so," he warned me at the outset. Keeping the holy fire alive was his responsibility so I kept my distance. Of lat,e he had become rather hostile and sullen. Rustom and Eruch had been his close friends, and them being killed in such a brutal manner, had hit Farehdun hard.

Soon after sun set the breeze turned stronger and cooler. There was no place for us to seek shelter as the mountain chain that bisected the two great deserts was still some distance away. If a storm did brew, we were totally at its mercy.

The desert was yet a sleeping giant to us as we continued our journey at its southern-most tip. Our silent march-past almost signified our respect for it, as though we were afraid of waking it up. It was as if it was sullenly watching us trespass its territory through the corner of its eyes, and was waiting for the right moment to announce its presence. We had braved through its reputation for five days, wary of its intents as it menacingly stalked us.

"The wind is getting stronger, father," yelled out Farehdun as his efforts to shield the Urn proved more and more difficult. "What should we do?"

"We will stop now and form a small and compact circle. Your mule will be in the centre of it. Everyone will sit down and remain as close to the ground as possible."

All hurried to do as ordered even as an eerie atmosphere surrounded us. Along with the mules and horses the circle thus formed was about fifty feet in diameter. The smaller livestock were quickly tethered to the ground. Father, Farehdun and myself, along with our mule, formed a semi-circle within this ring. Father came over to assist Farehdun as I tried my best to look busy and helpful. We, too, as everyone else had, made our agitated mule sit down, caressing him and soothing him with soft words.

"Make sure the Urn faces south," father corrected the mule's position.

Moments later the storm hit us. The wind swept past us soundlessly but its ferocity could be felt by its force as it pummelled us to hug the ground and remain rooted to one spot.

"Oh my God," Peshotan suddenly exclaimed as he shielded his eyes with his arms and forced himself to look northwards. The dark skies had turned deep red. "This storm is going to intensify further, and our fire will surely be extinguished."

That had to be the most demoralising prospect. Even as we prayed for fate to spare us that disaster, I saw Farehdun leave his mule in our care and head towards the northern side of the outer circle, where our other mule was with mother and Mahafrid. As he tottered forward like a drunkard, pushing hard against the wind, he fell down a couple of times. From the packages on the mule he removed a packet. But in doing so a couple of garments flew off the main package straight up into the air and disappeared in the darkness.

When Farehdun returned we saw what he had retrieved, a large piece of coarse cloth that we used as a cover over our tents. Through the darkness and the haze from the wind I noticed his face was covered with lines of blood. Before I could draw anyone's attention to it he opened the cloth and threw one end to father.

"You take one end at the mule's hind and sit on the cloth's corner. I'll do the same towards its head."

It was almost impossible to arrange the cloth the way Farehdun wanted, and at the same time keep the spooked mule down. As the cloth flapped about wildly, smacking us smartly every now and then, it was as though the wind was challenging us to complete our task.

When finally, both father and Farehdun were sitting on either side of the cover, they pulled the rest of it over their backs, over their heads and leaning forward, over the mule, and, most importantly, above the Urn. Instantly the mule and the Urn were safe from the winds. I had managed to get within the safety of the cloth and held on to the mule's tail, just to show my input in controlling the beast.

The red skies had now reached us and the winds were screaming down on us. Though everyone's back was towards north there were sudden screams and panic-laden cries for help. I prayed mother and Mahafrid were safe as they were managing the other mule, on their own. But knowing the importance of this mule, I knew they wouldn't mind being without the help of their male relatives.

When the eye of the storm rode over us it seemed that it had the backing of every devil in existence. It was not the sound of the storm that rattled us as we heard just a sharp shrill whistle. It was the fury and force with which it attacked us. It seemed it had been waiting for centuries for a group like ours to come by. Hungry for victims it now unleashed whatever it had.

I covered my eyes and face with the cloth, completely protecting myself from the ravages of the storm. As the storm intensified even further, and the wind became chillier I suddenly wished I was near mother. There was more warmth and safety in her arms.

A loud neighing sound and I lifted the cover by an inch and saw one of our horses within the outer ring suddenly spring up and bolt away, *along with the provisions it carried.* It would be next to impossible to catch him again once the storm stopped. Losing the horse was a serious loss to the family who owned it, but losing the provisions along with it may prove disastrous for them.

Every now and then our mule too threatened to get up and run away but we held him down firmly. Farehdun, who had tended to him for years, continuously spoke to him stroking its muzzle and regularly thrust his face in front of the beast's eyes, as if reassuring it that his master was still around.

In spite of the conditions and dispite being huddled within the cloth, we constantly kept an eye on the Urn. We can never let it die. Protected from all sides, except the south, it was glowing brighter than before and we derived a lot of warmth from it.

I once again peeped out of the cover and got the shock of my life as I could see nothing but a light grey curtain. It was as though I had turned blind. I instantly pulled back my head inside the cover again and was re-assured that my sight was still normal.

What amazed me a little later was the condition of the strong cloth we were being shielded by. It was being systematically torn to shreds, with long tears appearing in it. Why it should be tearing I couldn't fathom but I knew my father and Farehdun were taking a beating as their backs faced north. If the wind did not stop soon, I worried, we'll have no shelter at all and nothing to save us from hell's fury.

An eternity under the cover and the storm disappeared as suddenly as it had appeared, leaving us all shell-shocked and wondering what had hit us. I thought we were all lucky to get away from its fury with little or no damage. But when we got up and took stock of our situation I was shocked at what I saw.

The instant I tried to walk away I tripped over something and fell on my face. The 'something' was a layer of white dust, *a foot high.* It wasn't there when we took shelter.

When I got up and walked towards my mother and sister I was greeted by a volley of groans and cries of help.

What had happened?

"Dughdova! Mahafrid! Are you okay?" Peshotan came running from behind me.

No one from the outer circle was getting up or speaking. They all just lay there and groaned. It was quite dark and everyone seemed to be in a chaotic state of mind. We found my mother and sister and helped them up.

"It…it's burning," my mother whispered hoarsely. We couldn't understand till she slowly turned around. Her gown had been completely ripped off her back and there were streaks of blood oozing out. As the others picked themselves up, one after the other, we learnt the true source of their pain.

The strong winds had carried grains of salt from the desert and dumped tons of same beyond its borders. The salt flying at gale speed had cut through the clothes and the very flesh of the travellers. Though our cover cloth was also torn to shreds, father and I were spared the fate of the others. Even Farehdun's face was cut open when he had retrieved the cloth, but not that severely.

"God has forsaken us," bemoaned Minocher, setting a panic mood amongst the rest.

Suddenly a scream. A terrified Behruz looked about the group. We first thought her pregnancy was troubling her as she had lately bloated to a very large size.

"Where's Tehmina?"

God! I prayed, not another tragedy.

"I thought she had come to you," Tehmina's father said, hurriedly looking southward where a number of our things had been swept away. Could she have been swept away along with our supplies?

Everyone forgot their pains and aches as a frantic search began in the darkness.

"Where did you last see her?" Peshotan shook the poor father by his shoulders.

The young father pointed to an area with a trembling finger, "She was somewhere there."

Peshotan ran to the spot and started digging out the freshly accumulated salt deposits with his bare hands. Some of the other men realised what he was up to and immediately joined him in sifting handfuls of salt. The women brought out their bowls and used them to excavate whatever they could. When all seemed hopeless, Farehdun exclaimed excitedly.

"She's here!"

We saw her hand first, and when they dug out more salt, we saw the rest of her. She seemed to be asleep. Panic rode amongst all. She must have fallen unconscious during the storm and got buried by the accumulating salt.

Tehmina's hysteric mother snatched her in her hands and shook her violently. The mother was in a daze as she mumbled some prayers and kissed the child continuously. Mother suddenly grabbed Tehmina and held her upside down. She slapped the child's back and pushed her finger deep into her throat. A few small scoops of salt dislodged and suddenly Tehmina coughed and moved. More salt was dug out from her nose and mouth until she started crying aloud.

Relief poured out of every face and there were cries of jubilations. Momentarily, gone were the memories of the storm and the pain it had caused and opened her eyes.

"It's a miracle," said someone.

Peshotan turned to Minocher and softly reminded him, "God is with us. *Always!* Never forget that."

The rest of that night was spent as though in a military hospital. Amidst cries of pain and pathetic scenes we all assisted one another in applying whatever lotion and medicine was ready at hand.

By morning everyone was exhausted. But there was no rest as the sun had come out and it was best to move on. No one complained as we now fully realised that the sooner we get to the shelter of the mountains the better for all. It would be pure hell to get trapped in such a storm again while on this white desert.

❑❑❑

18

A few days later we saw the belt of low mountains. It rose directly from the desert giving it a weird appearance. It started as a series of rocks, one end stretching in a northerly direction, the other end southward. We altered our direction slightly and hit it at a tangent. The relief we all felt was palpable. Finally, we will not have the omnipresent white salt all around us. Finally, we were seeing nature more akin to what we were used to.

"On the other side of these mountains, and some distance away," my father announced knowledgeably, "is the other great salt desert of our country, Dasht-e-Lut."

Once into the range, father chose to snake along with it at its lowest elevation. It was mostly barren but we found some vegetation growing sparsely within crevices and in small patches.

"There must be some water flowing underground," said my father with satisfaction. "But I think we'll reach Darband any day now, so we need not dig for it."

"I thought we would have reached it by now," remarked Minocher worriedly, "I've noticed we've been moving in a north-easterly direction after the storm so…"

"That's the direction those brothers we met earlier told us to take," snapped Peshotan impatiently. "Don't worry we'll come across it any day now."

Darband was our immediate target. It was known to be a small trading centre, a meeting point for the districts in the east and the west, before the Arabs raided our country. But we had no idea if it still existed…if anyone still resided there.

Two more days passed in the mountains and the group was feeling exhausted. Ever since the storm we had taken no proper break, just short stoppages. With the lure of Darband approaching any day, Peshotan pushed all to continue and then take a long break at Darband. And as so often happens, a delay to an expected event meant anxiety and impatience, which translated to earlier than normal fatigue.

Another two days and yet no Darband.

"We were told that we'll touch Darband the day we reach the mountains," Minocher reminded Peshotan. "We must have gone too far north before we reached the mountains and missed the settlement completely."

Peshotan seemed worried too. Did he veer off northwards too steeply? It would be disastrous if they had really missed their target. The significance of reaching Darband was paramount. We desperately needed fresh provisions as a lot had blown away with the storm. And as desperately, we needed the rest and re-assurances. Our spirits had further flagged since the storm, and reaching Darband would have helped.

"Let's try for another day, and if we don't come across it, we'll revise our plans."

Next day a gloomy emergency meeting of the seniors was called for.

"We have definitely missed Darband," Minocher started off as Peshotan nodded glumly. "We cannot go back as that would mean a waste of time and energy, and we're short on both. I suggest we rest in this valley for a couple of days, replenish our spirits and the water supply from whatever sources we can and continue our journey thereafter."

"But we have already finished our water supply." An elderly lady raised the obvious point. "If we don't get water, we'll be dying one after the other… very soon."

"A little while back we passed some shrubs," responded Minocher showing more hope than the rest. "We'll immediately send back some of our younger men to dig in those areas and find the water."

"*If* it is there. So where do we go from here?" Somebody asked.

"Northwards, towards Naiband, another small settlement."

"How far would that be?"

"Less than a hundred miles from here. Thereafter we'll stick to the original plan as shown by Peshotan, and take things one step at a time."

Peshotan heard out his deputy who now seemed to take charge. He had nothing more to add and meekly submitted to the suggestions.

By that evening the boys had returned with some water, enough to see us through for a few days.

But I was worried. Were we on the right track? Moving northwards was okay, but was our line right? Because even if we travelled just a mile away from the right line we'll definitely miss Naiband, and God only knew how severely this would affect us. Were these our last few days before our valiant attempt came to a disastrous end?

I looked towards father for some encouraging sign, but his head was down. What happened to the hero I recently discovered? He seemed to have already given up. I wondered what bothered him more, his cardinal error of judgement in missing Darband, or the seamless change of leadership that was unthinkable till now.

❑

It was now over a month since Zahl and his men had occupied the mountains near the township of Shahr-e-Kord. They had moved away from the Zard Kooh Mountains after the initial attacks and settled down closer to the ranges around Esfahan. It was the influential township and its known affluence that Zahl was targeting. He knew that if the Arabs were hurt in this region, they'll come after him with all their might. And that was what he wanted.

"We have indeed stirred up a hornet's nest," said Noshirwan as he heavily plopped on the rock next to Zahl. It had been a very tiring month for him as he supervised the training of all his men, now almost numbering 50. "Not only the officer in charge of the garrison at Shahr-e-Kord is hopping mad, but the Commander of Esfahan is taking direct interest in our movements."

Noshirwan had already set up a small unit of spies and informers. Some were scared of getting involved but most were eager to do something for this unbelievable rag-a-tag army of Zoroastrians. And the rumour of the identity of its leader…well nobody believed it, but just the thought of it excited one and all.

"Good," said Zahl gruffly as he carefully supported his back against a tree. It was a hectic month for him, and he realised suddenly he was no longer that young. Strong, yes he still was, but this running around all day was getting to him. Almost daily they left this well-shielded camp before dawn. They travelled till mid-day to a point suitable for an attack, far away from their camp. Every time a different location. Their agenda for an attack was two-fold and simple: kill Arabs and collect provisions. Sometimes they got lucky and attacked two or three groups in a single day. Sometimes their day went eventless. But it was the return journey back to their camp that got to most of the senior fighters. A quick bite and bed was their fancy, even as the young frolicked on till late night. It was hardly a couple of months since Zahl's long trek to his son's village, but that was an easy trek…easy paced, his pace, and long breaks.

"They say even the Commander's father is with him," continued Noshirwan.

"His father? What's that got to do with us?"

"He is the Governor of Pars. His name is Sayyid Abul Yaser." Noshirwan thought the name would awaken his master from his slumber.

But Zahl looked at him blankly.

"So?"

Noshirwan looked about uncomfortably. Should he tell him who Yaser was?

"He's the man who cut off your hand," he suddenly blurted out.

Zahl looked at his lieutenant quizzically. What was he talking about?

"What? Who…"

Almost forty years of being single-handed, he had almost forgotten that someone had once chopped off his right hand. When it finally dawned upon him of what he was just told, he went silent. After much self-doubts he softly asked, "How do you know?"

"He says so. In fact, he's been boasting of it for the past thirty years or so."

"Does he carry a purple mark on his forehead?"

"He does."

Zahl gulped hard, trying not to look ruffled. "Still, could be anyone masquerading as my nemesis."

"He has your mace to prove it."

❑

Zahl excused himself from the next raid, and the next. He said there was a sudden pull of a muscle in his left leg and limped about to convince all.

The man with the purple mark…here!?

Ever since he heard Noshirwan mention that man, Zahl couldn't think straight. No matter what he tried to do to shake off the image of that man from his mind, it would stubbornly float back in focus. And when the shadow of that figure wouldn't go away he decided to skip the next raid. He knew he just wouldn't be up to it in a combat. He might endanger the lives of his men if he was not mentally fit. And how could he be mentally fit if his thoughts focussed on only one thing?

All day he sat, brooding over his next move. He never dreamt he would ever run into that man again. Is it good, or bad? Should he confront him now, or leave it for some other, more opportunistic day? He just couldn't decide. But why should he consider this as a challenge for him, he asked himself a dozen times? After all Zahl was a commander, a hero and an acknowledged warrior! And this man, if he remembered well, was but a foot soldier. He tried going back to that eventful day to recapture any details of his opponent, but all he could remember was the purple patch, the gloating and triumphant face, and his own bloodied limb in his foe's hands.

But why is his left hand shaking so much now? Was he nervous facing his nemesis? He hadn't felt so apprehensive before, even when facing a large army. So why had this man got him so uneasy?

"How's the leg?" inquired Noshirwan as he joined Zahl with a dinner plate. It was another successful raid that he had led today, but things were changing. One, he couldn't cope up with the youngsters and the regular raids. And two, the enemy seemed to be up to something. He could sense it. It was almost as though they, the Arabs, were leading them into a trap…enticing them to come closer to Esfahan.

"Better," said Zahl, uncomfortably. He knew Noshirwan had not fallen for his line for a minute.

A short silence followed as they pretended to enjoy their meal.

"Where does this Arab, what did you say his name was…?"

"Sayyid Abul Yaser."

"That's right. Where does this Yaser keep my mace?"

Good, mused Noshirwan. Straight to the point. "He never leaves it anywhere. It's always with him."

"Hmmm." It hurt Zahl to hear that. "We must get it back."

Noshirwan almost dropped his plate. "Wh…What!"

"That mace is the very symbol of our people's pride. *It cannot remain in our enemy's hands!*"

The last words were spoken with vehemence and aloud. The rest of the men turned to see their leader spring up from where he sat so docilely a moment ago. He paced angrily in front of Noshirwan, his 'pulled-muscle' forgotten. A sudden rush of blood had made his face red as he stared back at his men who suddenly lost all interest in the older men's conversation and concentrated on their meal.

"Don't you see," continued Zahl energetically, "half our battle will be won if we retrieve that mace?"

Noshirwan wanted to ask, "How? By walking into a highly fortified city and requesting the current owner to simply hand it over?" But he respected his leader too much to be sarcastic. So he simply asked, "How?"

"I don't know! But it must become our chief mission now. If we get it back, in one move we will have demoralised them to a great extent. It will not be enough to defeat them, but it will be a step towards salvaging our lost dignity. Something my people seem to have forgotten about."

Just as we got demoralised when they took it from you, thought Noshirwan, ruefully. "I fear a direct attack soon from the Governor and his father," he voiced his views.

Zahl reviewed his lieutenant. He always gave the impression of being just a strong man, but Zahl credited Noshirwan for possessing a good insight into many things, and a good judge of men.

"So keep ten of your men as sentries. Spread them around us, about ten miles away, and warn us if any intruders appear."

"I will, but Yaser will not rest till he has your head."

"Tell me, is this man from Esfahan?"

"Of course not! Don't you know anything of this man?"

Zahl simply shrugged. "He took my hand, and my mace. What else is there to know?"

"After defeating you, he became the most popular man in Arabia. He got promoted regularly and was soon the Governor of Pars. He has remained there ever since, reminding one and all of his victory over you."

Zahl nodded in appreciation. "Good for him."

"And he is the man that overnight killed your entire family and destroyed your house. Peshotan had just about managed to escape that massacre."

It was as if the cool air had suddenly frozen Zahl into a stone statue. He barely moved his eyes. Clenched teeth he hoarsely whispered, "Why didn't you tell me this before."

Noshirwan cleared his throat and looked the other way. "Thought you knew."

"I knew they were killed, but…not by whom!"

His dinner forgotten Zahl left the camp and wandered about aimlessly on the mountain slopes. They had earlier placed two sentries at strategic points, not to get caught totally unawares. But they were less than half a mile away from the camp. Not enough time to decamp and disappear from the area if they came under a full-fledged attack. It was good that they had now decided to cover the outer ring of defence too. He passed one of the sentries and was glad to note the man's alertness.

He always felt better when he was on his own. The night wasn't that dark as the stars shone brightly. He wound his way further away passing now somewhat unfamiliar territory, till he reached another slope. There he found a small boulder in a wide open space and finally felt the comfort he was looking for. He sat down on it with a deep sigh, as though the weight of the burden he was carrying was getting too heavy for him.

So what should he do now, wondered Zahl. A showdown with his nemesis was imminent, but when and where? His anger against the man had evaporated over the period of time but the news he just got from Noshirwan had set the mechanism running again. Why was this man so set against him? Zahl had done him no personal harm, so why was he so hell-bent in destroying everything Zahl had? And now, why did he still hound him, hundreds of miles away from his territory?

An hour later Zahl returned to the sleeping camp and roused Noshirwan.

"How did he know I was here?"

Noshirwan rubbed the little sleep that had gathered from his eyes. "It had to happen. You are very easy to spot. That is why the others at our small village were very apprehensive when you came to live with us. It was just a matter of time before the Arabs would come to know."

"You think they followed me here from the village?"

"I don't know, but that tax collector had certainly returned to the village on a suspicion. I had agreed to join you not knowing that Yaser could be involved in this. If I had known that, I wouldn't have left the village at his mercy. That man is dangerous and cruel."

Zahl held the front of his lieutenant's robe and pulled him up. Seeing the blazing eyes directed at him for the first time, Noshirwan felt weak-kneed. He stumbled up hesitatingly.

"You think he has harmed our village?" The words were spoken slowly and with distinct care.

"I…I…don't know…"

"Send back two men immediately to our village. *Now!*"

Within five minutes two men rode off with clear instructions. Make sure the village is safe and report back at the earliest.

❑

The next one week Zahl drove the renegade group to the edge. Noshirwan had never seen him so furiously single-minded and so energetic. Eight days since the two riders had galloped away for Mehrigard, and all eight days they were raiding, almost non-stop. And during each raid it was frightening to see Zahl going almost berserk as he tore into whatever group that had the misfortune to come across them and cutting them down with no mercy.

The two riders returned on the ninth morning.

"The village has been razed to the ground," they reported. "We saw no survivors."

Zahl let out a shattering scream and plunged his sword into a tree. The stout sword made by Noshirwan broke at the hilt.

"Could you see the remains of the victims?" Noshirwan asked.

"Only a couple that were lying out in the street…the rest must have been roasted within the houses. Difficult to recognise any of those bodies."

"How many?" Noshirwan still pried, hoping to hear what he wanted to.

"About ten."

So all were not caught. Most must have escaped.

Zahl rushed back to the two upon hearing their latest news. "Ten? But there were over fifty of them when we left. Where were the rest?"

"We didn't see anyone else."

Zahl whirled around towards Noshirwan. "What could have happened to the rest?"

"Maybe, they somehow managed to escape."

"*Escape?* To where?

❑❑❑

19

"Quhistan!!" Exclaimed Sayyid Abul Yaser. "Quhistan and Khorasan! That's where they must have gone. That's where all these cursed Zarthoshties seem to be going."

Standing in front of him was his captain, just back from his efforts of capturing the fleeing villagers. After hanging the two youths at Bafq he had spent the next few weeks trying to locate the remainder of the group. Returning to Yaser without the appropriate results he knew would tantamount to a betrayal. He had taken his troops first to Yazd in case the group had somehow managed to slip back into the city. When that brought negative results he re-shifted his focus southwards, rode back past Bafq and into Kerman. When that hunch failed, he dreaded his future. When he would report of his failed mission to Yaser, he knew there would be no future.

"But, Sir, there was no scope for them to go towards Quhistan from Bafq. The great salt deserts are in the way."

"The great salt deserts, you…you…*retarded donkey!* They have taken the obvious route between the deserts to Quhistan."

"But there is no route from there…"

"When you know that I'm on your tail, you'll try to find a route to hell!"

The captain knew his days as an officer in their army was over. He only prayed his days on this earth were not.

Yaser's younger son, Jamal stepped forward. Even as the Commander of the garrison at Esfahan, he knew he was outranked by his father and had remained in the background as the captain was impounded.

"Don't worry about that lot, father. I'll arrange a reception party for them, if and when they do reach Quhistan. I will send a large unit northwards.

They can circle Dasht-e-Kavir from above and pour into Khorasan. After they ride down to Quhistan, we'll be there, waiting for them…that is if they make it through the desert."

"Not a single man, woman or child must be spared…except Zahl's family. *I must have them all, alive!"*

❑

Our trek through the mountains towards Naiband was over a week old when we noticed the first change in the terrain on our route. It started with a few clumps of scanty bushes and that led us on to a wider spread of different vegetation. Nothing really to excite us in a big way, but it did give us hope.

And it was here that I learnt the biggest and the most important lesson of my life.

Of late, our weary group had slipped into a very depressive mood. One could not blame them either as ever since we had left our beautiful village (I never thought earlier that it really was a beautiful place), we had gone through a series of unpleasant and demoralising incidents. The latest in the list was the tragic loss of another senior citizen in our midst. Two days earlier she had tripped and fallen heavily on the rocky ground. She had shattered her hip bone. Excruciating pain that she was in we had no option but to hoist her on one of the mules and continue with our journey. That night no one could sleep as the old lady moaned aloud all night. By morning she was barely breathing as she struggled to suck in the air through her pain. Mercifully she passed away by mid-day.

The effect of this tragedy on the group was suffocating. All conversations had ceased as the future played heavily on everyone's minds. Our spirits had been dragged down to a new low as we waited for, what now seemed, the inevitable.

The mood was weighing me down and I intentionally started straggling behind all. Left on my own my fertile imagination lifted my spirits somewhat, as I started imagining the hero I would become if I could save the group from disaster. Lingering still farther behind, out of sight, of the others thanks to the twists and turns on the trail, my imagination became even more adventurous. Suddenly, I became aware of sounds far behind me. I looked back but saw no one. I couldn't identify the sounds but they were there. The sounds varied from a soft shuffle to a low growl and deep breathing.

A beast? But there could be no beasts living in this hell. Then it struck me. Could it be the horse we had lost during the storm in the salt desert? It was many days now since he had galloped off, but if he has discreetly followed us it would be a boon for the group as there were many elders who now needed to be carried.

I rushed forward to give the good news to all but then held back. If I pass on the news then someone else will be sent to re-capture the horse, and he will become the hero.

And it was my discovery!

No, I couldn't do that. I will bring back that horse.

"I saw something shining back there," I lied to my father after running forward to catch up with the rest. "Can I go back and check if it is water?"

Even a hint of a promise of water was enough to give it a try.

"Okay we'll rest here till you get back. And take your brother with you."

"No, no, no!" Why should I share my glory with him? "No need for that. I'll be back in a jiffy."

Before my father could reply I ran back down the trail, out of sight of them. I returned to the spot I last heard the soft steps and strained my ears to re-locate the sound. Sure enough, a moment later, I heard the low growl again to my left. I left the trail and climbed a short slope and whistled softly.

The growl was now closer and the sound of heavy breathing faster.

"Come here, boy," I coaxed in my gentlest voice and moved closer to the sound.

Loud sniffing came from behind me and I turned around. My blood froze and I stopped breathing. Three wicked looking wolves blocked my way. They were all very lean and eyed me hungrily. As there mouths drooled continuously they menacingly crept towards me.

"Help!!" I tried yelling but the sound was no louder than a whisper.

"HELP!" Much better, but the wolves were inching closer.

"H E L P!!" I screamed with whatever I had in me, and the result was there to see. The wolves stopped in their tracks. I hoped the clear mountain air had carried that desperate cry far enough for my people to hear. But even if they did it was going to take them some time to reach here. And the wolves had recovered from my sudden row and now were a mere 20 feet away.

I picked up a stone and flung it at the leader of the pack. It struck him hard on the snout. A sharp yelp and their advance was once again arrested… for the time being. I looked about for more effective weaponry but found only a larger stone. Threatening to throw it in their midst I managed to get them thinking…for two seconds. Then I saw their tactics change. Two of them got to either side of me as the third advanced. I let out a series of 'help' and took evasive action. I moved backwards and at the same time raised my arm with the stone. They hardly blinked.

The wolves were now growling loudly and their fangs were open for inspection. I didn't like what I saw and simply made a tremendous racket, even as tears fast approached the rim of my eyes.

Where were my people? They should have been here by now.

Another mild charge by the wolves and I tried taking another step back. But I had reached a huge boulder and there was no more stepping back. One of the wolves evilly licked his lips and my tears burst out and I started howling loudly. Five feet away from me and they crouched before the final leap.

"Jamshid!"

It was Farehdun, shouting as he charged towards us, a large stick raised above his head. Two more of his friends joined him and together they chased the wolves away.

My knees could not support my body any longer as I crumpled in a heap at the foot of that boulder, sobbing and shivering, all at the same time.

By now a small group had come up and stood around me. One of them, my father.

"Are you okay?" he first wanted to know.

When I weakly nodded in affirmative he asked, "So, where is the water?"

Tearfully I confessed to my lies.

That was the first time I saw my father so angry. First of course came the slaps and blows at my conveniently placed head. And when that stopped he tried tearing out my ear.

"LIES? You dared to lie?" The action over, I prepared for the lecture. But this was one lecture I will never ever forget. I vowed at that time itself that I will carry this lesson till the day I die.

"Don't you know the first thing about being a Zarthoshty?" he raged uncontrollably. *"We never lie!* That is our first and most important commandment! It is Gods law, *and we never break it! NEVER!! No matter what!"*

I bowed my head in shame for angering my father to such an effect. Even when the tax man had humiliated him, he had never shown his feelings. But today, for something I thought so insignificant of, he had lost control.

Truth!

It had to be the most important commitment in his life. And, as of now, it will become the most important commitment in my life as well.

❑

Later, as we trudged on, with me at arms distance from my father, Minocher remarked, "Wolves, here? Hard to understand. How do they survive?" The three wolves had not given up on us as they slyly trailed us, letting out an eerie howl every now and then.

"It is the fertile patch that we have reached," explained my father. "Where there is vegetation there is water. Where there is water there is life. And where there is life, there is hostility, hatred and the hunt for survival."

Later that afternoon we saw another pack of five wolves. And before nightfall two more packs had joined the cavalcade. In the faded light of dusk we counted over twenty pairs of hungry eyes, *all around us.*

Till now they had maintained a healthy distance from us with just on a couple of occasions an adventurous wolf got closer to us than was comfortable. Both the occasions they were chased away.

It was time to settle down for the night and a nervous group searched for a likely place. Peshotan saw an opening in the mountains and investigated it. It led into a valley that narrowed down as it went deeper.

"We'll rest here for the night," he called out. "It should be safer than out in the open."

I was glad that no one objected and all followed his instructions. Had he got back his confidence? I hoped so as he was my natural leader.

Even as stars sprang into view, we could see the wolves sneak into the opening, one at a time. It was impossible to stop them as they didn't use the ground but came in from different heights of the slopes around us.

They didn't bother us during the initial part of the night but made sure we knew of their presence. Every now and then a low howl was let out even as some of them growled deeply. Scary, yes, but still scarier was that we couldn't see them except their shining, unblinking eyes, as they surveyed their prey with suspicious patience.

An hour of uneasy slumber and suddenly we were awakened by a shout. *"They've got very close!"* our sentry cried out aloud. When we awoke we saw the wolves in a circle around us, barely thirty feet away. Some were snarling and didn't seem to be intimidated by the presence of so may people.

"Burn a few torches and push them back," father called out reaching for a stick and lighting it in the common fire.

A few minutes later we did push them back in some disarray. But only for a short time. Soon hunger and excitement reminded them of their strength and our weakness. So they were back, noisier and more daring.

"It's no longer easy scaring them," called out a young man in panic as he actually used his torch like a sword.

The wolves were certainly making progress as their ring had closed in within twenty feet of us. As we sat in a tight circle and the men tried all the tricks they knew of scaring a beast, we soon realised it was a losing battle. The wolves were using any gap in the men's defensive circle and charged almost on top of us. It seemed they were more inclined towards the little children as they singled them out.

"Shout and scream!" ordered father and we immediately pretended the devil had dropped by and hollered our throats out. It confused them for a while but how does one convince a hungry beast that the sumptuous meal laid out in front of him, was really not meant for him?

"We can't control them any longer!" The desperation in the voice was obvious. Some of the wolves had broken our line of defence and were in our midst now.

I saw our men grappling them with their bare hands and sticks. One of the men was down and a couple of wolves were atop him. I saw my father run to his rescue with a stick. A few hefty swings and the two wolves yelped in pain and withdrew. I saw another man struggling with a larger beast, even as a second wolf had sunk his fangs into the man's neck. I saw four of the beasts heading for the women and children. Some of us youngsters pelted stones and brickbats at them but that hardly bothered them.

In the midst of this wild scene we suddenly became aware of another situation. A group of women had surrounded Behruz and were animatedly encouraging her, just as she was writhing in pain and screaming.

"What happened?" Peshotan took a moment off from the wolves.

"She's having a baby," mother informed him. "The excitement and action triggered a pre-matured delivery."

More screaming from Behruz and suddenly we heard the cries of a baby. Before we could somewhat cheer, the wolves also heard the baby's cries and became even more frantic and violent. The intensity of their attacks increased and it seemed it was only a matter of time before they completely overcame us. The women folk who were helping complete the delivery screamed for help as a couple of wolves reached within ten feet of them, hell-bent on feasting on the new-born. A few men went to their rescue and chased them out with a few well planted kicks.

Was there no escape from this horrible fate? Why don't the wolves leave us alone? But I knew the answers. They were hungry…and the rest was nature.

It was a wild scene, something straight out of a nightmare as man and beast almost fought each other with hands, claws and fangs. Shouts from men, screams from women, shrieks from children…and in the middle of this, the continuous howls of the wolves and the gnashing of their teeth as they tore into a few people.

Suddenly Behruz screamed again, and the team of mid-wives were around her immediately. Was she going to die? But a few moments later the cry of another baby laid our worries to rest. *Twins!* And the wolves went completely berserk with the scent of another new-born baby.

This had to be the end.

Through this maze of frenzied action, I had seen Farehdun busy by his mule. He had hoisted out the Urn from its shielded home and placed it on a wooden plank on the mule's back, securing it with some strings. He fed a whole lot of wood into the fire till the flames reached five feet high. All along he was talking to the mule and caressing it. Now he covered himself with a large dark cloth, jumped behind the Urn and rode the mule.

As the mule started walking Farehdun half stood up on it, raised the cloth high above and around him and screaming on top of his voice, charged straight into the wolves. When I saw him in such a stance, with the glow from Urn lighting his face in a strange way, I nearly wet my clothes. Moments later the mule joined his screaming and started braying like never before. Before long the other mules joined in the chaos and the mountainside reverberated with the weirdest blend of sounds.

What the wolves must have seen was a wild mule on fire and a devil with wings riding him. When Farehdun shouted his battle cry and unexpectedly the other mules joined in, the crescendo was so deafening and high-pitched, that the wolves finally turned tail and ran away in one direction, the opening the group had come into the valley by. Ten feet behind them, the Satan himself, and all the devils under his command, chased them straight out of the valley.

When Farehdun returned a few who still had their voices, including me, cheered him tiredly. Somehow, I felt jealous of him. Once again he was the hero and I was still on the applauding side. *When will I be the hero?*

But the rest of the group didn't pay attention to us as they went about licking their wounds…and there were quite a few of them. Eight of our men were bitten by the wolves, three of them quite grievously. The women helped in treating the injured, wherever they could. But the three that were mauled savagely, seemed to be beyond help. Chunks of their flesh had been ripped out of their legs, hands and body and the raw wounds were fatal. We tried comforting them, their families tried looking brave, but we all knew it was to be their last night.

One of them died within the hour, and the other two succumbed to their injuries before dawn.

And the babies, both boys, were named Eruch and Rustom, in honour of the two valiant boys who had given their lives so that we could have ours.

❑

Two days later, we stumbled on to the most beautiful sight under the sun. A small lake.

It was like a mirage, seeing the shimmering waters. The water was clear and clean, though not for long. Everyone in the group, man and beast, after drinking the water hungrily, plunged into the lake. After a brief soaking the rest got back on land but we youngsters enjoyed ourselves to the fullest and remained in the lake for hours.

Though the terrain was rocky, there was soil in patches where tall trees stood sheltering bushes and other vegetation on the ground.

"I don't believe it," exclaimed father, staring high up at the trees. "They're date palms! I can see bunches of the fruit up there."

It was like the king had suddenly proclaimed that every citizen in his kingdom will be gifted a sack of gold. We went wild. What an unexpected bonanza. The task of bringing down the dates was left to us youngsters.

It was a game for us as we scurried up the trunk, as if in a race. No one was an expert at it, but we wanted to impress the elders with our special skills. God be blessed, I was the first up, the one who plucked and threw down the maximum dates, and the fastest. Finally, I was a minor hero.

Peshotan, now back in his place as the leader, decided to have a longer break at this oasis.

"We'll recoup our strength and spirits here for the rest of the journey. We cannot forget what happened to our fellow-travellers who are no longer with us, but try not to think about it. Think of the days ahead of us, the travails we still have to face and the ultimate reward that awaits us when we reach Quhistan…the right to follow our religion."

The speech over, another howl of a wolf reminded us it was never going to be easy. The wolves were still seen now and then, but they maintained their distance at day time. When night approached, Farehdun was ready for them.

❑❑❑

20

"Sayyid Abul Yaser was seen today by our observers, along with his son, Jamal," reported Noshirwan to his commandant, a week after receiving news of Mehrigard. "And they were seen quite close to our camp."

Zahl's pulse raced faster. The time had come for him to square his account with this man. Till now he had maintained little enmity or hatred towards Yaser. It had happened in a battle, and it was his duty to kill and win. But when Zahl learnt of the decimation of his family by the vengeful hand of this man his blood had set boiling. When he found out about the sacking of the peaceful village, Mehrigard, his patience had spilled over. He had cried out, "That man and I cannot breathe the same air! *One of us has to die.*"

"Good," said Zahl not displaying his foul mood.

"They were with a very large contingent of soldiers," Noshirwan continued. "Seems they have confirmed news of you being here."

"Better," said Zahl, unperturbed. "Now we'll not have to go around looking for them. So gather the men and let's go after that Yaser."

Zahl got up enthusiastically and buckled his sword belt, He realised Noshirwan had still not moved and looked at him inquiringly.

"Sire, I must remind you," Noshirwan spoke with hesitation, "let this not be a dual between yourself and Sayyid Abul Yaser. This is a war between the Zarthoshties and the Arabs. Else it will be a lost cause for the men, and it is their lives we are playing with."

As usual, thought Zahl, this man is out-thinking me. Of course, he's right and I'm mistaken. This has to be a fight against all the aggressors and not against one man only.

"We will do as you say. No more of personal vengeance. But if that man is spotted, he's mine. Now get ready and let's go and attack the enemy."

"Again Sire, our strength lies in taking them by surprise. With just fifty men under your command we must select our target. We must hit them when and where it hurts them most. Till then, let them worry about us."

This man wants my place, thought Zahl suspiciously. But, he had to admit, his strategy was absolutely right. Attacking them now would be playing into their hands.

"Okay, so let's break this camp and move further up into the mountains. We'll attack them as and when it suits us."

And that didn't take too long. Two days later a small group of Arab soldiers were spotted scouting the land ahead of the main force. Overcoming them presented little problem and getting the required information out of them, even less.

"They're five miles behind us, behind that mountain. There are about two hundred soldiers. And yes, the governor and his father are at the head of the unit."

That night Zahl lay awake as his troops rested.

So, the man behind his downfall, the man who could lay stake as the champion for the defeat of the Persian Empire, the man who massacred his family stood but five miles from here. After the long and treacherous journey, after reliving his distressing past, five miles meant the man was at his elbows. If only they could face off now, he'll be relieved of a tremendous build-up of tension.

But Noshirwan was wise. If they suffered a loss, and that was very possible as they were up against a much superior army, superior in numbers and skills, then the rebel movement he has started will perish prematurely. And worse, it will act as a catalyst to put a stop against all future movement.

Zahl flung a large stone across the open grounds in frustration. "But I wish we meet soon…very, very soon!"

Suddenly an idea struck him. He can make it happen very soon, and yet not risk the lives of his men. He looked around the sleeping men and found some of them still shuffling about. "I'll bide my time," he told himself with a satisfied smile.

A couple of hours later all was silent as Zahl got up. He checked on Noshirwan, heard him snoring loudly and he knew his coast was clear. He knew where he had posted his sentries and without much ado, managed to sneak past them undetected. Once in the clear he hastened his steps, as though there was an urgent call.

It was not difficult to locate the enemy camp as their fires blazed away without any pretence of shielding them. They were the rulers of the country so why should they hide? Their sentries posed a problem, Zahl found out as he scouted the outskirts. There were too many of them, posted at regular intervals. There was only one thing to do in Zahl's mind. He eliminated two of them and that gave him a wide enough berth to sneak into the camp.

It was still dark, at least an hour before dawn. Identifying the commander's tent was not difficult. Another sentry stood guard at the entrance, but at this hour nobody maintains full alertness. After breaking his neck with a single blow, Zahl eased the sentry's body out of sight. He took a quick glance around. Good, no one had seen him yet. Now to complete a long pending duty.

He roughly pulled aside the flap covering the entrance and boldly walked into the commander's tent.

❑

The break the weary group took at the lake site, stretched for five days, much beyond Peshotan's liking. But he didn't have the heart to push them any further. There was plenty of water now and with a little control on the food supply, there really was no necessity to hurry them.

"How much longer before we hit Naiband?" Minocher slowly strolled up to Peshotan, who was resting with his wife, Dughdova. He seemed to have overcome the loss of his son and wife, as his concentration was centred over the well-being of his fellow-travellers.

"It's less than a hundred miles away and we're doing just five miles a day on these mountains, so maybe fifteen to twenty days."

"That's not too bad. After this rest, I'm sure we'll move faster and cover that distance in 2 weeks itself."

"And once we reach civilisation," added Dughdova, "we must have a *jashan* ceremony. It's been many a day since we left home, and we've overcome a lot of hardships, so it is time to thank God for it."

"Yes," agreed Peshotan, "But not at Naiband. It is but a small trading settlement… and not the end of our journey. From Naiband we'll move on to our next destination, Birjand... another hundred miles or so away. It is from Birjand that we'll branch off eastwards, directly towards Quhistan in Khorasan. We shall have a proper ceremony after we reach Quhistan."

Minocher was studying Peshotan as he revealed his plans. Suddenly, he asked, "How did you know the complete route, when neither have you ever encountered it, nor have we ever discussed it before. We have spent most of our lives together, but I know nothing of the route we have embarked on."

Peshotan smiled. "Because you have not been listening. I have pieced together this route through a number of snippets from a number of people who had either heard about, or experienced a small section of it. For example, do you remember Shehriar, our old neighbour at Yazd?"

"Of course. But he had never ventured out of Yazd in his whole life."

"True, but his brother from Kerman had once visited him. He had talked of the ancient road we had taken first after leaving our village. And he knew of the Zoroastrian families scattered beyond Bafq, right up to Dasht e Kavir. You were there too that day when he spoke."

Minocher tried remembering the incident, mumbled something and returned to whatever he was doing.

❑

The journey to Naiband was thankfully, uneventful. We were well enough stocked with water and food and no untoward incident bothered us. As predicted, we reached the small settlement in two week's time.

The settlement was comparatively large, a hundred families, where fifty years ago over five hundred families flourished. Trade was good as the inhabitants indulged in a number of activities; from weaving carpets to manufacturing expensive cloth to livestock trading. They could have carried on their business in Khorasan itself, but here they were away from the prying eyes of the Arabs. They encountered very few travellers so the bulk of their trade was in the cities outside Khorasan. As we had previously encountered, these settlers visited the cities, sometimes over a hundred miles away, and traded their ware with essentials they needed. A very secluded way of existing, but it gave them what they prized most…freedom.

It didn't take us long to locate their leader, Behram Khosravi. He was said to be the biggest trader amongst them and he had the land and cattle to prove his wealth. He stared at us as though we had dropped in from the sky.

"You have actually made it? We have heard of your endeavour, and we have all prayed for your safety, but in truth and in our hearts we didn't expect you to make it."

"You say you have heard of our endeavour," Peshotan asked concernedly. "How? Nobody but us knew of it."

Behram looked around uncomfortably. "You're wrong! The Arabs know of your attempt and have covered all points leading to Khorasan, including Quhistan. They suddenly came from the north, questioned and harassed all to give information of your arrival, and when they felt convinced that you still have not reached this area, they set up posts across the border to Quhistan to catch you when you arrive. We have all been warned against assisting you."

Behram had allowed all of us to settle down comfortably on his vast grounds. We were served refreshments and the travails of the journey were fast receding to unpleasant memories. Now we were once again jolted to reality.

Peshotan sat as though the sky had fallen on his head. He had convinced all about this impossible journey with dreams of freedom and happiness. And now he was told he could proceed no further.

"So what should we do now?" Minocher asked the obvious question. "We can't go forward, and we certainly can't go back."

Peshotan could only hunch his shoulders and remain quiet. They looked at Behram for the obvious conclusion.

"I don't mind you staying back in our village, but I'm not the only resident here. We must consider the danger you'll be putting the entire village in, if the Arabs find out that we're harbouring you. They could do anything to us."

There was no need to illustrate further the dangers of sheltering a fugitive. It was a hard lesson they had learnt recently. As worry lines appeared deep on the traveller's forehead, Beheram felt genuinely sad for them.

"There is no hurry for you to decide," he said trying to infuse hope in their broken hearts. "You can stay here for the time being. The Arabs come here once in a while, so you'll be safe at least for a few days."

That night the euphuism that had engulfed us all had receded. Had we come such a long way only to be sent back? What now, I wanted to ask the wise old man in the mountains. He had advised us to seek new pastures where we could follow our religion. We did just that and yet we were in exactly the same position we were earlier in. I wanted to ask Zarthushtra why his religion was so despised by the Arabs as to instigate them to eliminate us one by one. I wanted to ask God why he created mankind if all they wanted to do was hate one another and fight.

Early next morning Peshotan called for a meeting of the elders. "There is a way for us to survive the dilemma." Hope once again ignited in their hearts, they attentively listened to their leader. "The Arabs who have spread out along the border of Khorasan have been ordered to look out for a group of villagers coming in from the west, the salt deserts. I feel if we disintegrate into individual families and slip across into Khorasan from different locations, they will not suspect us of being the renegade group."

It took some time for the others to digest this new approach. "You mean we must separate here and be on our own for the rest of the journey?" inquired the pessimistic Minocher. "How could you suggest that after all we've been through together, after all the sacrifices we have made for the group to successfully complete the journey together?"

All eyes back on Peshotan. "This is the only proposal I can make. If you come up with a better plan, let us hear it."

Again a long deliberation and finally everyone submitted to the plan. They asked for Behram's suggestions as to the possible destinations the individual families could head for.

"Your target of Herat needs to be revised. It is north-east of here and about 200 miles away. I would suggest you forget Herat for the time being and move directly eastwards…into Quhistan, the southern district of Khorasan. Not only is it less than half the journey to Herat, but the borders are mostly free of the Arabs. Thirty miles before Quhistan, disintegrate into families and head forward at different angles. You are just about 15-20 families, so it shouldn't be difficult to manage. Cross over discreetly, and then spread out to different cities and smaller towns. And if an Arab petrol catches any family, they can excuse themselves as residents of Naiband. We go through those patrols now and then."

Nervous looks were exchanged all around.

"What places we should head for in Quhistan?"

"Baijand is a big enough place and more than one of your families can eventually settle down there. There are other smaller places with Zarthosties, so you'll have no problem. The important thing is to get across the last hundred miles. The mountains here are high and treacherous."

"How long you think it will take us to cover the distance?"

"We use horses on our trips to Baijand. These are sturdy creatures quite used to climbing mountains. It takes us roughly five days to get to reach the Quhistan border. Seeing how you are heavily burdened, it should take you about three to four weeks."

Long faces all round, but everyone understood they didn't have much choice. We decided to rest at Naiband for a couple of days before attempting the last stage of our quest. A quest I was beginning to equate with the rainbow…easy to see, but impossible to reach.

Later that night we had another well-wisher visiting us. His name was

Xerxes and he was also a supplier of provisions to the town's citizens and a leading business rival to Behram. He was a short, robust man with an easy-going, hearty attitude. He laughed a lot and mixed with all and sundry.

He came with a bagful of goodies and chatted with us till late into the night. He encouraged us with our mission and gave us a more detailed account of the road ahead. There was another route to Quhistan, he explained, that could reduce our journey drastically.

❑❑❑

21

When Zahl pushed aside the flap of the tent, he was not sure what to expect. He had his sword in his hand…and the rest he left to his maker.

Inside he saw a man in deep sleep, on a make-shift bed. Next to it was another bed, unoccupied. Good, handling one opponent made things easier. A low lamp was burning at one corner and he noticed the finery draped around the sparse furniture. He walked up to the sleeping man and placed his sword on his throat.

The man opened his eyes in irritation and felt the sword. Slowly his eyes crept up the hand holding the sword till he saw the face of the intruder, and his head swam. He spluttered as words refused to form on his lips. He knew his time had come.

Zahl immediately noticed the purple mark on the forehead of his captive. So this is Sayyid Abul Yaser! The man who had crippled him; the man who destroyed his family; the man who still wanted more from him.

"Where is my mace?" he asked menacingly.

Yaser's trembling finger pointed towards a corner. Zahl took in a quick breath on recognising his beloved weapon.

"Bring it and put it at my feet," he tersely ordered.

Yaser did exactly as he was told and took a couple of steps back. *Is he going to kill me with it?*

Zahl replaced his sword under his belt and bent down to lift his mace. Ahhh, the power that rushed through his veins the minute his fingers curled round the cylindrical base. He never dreamt of this moment so he didn't know what to do next.

Suddenly a movement behind him and a voice. "Father, the sentry…" A young man had entered the tent and stood gaping at the giant in front of him. When he overcame his shock he moved to call out his guards.

At the same moment Yasser yelled a warning, *"Jamal! It's the..."*

Zahl didn't wait for more. He swung his mace and hit the young man squarely on his head. A cracking sound and the young man crumpled to the ground soundlessly.

Another sound behind him, but this time Zahl was too late. Yaser had retrieved his sword and plunged it deep into Zahls's back. Even as the hot metal was pulled out for another attack, Zahl once again swung his mighty mace and caught a passing blow at Yaser. But it was enough to send Yaser sprawling across the tent and momentarily knock him unconscious.

His head spinning from the shock attack Zahl tried to steady himself. He stumbled against a stool and another sharp jolt of pain ran through his body. This was not good, he sensed. *I must get back to my camp.*

He stepped over the body of the young man and peered outside. All was as it was a few minutes back...quiet. He left the tent and keeping himself in the shadows made his way to the fringes of the enemy's camp. He went in the same direction he had come from, found the gap he had created in the line of sentries and made his way towards his own men.

He must have covered half a mile when suddenly from the Arab's camp he heard a shrill and spine-chilling cry.

"J A M A L!!"

An alarm of some sort sounded and Zahl realised he'd be better away from this place. He realised he had killed Yaser's son, the Governor of Esfahan. He felt assured that they wouldn't try to catch him in this darkness, but at first light Yaser will come after him with all the men he could muster. He tried to hurry but faltered and crashed on to the ground.

What was happening to him?

He had never felt this way before...since the day he fell at the Battle of Qadisiyyah. He reached towards his back and got his answer. He was bleeding profusely.

Must get back to camp before I pass out.

He managed to pull himself up, but immediately collapsed again. He needed some rest. But if he wasted time here, he'd keep losing blood. His mind in a whirl he again stood up and forced himself to move on.

My only chance lies in reaching my camp.

He stumbled over numerous stones, barged into unseen trees and crashed on to dark rocks...but he moved on. Twice he fell unconscious, each time losing valuable time. But his immense will power brought him back to consciousness. The minute his eyes opened he picked himself up and continued his impossible journey. He knew it would get light soon, and he had to warn his men of the imminent attack. Yaser will not spare a single man if he caught up with his men.

But the five miles seemed to be fifty!

When he finally reached the last hill he gave up. He just couldn't move on. He must have lost all his blood and there was no hope of him continuing.

The crack of a twig and he knew it was all over. But the sound came from ahead of him, not behind. A moment later one of his sentries found him.

With the help of another sentry they half carried him, half supported his weight. It would be impossible for them to fully carry him. As they reached their camp the sentries called out aloud for help. Next moment fifty pairs of arms rushed forward to aid their hero.

"He said the Arabs will be here in the morning in full force," the sentry announced excitedly as Noshirwan examined Zahl's wound. "He said we must be away immediately and retreat far away from here. He has killed the Governor of Esfahan!"

Noshirwan immediately assessed the condition of his leader. The wound was too grievous, and he knew nobody could help him now.

"How did this happen?" he asked in anguish as Zahl looked up at him through hazy eyes.

Zahl smiled and raised his mace above his head. "I got it back."

So saying, he breathed his last.

❑

There was no time for mourning as Noshirwan ordered to break camp. In ten minutes the stunned men were ready.

"We cannot leave Zahl's body here," he announced to the shocked men. There had been no chatter amongst them as they tried to fathom the depth of the tragedy. "The enemy will dishonour it in every way they can."

Zahl's body was placed on a make-shift stretcher and a team of six men carried it. They would take turns in carrying him as no team could manage his weight for more than a few hundred yards. As the first light hit the mountainside the sombre procession made their way out of that valley, leaving behind their hearts and their spirits. For a short distance ten men swept the ground behind them, obliterating whatever tell-tale tracks they left behind.

Five hours of non-stop trekking before Noshirwan called for a halt. He had been surveying the landscape of every slope and mountain they traversed and now he seemed satisfied.

"We'll bury Zahl here," he announced.

"Bury?" some of the men responded in disbelief. "Aren't we going to give him a proper Zoroastrian farewell…put him on a mountain top and let nature take its course?"

"No, we cannot afford that luxury." Noshirwan's face was set in a grim expression. He didn't like this decision either. "We just can't afford to take the chance of the enemy stumbling on his body. It will demoralise what ever hope we have instilled in our people. And the Arabs will make sure of taking whatever advantage they can from the opportunity. Zahl's body should never be found for his legend to live on."

The gloomy group looked on unimpressed. Zahl was a Zarthosty and his last rites ought to be of the Zoroastrian tradition. It was not going to be easy convincing this lot, Noshirwan knew, seeing the mood of his men.

"So where do you want us to bury him?" Ardeshir came to his rescue.

"See those rocks on this slope?" Noshirwan pointed to a large formation of rocks about 200 feet above them. There were hundred's of loose rocks below them too. "Just one rock is supporting the entire lot. Remove it and we'll have a minor avalanche."

Ardeshir examined the slope and agreed on the surmise. "But how is that going to help us?"

"We'll place Zahl's body between these two rocks, directly below that formation. When we trigger the avalanche, Zahl will be buried forever under a huge pile up. Yet, his body will not be crushed thanks to these two supporting rocks on either side of him."

The men saw the wisdom in the plan and set about implementing it. One large rock was already in place below the targeted slope. They found another rock of the same size and tumbled it five feet away from the first. They next carried Zahl, placed him between the two rocks and covered his body and face with a white cloth.

Five of the men climbed to the spot where the dangerous formation of rocks stood. Below, the rest of the group moved away from the spot and stood in respectful silence. It all just didn't seem real to them. There lay a man they thought could never die. There was the man they'd follow to hell and back, the man they were sure will win back Persia for them. And now he lay there just like any other mortal…dead!

Just as the men above were about to dislodge the supporting rock, Noshirwan stopped them.

"Wait!" he cried desperately and rushed forward. "The mace! He should have his mace with him."

Ardeshir, who was carrying the mace, immediately protested. "Why? Let the enemy fear this symbol even after his death."

"No!" Noshirwan spoke empathetically as he took the mace from Ardeshir. "Nobody, and I mean *nobody ever*, can own it, but him."

With that he placed the mace on Zahl's body and put his lifeless hand over it.

"Okay!" he called out. "Remove that rock!"

Removing the rock was not easy. With the weight of tons of heavy rocks on it, it wouldn't budge. From below it looked a deceptively easy job dislodging that single stone.

"We'll have to break it," one of the men suggested. So they began hammering it with whatever weighty instrument they could lay their hands on. Just when they were about to give up, the stone cracked. They scampered out of the way as it crumbled and allowed the heavy rocks above it to slide down. Soon the avalanche gathered momentum as other loose stones got dislodged and together made their journey down the slope. The result was beyond Noshirwan's calculation. What came down was almost half the mountain, the five men barely escaping being pulled down. What came up was almost another mountain, clinging to the original one.

When the dust cleared the men were surprised at their handiwork. There was naturally no sign of the two rocks Zahl was buried between, as above them, and all around them, there was a pile-up of over fifty feet.

It was a great monument, befitting a king.

"Let them try and find Zahl and his mace again," Said Noshirwan with a pang. They won't find him, but neither will he or anyone else, ever see their hero again.

❑

When the group departed from the avalanche site, their thoughts were a mixed lot. Some found it impossible to leave behind the memories of a great soul. Others, the more practical ones, knew of the predicament they were in. The Governor of Pars, the ruthless Yaser, would not let the death of his son go unpunished.

"We'll completely vanish from this area for some time," announced Noshirwan. "For the next few days our plan is to cover as much distance as we can from here."

So for the next five days they travelled all day, and sometimes into the night, careful not to be seen. When finally Noshirwan found a suitable place, fifty miles north of Esfahan, in the wilderness of the Zagros, he set camp. Then for a month they remained hidden.

When the patience of his young army ran thin, he decided to come out of retirement. Less than ten miles south was a small road, leading to Esfahan. Not frequented by travellers it still was ideal for their purpose, for Noshirwan had a plan.

Amongst their recruits was a very tall man, Hormuzd. Thin and scrawny he hardly enthused the other fighters. He was bullied by the smallest man and never displayed any nuance of a warrior. But he had vowed to fight alongside Zahl, and that's why he had joined the group. In him Noshirwan saw his plan materialise. Just before a raid Hormuzd was made to wear five pairs of clothing, one top of the other. Further layers of vegetations were padded under those clothes until he looked almost as broad as he was tall. His right arm, too, was strapped under his clothes, giving him the impression of being a one-handed man. A wooden club in the shape of Zahl's mace was handed to him with instructions that when they attacked the next party he should create a ruckus, but maintain a good distance from their victims. The victims should see him and hear him, but not get near him. The arrangement suited him well.

So that night they attacked a small party of five men, returning to Esfahan. They didn't kill anyone but made sure they noticed the tall figure on a close-by knoll, hollering his throat dry and frantically waving the club in his hand.

"Kill them!! Kill them!!" the tall man shrieked, freezing the blood of the victims. Noshirwan's men robbed the five of all their valuables and allowed them to be on their way.

Next night a group of seven soldiers used the same road. A battle was fought and the soldiers were defeated. Five were killed and two allowed to escape...after they had a good look at the terrifying figure atop the knoll. This time Noshirwan had made a short rebel stand next to Hormuzd. Now he seemed much taller than his actual height.

News spread like wildfire that Zahl and his men were still fighting the Arabs. But the best part of the news was that Zahl had retrieved his mace. The people needed that confidence and belief, and Noshirwan provided them just that.

When Yaser heard about it, he went into a blind rage. *Was this man indestructible?* He was sure his sword had done the job. After his son Jamal was killed by the tyrant rebel, he, along with his troops, had immediately set off for the mountainside they suspected Zahl's camp to be on. But he never caught up with them. A few days later they were spotted on another mountain range, but when he rushed there, the rebels had already left that area.

He never recovered from the loss of his son and vowed vengeance against Zahl, and the villagers who had escaped to Quhistan. He had little confidence in his men so he called his other son, Mohammed, from Arabia to assist him completing his now only mission in life…destroy whatever remained of the Mahrespandan family. He would keep hunting for Zahl wherever he went, and his son could bring down Zahl's son's family at Quhistan, if they have survived the salt deserts.

Meanwhile Noshirwan and his men continued their fight against the Arabs in the mountains of Zagros. But the zeal of the earlier days was missing. The magic called Zahl was not there, and without him the new recruits slowly lost their enthusiasm to fight. Soon they started leaving the group. A year later, just ten of them remained. And then Noshirwan was killed in action.

Ardeshir kept the fight on for a little while longer, but it was a lost cause. They attracted no new recruits and the few who remained, showed signs of fatigue. The movement had come to an end, and soon Ardeshir disbanded the group and all went back to their normal lives.

Only Hormuzd remained loyal and enthusiastic. Zahl's very soul seemed to have entered into this man. After the group had disbanded he used to sneak out of his village once every month or two, dress up in his now trademark attire and intentionally be spotted by the locals in the mountains. Sometimes, when just a couple of soldiers passed by, he would pretend to give chase. The soldiers, knowing Zahl's reputation, never tried to retaliate.

Thus the legend of Zahl lived on in the hearts of the Persian people for generations to come, and instilled fear and dread in the hearts of the Arab invaders.

❑❑❑

22

The morning after our arrival at Naiband we got the shock of our lives. Peshotan was talking with Behram when the topic once again turned to our immediate route.

"But Xerxes thought that was the more difficult route," Peshotan said after hearing Behram's plan. "He suggested an easier way."

"Difficult yes, but safer...what did you say?" Behram looked alarmed. "Who advised you against it?"

"Xerxes. He said..."

Beharm shot up from where he was sitting and rushed out.

A few minutes later he returned with a worried look.

"He's gone," he announced. "You shouldn't have spoken to him about your plans. He's friendly with the Arabs in Khorassan and we fear he is their spy in our camp."

"But surely he won't turn against his own?"

"Yes, he can. The Arabs give him a lot of business, and, in return, he does them favours. The fact that he's left the town is self-explanatory. He's off to report your presence."

"God? Have we come thus far, only to be betrayed? What can we do now?"

"There is no immediate danger as it will take him about five days to reach the Arab posts and another five days for them to reach here. By that time you can be half-way home. The danger will be the chance of crossing them en-route. Keep away from the main route and you should be safe. Once Quhistan is in view, follow our original plan."

"And what about you people? Won't the Arabs heap revenge on the village for assisting us?"

"We can always say we were unaware of your true identity. And Zerzes will make sure we won't be harmed...if he wants to continue living with us. Sooner or later," he said with a set mouth, "we'll make him pay for this treachery."

With little options left we agreed to follow the plan as laid by Behram. We stayed back another night and left the town early next morning. ❑

Two days into the mountains and we understood the warning Behram had given us. The mountains in this region were the tallest we had encountered so far and difficult to negotiate. We had left most of our livestock at Naiband as we were warned of the tall mountains, and, in return, we were given sufficient provisions to last out the rest of our journey.

It was two days of silent march, our thoughts constantly on our new predicament. Were our hardships not enough that we now had to contend with betrayal? Were our eyes not weary enough constantly searching the road ahead of us for deliverance, that we now have to continually look over our shoulders for danger from behind?

"Luckily the route is well marked by the frequent trips the villagers make to Khorasan." Minocher said, trying to look at the positive side. He was holding his sides in obvious discomfort and his tongue was half hanging out. But he asked for no leniency as the group tackled the high slopes.

"Yes," conceded Peshotan, panting loudly. "But with the load we have, I don't think we are going to complete this stretch as quickly as Behram predicted."

Five days of climbing up and then down made the weary group demand a halt. So that evening we found a sheltered patch within the shadows of the valley.

"Xerxes must be returning any day with the Arabs, so it is just as well that we are not on the route. Once they pass us, we can continue our journey for another few days...and hope for the best."

Not a very encouraging speech but we were learning to live with the devil at our side. Each day of survival was a bonus, and each mile, a mile closer to safety.

"Brrr...why didn't Behram warn us of the cold?" grumbled Minocher, getting back in his stride. It was almost four months since we left home and summer was over. We were thankful that we wouldn't have to spend the winter in the mountains, as it would be near impossible to survive. In fact, the seniors were already bothered by the chilly evenings. And the nights particularly were beginning to be miserable. The sooner we leave these high altitudes, the better. "Aren't there any caves around? Besides warmer, it would be safer too."

Four youngsters were despatched to make a survey of the nearby slopes and try to locate a proper shelter. A cave was found away from the route and we all crowded into it. In an hour's time we were comparatively cosy...but, of course, there was little bonhomie.

Fugitives in our own country! It was a punishment and humiliation no people should be made to experience.

It was my birthday, too, but I've never had such a drab and forgettable birthday. Forget about celebrations, there were no gifts, and no special food. All I got was a kiss or two from my family, painful pinches on my cheeks from the elders, and heavy thumps on my back from my friends.

Dispirited by the glum atmosphere I stepped out of the cave. It was dark and cold, but I felt happier being on my own. I breathed in deeply and the fresh crisp air revived me somewhat. Now I must find a secluded spot to contemplate the vagaries of life. Every time I grew a year older, I felt I was wiser than the day before, and that I should behave as such. Today I was eight, and I felt it my duty to upgrade my intellect and live my life as an eight-year old. For the past two years, at the end of each birthday, I would sit down and try to figure out the mysteries and enigmas surrounding my life with the broader, more advanced mental power I perceived I now possessed.

Careful not to venture out too far I found a small tree twenty feet below the ledge I was on. Balancing on the mountain side its top branches scraped the slope. A good place to be by myself, I thought. I slowly climbed down to it. It didn't take me long to settle down comfortably on a stout branch. There was no difference in the view from here, but I was happy. Definitely no one will bother me here.

So, I reflected, we were headed once again towards the proverbial wide open mouth of a hungry lion, and now, with the ever-persistent wolf snapping at our heels. Knowing the Arabs were waiting for us, knowing there'll be no peace in Quhistan either, why at all go there? I just couldn't figure out our elders, particularly my father. Quhistan is obviously not going to be a paradise for us, at least not till that evil man Yasser existed, so why not accept the fact and change our destination?

Why not leave this land altogether, as the wise old man in the mountains had suggested, and go where the Arabs will not bother us?

Did other people from other countries go through what we were going through, I wondered. I knew other religions existed, but were they, too, under the same threat we were experiencing? Did they, too, run away so they could follow their religion in peace? *Or did they fight for their right to follow their religion?* We were past fighting our rulers and were no longer a nation of one people. Even a man with the name of one of our historic heroes, Zerxes, chose to betray us.

And were we really saving our religion for posterity? *How?* We followed it in secrecy, as though we were concealing a disease. Wouldn't it be better to follow our religion with conviction, in a place that would allow us?

I suddenly thought of my grandfather and immediately felt guilty. If he knew how his grandson thought he would die of shame. *Leave Persia?* I wondered how he had progressed with his dream of pushing the Arabs back where they came from. Or, had he given up and embraced reality. No, I was sure he would rather die a thousand deaths fighting for it.

I looked eastwards and imagined my grandfather, far away on some mountain, still fighting the Arabs. If only he was around I wouldn't mind walking into the jaws of a hundred hungry lions. I unconsciously fiddled with the Asho Farohar around my neck and felt more at ease.

But why wasn't grandfather with us? Hadn't he suffered enough of loneliness and pain?

To be more precise, why *do* people suffer, I wanted to know. If their *Manashni, Gavashni* and *Kunashni* were unblemished why couldn't they live a happy life? Zahl was a warrior, so he must have killed people, so his Kunashni may be tarnished. So he may have suffered. I could understand that. But why were my parents suffering the way they were? Why were little children made to go through a living hell? There was no questioning their *Manashni, Gavashni,* or *Kunashni,* I was sure!

Zarthushtra had preached that the world was a battlefield between the good and evil forces, and the day the evil forces were conquered the world would come to an end and all souls will merge with Ahura Mazda. That's fine but what about the interim period, the period we all are living through? Why aren't the good, who are living a just and peaceful life, be suitably rewarded while in transit in this life? Why do we find the good forces being meted out the same fate as the bad...and sometimes, worse? If God wanted the world to be good the obvious solution should be to reward or punish, in this life itself. Else, the good may see no point in being good today, if he is to be rewarded later. And even that is not guaranteed. On the other hand the wicked go about their wicked ways confident that God is not going to retaliate till, maybe, after they die. And if that's the case, why should they worry?

Somewhere, somehow, I was sure, God was missing a trick or two. If…

"Jamshid?"

Alarmed that God may have read my thoughts I shakily looked up at the ledge above me. Farehdun stood there with his hands on his knees and staring keenly at me. How did he find me?

"What are you doing sitting on a tree in the middle of the night?"

That's the problem with close-knit families. They won't let you be on your own for a minute…particularly on your birthdays.

"Just sitting." I didn't want to encourage him or he'd join me and ruin my solitude.

A minute later he scrambled down to my branch and sat looking around. "Not much of a view from here."

"I didn't say there was." I didn't start any conversation as he never said anything that excited me. He was a hero to all, I know, but my brother was a boring person. Talk about his mule and you'll get an animated discussion on the importance of raising one. Talk of anything else and you'll get respectful silence. And whenever he started on a subject he would easily detour and talk of a dozen other things not relevant to the subject matter.

But he was the acknowledged hero, and my elder brother and much stronger than me. So though I found him aloof and uninteresting, I had little choice but to respect him and his ways. Maybe, if I cold-shouldered him he'd go away.

"Did you hear about Zahl?" he asked casually.

I immediately became attentive.

"Behram was saying they heard a lot of rumours from the towns they visited. You know there are several interesting towns ahead of us, they say. Some are complete weaving towns, some are…

"You were talking of grandfather," I gently reminded him.

"Yes. They say he has successfully raised a small army and they are already a thorn in the sides of the Arabs."

I sat bolt upright. So my grandfather's fight is on! So my family is still fighting for the honour of Persia, like they had been for centuries. And here I was contemplating abandoning my country.

"What else he said?" I asked eagerly, leaning forward and hanging on to every word my brother said.

"He said Zahl's army was located in the Zagros Mountains around Esfahan, and that Yasser is also there, still trying to catch up with him."

He'll never catch my grandfather, I was sure. If Zahl's army survives for just another dozen years, I'll go to the Zagros and join him. I caught myself in a quandary. A minute ago I was thinking of running away from my motherland, and now I wanted to fight for it. Where do I really stand? I decided to let time pass by and…

"What are you boys doing down there?"

It was mother.

It was no use trying to be alone, so I climbed up the slope again and joined the rest in the cave. When I finally dozed off I was in a fancy uniform astride a beautiful steed and grandfather was watching with envy as I knocked down five enemy soldiers with one stroke.

❑

On the twentieth day of the last stretch of our epic journey, father called for another meeting of the elders. With the additional provisions we were carrying from Naiband, the period was covered comfortably enough.

"I think we have now reached the point Behram was talking about. We have climbed down the last of the tall mountains and the Quhistan border should be about 20-30 miles away. We have managed to elude the Arabs so far, but there is no saying when and where the reinforcements Xerxes must have alerted will be upon us. We are not sure if they have already returned from Naiband...or they're waiting for us somewhere up ahead. So we'll continue to be on our guard, even as we approach freedom."

It was a statement not many were overjoyed to hear. Yes, we were near completion of what we had set out to do, but it also meant we were near a heart-wrenching separation after a period of complete togetherness, support and protection. From hereon we were to move on as individual families, and prey that Xerxes's treachery remains ineffective. In smaller groups we will be moving faster, but the advantage of a larger force will be lost.

"Who goes where?" someone wanted to know, as the weight of separation mounted..

"Ahead of us we can see three rough routes, all heading eastwards towards Quhistan. We'll divide ourselves into three groups from this point on. As we proceed we may come across roads branching off. We should divide ourselves further by using these off-shoots. All will be eventually leading to Quhistan so it should be okay. If you have not sub-divided in the next couple of days, then break up and proceed in stages, one family each day. Avoid a larger group under all circumstances."

Some wanted to hold back a little longer, be together for some more time, but others wanted to get over with the pains of separating. The distribution of the three groups began and all wanted Behruz's family with them. But only one group got them. Ours.

Before the moment of separation came Peshotan held a short meeting with the head of each family present. He handed over three large gold coins from his collection to each of them. "This will see you through for over a year," he said.

So six families got together, hugged the rest, wiped their eyes dry and set off for Quhistan immediately. It was sad to see the people we had spent our lives with together, wind their way between the rocks strewn beyond the mountains. Soon they were out of sight, but never out of our minds and hearts.

Father was the one most affected by the separation. He had seen through countless hardships and happy days with the entire group. He was after all a godfather to one and all. Careful no one saw him wipe a tear from his face he tried to infuse encouragement. "Well, the rest of us are still together…at least for another day. Tomorrow we will as well take our own road. Minocher will be part of our family."

The statement raised a few eyebrows, particularly mine and my mothers. I looked at father with disappointment and anger for taking this decision without consulting us. Mother had an eyebrow raised that refused to come down again. We knew Minocher's family had raised father, and he was now alone, but he was such a difficult person.

We thought an additional day together would be fun but no one seemed to enjoy it. A third of our group was missing and the rest missed them sourly.

We all were up early next morning, eager to get over with the second separation. Without much fuss or fanfare the two groups took their separate routes, and we were alone…just the twenty of us from six families, and Minocher...and a pack of Arabs on the tail of one of our groups.

❑

It was a month since his son Jamal's death and Sayyid Abul Yaser had lost all interest in life…all except one. He wanted the head of Zahl.

He remembered that fateful night and flinched. How did he let the champion warrior slip through his hands? When he had opened his eyes and saw the giant looking down at him he thought all was over and he mentally prepared himself to meet his maker. But he knew the giant was desperate to get his mace back, and Yaser saw a glimmer of hope. To survive, he had to trick Zahl, somehow, for fighting him individually would be futile.

But just then Jamal had walked in.

Momentarily Zahl's attention was divided and Yaser saw his chance. He grabbed for his sword that was hanging from the bed-post. But next instant the deadly mace moved with lightning speed and he saw his son fall. Same instant he plunged the sword into the enemy with all his might, certain it was a mortal blow. Next moment his head exploded into darkness.

When he opened his eyes again the giant had vanished and his son lay in a large pool of blood. He felt a sharp pain on the side of his head and instinctively touched it. Blood trickled down his fingers He ignored it as he concentrated on the bigger issue. When he found no life in his son's body he could control no longer. He let vent his frustration and anger by screaming with whatever power his lungs possessed. That very moment itself he made a promise.

He will hunt down the giant, or die doing so. And he will do *nothing* else, till his death wish was fulfilled.

They soon set off against the giant. Yaser was sure to find his body somewhere near the Arab camp itself, as he felt no man could survive for long carrying such a wound. But the giant seemed to lead a charmed life. There was no trace of him.

A week later he returned to base camp and handed over his resignation as the governor of Pars. The post meant nothing to him any longer. He next sent an urgent message to his elder son.

Mohammad,

You or I can breathe no longer, till the killer of your brother, and his entire family, breathe.

I forbid you to spend another moment in Arabia, I forbid you to think of anything else, but the sacred duty we are now bound to. Come to Persia immediately, or never show me your face.

Your Father.

Yaser knew his son was no soldier, but he needed a man with conviction to carry out the task he had in mind. He could have entrusted the job to his second-in-command, but it wouldn't be the same. His family had been humiliated and it had to be a member of his family who would bring down the accursed Mahrespandan family.

Mohammad stood in front of his father in less than 40 days. He had heard about the death of his brother but he had no idea where he fitted in. The sword was not his tool of trade and he felt uncomfortable guessing what was in his father's mind.

Yaser wasted no time mincing words. The last 40 days had been a personal hell for him as he got regular reports of attacks by Zahl and his men. He just couldn't figure out how a man so grievously wounded could still stand, let alone fight.

He had to be the devil himself!

"But the giant is not your worry," he instructed Mohammad sternly. "He is marked for me and is destined to die by my hands, *and mine alone!*"

Mohammad had seldom seen a man so consumed by grief and anger, both at the same time. He waited for his orders.

"And you shall go east, to Khorasan. That's where his family has escaped to. Our men are already there, but they've been unsuccessful. You are no soldier so leave the fighting to the men, but use your mind and body fully to trace that family. Leave no stone unturned as they are a crafty lot, *but find them!* When you have them in your hands, make an example of them no Zarthosty will ever forget."

Yaser didn't let his son rest even for a day, after his long journey from Arabia. The same afternoon Mohammad left the Esfahan valley with a team of twenty hand-picked men.

❑❑❑

The Arabic ambition of ruling the world and imposing Islam as it's religion, took a setback when the Muslims divided themselves on an internal matter, and faced each other in the Battle of Karbala in 680. The second Islamic civil war followed soon after. Their energies divided, they concentrated more on the problems at home. Their dream of continuing into China and Hind was put on hold. Shortly, in 690 C.E. Wu Zatian, a concubine of Emperor Taizcng, became the Empress of China and converted to Buddhism. A year later Buddhism became the official religion of China.

The Zoroastrians of Persia by now accepted that there was little hope of them pushing the Arabs out of their country and reviving their religion. Many converted to Islam, some escaped to nearby regions like Central Asia. A few still practiced their faith discreetly, stubbornly holding on to a hope that they will someday succeed in reaching a more permanent and acceptable solution...and they prayed to their God, Ahura Mazda, for that day to come.

23

The countryside here was in stark contrast to the rest of the land. The greenery was lush, the climate cool and an abundance of flora and fauna scattered all round. The altitude was high, along with the spirits of the people residing in the area. They boasted of being the only free district of the country.

Sayyid Abul Yaser cast a lazy eye over the surroundings and was unimpressed. His mind had long ago proved to be unreceptive to nature and its beauty. For that matter, he was unreceptive to anything on earth, except news of Zahl and his family.

"Even Esfahan was not as beautiful," his lieutenant remarked, enjoying the cool breeze that caressed his face gently. "Why don't we rest in these parts for another month?"

Yaser looked at him as though he was the leftovers from the cat's dinner plate. He scowled, grunted and shook his head in despair as though the suggestion was the most ridiculous thing he had ever heard. No commitment amongst his men; that was the problem. They all wanted an easy life with no responsibilities; they dreamt of being rich, without working hard. *That was not how this country was conquered!* The men who achieved that impossible dream were made of a different mould. When we fought, he remembered, it was not for money or praise. It was for the glory of Islam, *and nothing else!*

They were passing through Rhagae, also known as Rae, a city in the north of Persia. It was an ancient city with a glorious past, but Yaser didn't notice any of the historic relics. They had just passed the famous Sokout Tower, the 'Tower of Silence' of the Zoroastrians. Twenty feet high, circular in shape and open to the skies the 1600 years old structure was used by the Zoroastrians as the place to leave their dead. Built of mortar and stone it had survived the ravages of time, and Alexander the Great. But it failed to even raise Yaser's tired eyebrows.

"I would have liked to see the great Hyrcania Ocean." Yaser finally showed some interest in the country he had helped conquer. "I believe it is the largest body of water anywhere in the world. But to reach there we'll have to cross the Alburz Mountains, and we don't have the time. I shall come back and spend time there, only after every Mahrespandan in existence has been eradicated."

"It's not only the Alburz that we'll have to worry about," his lieutenant reminded him. "Don't forget the land between the mountains and the ocean is still controlled by the Zoroastrians."

Yaser jumped to his feet in anger and asked his men to get ready for continuing their journey.

It was ten years since he had last seen Zahl. Ten long and fruitless years. All that time he had scoured every inch of the Esfahan valley, up-turned every stone on the Zagros Mountain, traversed every field beyond the mountains, *but there was no trace of Zahl*. The fact had brought his mind to the edge, and his men feared he would soon lose his sanity.

"Where could he have gone?" was the question foremost in his head every morning he opened his eyes.

"He couldn't have just disappeared!" He was too huge a man not to be noticed. Who was shielding him, and where? And what about the rag-a-tail army Zahl had gathered? Where had they all disappeared? In the initial months he used to boast that they had defeated the rebels and chased Zahl and his army out of the country. But when he couldn't prove it with any evidence the claim was doubted, and Zahl's legend of invincibility grew. Even his men spoke in whispers when his name was mentioned. This maddened Yaser further and made him widen his search radius. He searched outside the realms of Persia, in the mountains of Khvarvaran and the city of Ctesiphan that they had captured. But to no avail. He returned to Esfahan and resumed his search, evenly distributing the men under his command. The most defeating fact that made Yaser climb walls was that Zahl was spotted every now and then.

But by now the new Governor of Esfahan had grown tired of the personal vendetta Yaser had got into. A lot of the province's men were being deployed chasing a shadow. He ordered them back to their regular duties and Yaser had to stop his madness.

One day it dawned upon him that Zahl must have left the valley and gone east to his family. So began Yaser's new quest…to go to Khorasan and kill two birds with one stone, kill Zahl and teach his family a lesson this country will not forget. He was joined by his faithful lieutenant and five enlisted men and together they set off for the North, en route to Khorasan.

Yaser had asked his son, Mohammad, to meet him at Herat, the city he felt the Mahrespandan family was most likely to make their home. Part of their journey was already over and it should take another month or so to reach Herat. He learnt the hard way that he was now old, and his body could be punished no longer. A year ago he tried intensifying his search for Zahl but ended up spending the next six months in bed. He felt his end was near, and sadly his mission in life was left incomplete.

❑

"Almost ten years in Khorasan and all you have achieved is the capture of three of the twenty families you had set out to destroy."

"Plus the two families we caught before they reached Quhistan," Mohammad corrected his father.

"*But none that mattered!* Not a single member of the Mahrespandan family amongst them. And that success was not your doing either. That was thanks to a traitor in the Zarthoshty's ranks. That is the quality of their patriotism...wave gold in front of their eyes, and they'll sell their mothers." He sneered and turned sharply towards his son. "Couldn't you have similarly bought their co-operation? You had all the resources in your hands."

Yaser was beyond anger and he let his son know he wasn't pleased with the progress. They were just outside the city limits where Mohammad had set up his camp.

"It isn't easy," said Mohammad, not too happy either to see his father. He missed Arabia but life was easy in these mountains, and the city of Herat had been good for him. It boasted of diversity and abundance as people from other parts of the world, particularly the east, converged here to trade. "And tracking down those families was not my only achievement. I've regularly preached our Islamic convictions and have succeeded in converting some of these Zarthoshties into Islam."

"That was not what I had asked you to do." *Why can't people follow simple orders,* Yaser wondered. And he had called his son from Arabia as he expected unwavering co-operation from him. "And how many did you convert?"

"About seventy families," Mohammad proudly answered. He was God's son and had spent a lot of time spreading the good teachings of Islam.

"Seventy families? In ten years? BAH!" Yaser was slowly losing his cool. Did he make a mistake depending on his son? "I had converted seventy thousand families in Pars, *in ten days!"*

Yaser stomped about as he ran his fingers through his hair. His son had failed in his mission and now he, Yaser, will have to complete it on his own, and he was not getting any younger. He was soon to be eighty years old.

"And any news of Zahl in these parts?" he suddenly asked.

"Zahl? I thought you were after him in Esfahan?"

"I was," Yaser's voice was barely heard. His own failure was being pointed out. "But he escaped."

"I heard people still come across him in Esfahan, every now and then."

"I know, I know," said a frustrated Yaser. "But they're all hearsay. I believe he's actually somewhere out here, close to his family, *and I'll find him!* Tomorrow we'll leave for one of the villages the three families you caught had made their home. Maybe I'll find something more than you did."

"Why don't we simply leave them alone? They are harmless people who work all day, pray at their fire temple and mind their own business."

"*Pray at their fire temple?* What do you mean?" Yaser couldn't believe his ears.

"There is one fire temple functioning in the city, and that is…"

"*WHAT?* You mean we haven't destroyed it yet?"

"Well the rest are destroyed. As a mark of goodwill the governor has allowed this one to remain intact."

"I don't believe this! Hasn't the governor heard the Caliph's orders that every fire temple in the country has to be destroyed?"

"Yes father, but I told you this has worked better for us as the Zoroastrians show their appreciation by collaborating with us on all other matters." Mohammad didn't care for the look in his father's eyes.

"Collaborating? Who wants their collaboration? *We demand their obedience!* I will meet the governor immediately about this."

The governor disagreed with his views.

"I shall write to the Caliph about this," Yaser threatened and made a dangerous enemy for himself. *"That fire temple must come down!"*

❑❑❑

It was winter and very cold. I ambled along the narrow lanes of Herat, quite adapt with its many twists and turns.

Ten years! That's how long back we had come to this area. After crossing over the salt deserts we had tried to settle down at a number of villages, but something or the other made us move on northwards. When we reached Herat we knew we had finally arrived. Now, we felt, we could finally live in peace and safety.

The first year went by fast. I made quite a few friends and was happy that we had travelled such a long distance to be here. There were many Zarthoshties, all moving around freely. And even the Arabs, who had settled there, were no problem. It was a 'live and let live' atmosphere where everyone benefited.

Father bought a house on the outskirts of the city with plenty of land around it. In spite of the gold used for purchasing the place, we maintained that we were basically a poor family from Quhistan in search of a proper livelihood. As farming around Herat was more practical, with a ready market in the vicinity, we had made the change. Mahrespandan may still be a dangerous name so after much deliberations and protests we assumed Minocher's family name, Athavian.

Minocher passed away within a year of coming to Herat. The poor man never really recovered from the loss of his family.

In due course of time Farehdun found a girl and got married. He and his family, now extended with a son and a daughter, lived with us. We, the men folk kept busy in the fields, growing seasonal crops and fruits.

And then we heard of Yaser's son. At first we heard good reports about him but soon learnt of the massacre of one of the families we had travelled with. They lived in a village close to Herat. Mohammad's men had given them no chance, butchering them in their small house. We also heard of the capture of two more families by him, but he was more lenient with them. He handed them over to the local authorities and ensured that they'll remain slaves henceforth.

"They say, the men were looking for a family who went by the name of Mahrespandan," were the rumours that filtered through. It saddened us deeply of their loss, but were immensely proud of them. They knew we had settled down at Herat, but didn't inform the Arabs.

What had traumatised us most was the ill-fated group that was captured before they reached Quhistan. There was no news of their destiny as they were never heard of again. Luckily that group had just divided into three smaller groups of two families each from the original six. The rest were safe.

A year had passed by before we got the news that a man by the name of Xerxes from the village of Naiband was attacked by a pack of wolves and devoured. The strange part was that no wolves existed within a hundred miles of that town.

❑

I was now eighteen years old, very tall, very thin…and very ugly, according to Mahafrid. I admit I could be a little gangly and maybe my face was not looking matured enough as my beard was taking its own time coming up. But I wasn't ugly. Problem with Mahafrid was she found something wrong with every man she met. That's why she was still a spinster; a fact that horrified my mother.

"Fifty boys we've shown you and yet you are unmarried," she lamented regularly. "Back in Mehrigard you wouldn't have had the choice of two boys, and would have had to settle choosing one of the two. But here you suddenly think you are a queen, and want a prince for a husband."

"But mother, you want me to be happy, don't you?" She knew how to cajole mother. "None of these boys was fit to be your son-in-law."

She was now twenty four, and it was an alarming age for a girl to remain a spinster. Mother was desperate and I was the scapegoat. "You move around with so many boys, why don't you select one?" Which I did, and which was why I was in the market. An elder brother of a friend of mine had impressed me with his maturity, and his wealth and I had invited him to our house to introduce him to Mahafrid.

"Go to the bazaar and get the best sweets and the best meat for him," mother had instructed me. "I'll make some *kebabs* he'll never forget, and give the credit to Mahafrid."

I was selecting a particularly flavoured sweet from Hind when my eyes fell on a man at another stall. He too was tall and very thin. He was shabbily dressed and seemed to be aimlessly wandering around. Suddenly I knew who it was.

"Ardeshir!" I called out softly.

He must have heard me as he swung around towards me, his fists up, ready for a fight. He didn't recognize me and surveyed me with suspicion and aggression.

"Ardeshir, it's me, Jamshid."

He still looked confused and then he broke into a huge smile. "Nosy midget?" he said, rushing to me and clasping me hard in his bony arms. "You've finally grown taller."

I was a clear inch taller than him, but didn't point it out. After the initial burst of greetings I asked him, "But you were fighting the Arabs with grandfather?"

"That was long ago..."

"How is he, my grandfather?"

Ardeshir looked about uncomfortably and then told me. I was shattered. All those stories we were hearing about grandfather had acted as moral boosters for us, keeping our spirits and hopes alit. To learn that, in fact, he had died ten years ago was as heart-wrenching as it was unbelievable.

"I believe Yaser is in Herat with his son," said Ardeshir, trying to draw my attention on to another subject. "He is determined to track down your family."

"I know, but there is nothing to fear. Too many years have gone by, and we've changed our name too." I didn't want to discuss anything at this point of time. I just had heard the saddest news of my life and I needed time to grieve the loss of my grandfather.

"Maybe, but he is determined man." Ardeshir reminded me. "He has almost lost his mind with this single-minded pursuance in his life. But they say he won't last long."

"Where do you stay?" I asked, forcing the picture of grandfather out of my mind for the time being, to bring it out again only when I was alone.

"Oh, here and there," he said, trying to sound casual. "And you?"

I was beginning to understand the situation Ardeshir was in. He was down and out, and needed help.

"What happened?" I wanted to know.

"Still the question mark you always were," he said with a smile. "What didn't happen would have been the more appropriate question. Ever since I left the Esfahan valley and came over to the east, I have had no breaks, no stability. I tried my hands on a number of things, but nothing worked. Today I work as a servant in the house of an Arab." He looked down ashamedly and turned his head.

"Not to worry, I'm sure father can use you in the fields. Come, I'll take you home. We stay a little distance away, but the family will be very pleased to see you again. But first I must complete the purchases I had come for."

Later at home, after the euphoria of meeting an old friend, the news of grandfather brought everyone back to reality. Father simply excused himself and went to his room. He had never forgiven himself for letting his father leave our home. The years had been harsh on him too and now he was but a shadow of his old self. His prematurely white beard still stamped his authority wherever he went, but he had become frail and spoke little. I feared the news of his father will certainly add to his failing health.

"No wonder Yaser is so determined to take revenge," said Farehdun slowly. "Grandfather killed his son."

"Yes, but don't forget Yaser wiped out grandfather's entire family," I reminded him hotly. After marriage Farehdun seemed to have changed. He had become meeker and too careful about his ways, and it bothered me to no end.

In the excitement I had noticed the sudden silence that Mahafrid had got into. I presumed it was due to grandfather's news, or maybe, she was nervous about meeting her new suitor who was due any minute now…but she was an experienced rejecter, so that couldn't be the problem.

The suitor came at the appointed hour and impressed one and all…all except Mahafrid. After the show was over and the suitor had left, mother tackled her.

"What in God's name was wrong with this man?" she demanded to know. "He was handsome, courteous and he has money! If you don't find him up to your high standards, *whom will you marry?"*

"Ardeshir," was her simple but determined answer.

Mother fainted.

24

The marriage took place a month later. But not before mother threw a series of tantrums.

"He was a loafer ten years back, and he's a bigger loafer today!" she maintained.

But Mahafrid wouldn't budge. "He'll change."

"For the worse!" mother promised, tearing her hair out. "And where will you both stay? On the roads of Herat?"

It was a private ceremony with father doing the honours. A section of the house was allotted to them and Ardeshir kept busy on the fields with us. Soon he was adapting to his work better than us and was capable of putting in more hours than us. And yet he had time to help mother maintain the house. He could fix anything. When a year later a boy was born, mother became Ardeshir's biggest ally.

That Ardeshir had changed was not a matter of doubt. He had changed dramatically…for the better and for the worse. He was far from his wild ways of Mehrigard, and far from the carefree and unproductive life he had led. But he had also lost his flamboyance, his dash and, I hate to say this, his courage. He no longer wanted to take any chances, walked away from potential fights and refused to be involved in anything remotely dangerous. *Worse*, he said he no longer wore the *Sedra* and *Kushti,* as he no longer believed in Zoroastrianism. For a man who had fought alongside Zahl for the honour of his religion, his new stance was most bewildering and illogic.

I was not sure I liked the new Ardeshir. Give me any day the fun-loving, head-clipping, arrogant Ardeshir we knew. Don't know what could have happened to him.

But Mahafrid loved him, and he was devoted to her. And that was what mattered the most.

One day not much later I cornered him. We had finished our dinner and Ardeshir announced he was going out for a short walk.

"I'll join you," I said and walked out with him.

It was a starry night and the fresh air was a balm to our tired bodies. My friends in the city lived a much more balanced life, with a decent quota of fun filled onto their daily lives. We lived a more work-oriented life with little time for leisure or entertainment. And father was never happy about us visiting the city. Too dangerous, he said.

"Ever since you've come back," I started, not wasting a minute, "you look sad and thoughtful. That is not how I remember you. Did your time with Zahl make you so?'

"No, no," he said hastily. "In fact, that was the time of my life that I enjoyed the most…being with your grandfather."

"Then what has changed you?"

He looked uncomfortable and was hesitant to reply. One more push from me and he opened up.

"After my days with your grandfather and the Esfahan valley I travelled north, towards the Hyrcania Ocean. As you may know, the Hyrcania region is still a free area and the Arab presence there is minimum. I was happy there and seriously contemplated settling down. There was a girl, too, whom I loved. She had a large family with seven brothers and a sister. The sister fell in love with an Arab from a small neighbouring village, much to the family's dismay. They tried their best to stop the relationship but the girl had made up her mind to marry the Arab. One night the Arab sneaked into our town and eloped with her.

"The brothers, in uncontrolled rage raided the Arab's village with a large group of friends and trouble-shooters. They found their sister there and one of the brothers forcefully took her back home. The rest indulged in a carnage I never could imagine. They killed everyone in sight, man, woman and child. They say over twenty civilians, all Muslims, died that night."

I digested the tragedy with little emotions, as many such incidents had been witnessed where the Zoroastrians were similarly butchered. What I had heard was ugly and detestable, but these days we heard little else.

"And so?" I prompted after a while.

"SO?" he asked incredulously. "Is that all you can say? There were five little children killed in that attack! Women and elderly people were not spared either! And you ask 'and so?'"

We walked on in silence as an owl flew overhead and settled on a low branch of a tree, observing us suspiciously as intruders in their space. I wondered if our feathered friends ever have to deal with tragedies of this nature. Maybe, the pressures of scrounging for their daily food didn't give them the time for such atrocities. Maybe, it was better to remain basic and in need.

"And what about the thousands of children and elderly people the Arabs have butchered of our people?"

"That's it!" he turned at me vehemently. "That's exactly what my point is! Just because they did it, *did we have to do it? Then we are as evil as they are!"*

I was getting to understand his logic, but not necessarily agreed with him. Though now was not the right time to prove him wrong. He looked so distraught and broken that I wondered what happened to the brave fighter I always thought him to be.

"Just one of their men gave vent to his love," he continued as an after-thought, "and a massacre was the result. We are as big a lot of barbarians as them…if not worse!"

"What happened next?"

"I wanted to give up everything I loved, the girl, the region…and my religion. I was a fighter too and have killed many, *but never children and women*. Zahl would have condemned that attack, too."

"You wanted to give up on your religion?" I stopped walking and stared at Ardeshir. "How could you ever think of doing that? *The massacre didn't take place only because of the religion!*"

He looked about helplessly, almost in tears. "I know it didn't, but if our teachings were strong, it could have prevented the killings."

I wouldn't go to the extreme of saying he had a point there, but yes, he did make me think.

"In any case I didn't lose all my faith due to that episode. I still followed my faith, though less fervently."

More was to come so I suggested we sit on a rock and continue our conversation. He let me sit but remained standing. I didn't need to prod him further as he seemed anxious to get the burden of his past, off his chest.

"Disappointed I left Hyrcania and came over to Herat. It was difficult to forget the slaughter I had witnessed but a few months of a steady job helped me a great deal."

"You, with a steady job?" I asked with a laugh. "I find it hard to believe that the cavalier Ardeshir I knew could actually work as an employee."

"It was okay. It kept me busy and finally there was some regular income for me. He was a Zarthoshty businessman and my job was to supervise his stock movements. Then one day there was some shortage in the inventory and he immediately charged me with cheating. I could be blamed for negligence, *but not for cheating.* Not only did I lose the job, but my employer spread the word in the market that I could not be trusted. Thereafter no Zarthoshty businessman hired me. I was prepared to do any kind of work but it was the same story, 'No work right now. Come back some other time'.

"Soon I was penniless. I appealed to many Zarthoshty families I knew to let me do household chores, but none came to my support. But that was not punishment enough for that businessman. He had some powerful friends so he made sure I was arrested and imprisoned. I was in a miserable prison for five years."

Now I understood why this man had lost his zeal for life and why he no longer cared to be called a Zarthoshty.

"After I was released from the prison I found it even more difficult to secure any work. No one would touch an ex convict. I steadily slipped downwards, from being a labourer I was shunted down to being a household servant to finally a toilet cleaner...*in Arab homes.* Yes, they at least allowed me to work in their houses. I ate once a day, slept with the cats and dogs in the streets and had no shelter over my head, *even in the winter when it snowed heavily*. That's when I met you, and my days changed."

Would I have done the same thing, lose faith in my religion and my people, if I had faced a similar situation? That was the question running in my mind. I wondered if under similar circumstances I would have become insane, for there is no greater tragedy than that of an innocent man branded guilty and made to live the life of a criminal.

At that time, I had no words of sympathy to offer him. Hearing of his experiences I had become quiet and reflective. No man deserved to be treated such...certainly not a courageous hero that Ardeshir. I wanted to remind him that one wicked Zarthoshty should not constitute as the benchmark of an entire community, but I hesitated. I felt he rightly condemned the community for not being with him in his hour of need. And he rightly condemned the community for not having the conviction of restrain when they went on a rampage at Hyrcania.

I finally surmised that, after all, we were not that special a people we considered ourselves to be. We were part of mankind and we possessed the same weaknesses, the same faults, as others.

We lingered on for some more time and then silently made our way back home…and sanity.

❑

"Father we must move on," Mohammad reasoned unsuccessfully. "I've been in this country now for too long. And all for what?"

"For what?" Yaser exploded. "Isn't pride and honour reason enough?"

"Yes, but there has to be an end to everything." Mohammad loved his father and was immensely proud of his earlier achievements. But today he knew he was talking to a man not totally in control of himself. Insanity had intruded where earlier only pride and power had resided. Two days earlier they had found Yaser clinging to the neck of a tall Arab, yelling *'It is Zahl, I tell you, it is Zahl.'* He had taken to scrutinising people at will, barging into houses that belonged to respectable Arabs and even apprehending them and getting into regular scuffles. He would remind them that they were dealing with the foremost hero of Arabia, but no one really remembered who he was. The crunch came when he insisted that the local Governor was shielding the Mahrespandan family in his palace. "I have to be right," he reasoned. "We have checked every other inch of this district." It took all of Mohammad's guile and influences to get him out of the brouhaha that ensued. After the threat Yaser had given of informing the Caliph about the fire temple, the Governor was itching to come down heavily on him, and this was his opportunity. But by now Mohammad with his religious commitments, was an influential man. So just a clear warning was given. One more such incident and Yaser will have to pay for it.

Yaser glared at his son, as he often did to dissuade any resistance to his ideas. "It will all end when we have them, *and not a minute before!"*

"But this is insane! We don't even know the family is still in existence. Father, I have had enough of this. I want to go home…back to Arabia."

It was as if a knife had been plunged into him as Yaser gave a short cry, clutched at his heart, and staggered to his stool. Mohammad hated to see his father in such a vulnerable state as it happened so often these days. It had become so easy to hurt him.

"Not immediately," said Mohammad quickly, resting his hand on the shoulder of the man he loved so deeply. "I meant if we don't find the Mahrespandan family soon, we must plan to return home, together. You are now almost eighty years old and need rest."

Yaser nodded submissively, but whispered, "Yes, but we'll get them first."

❑❑❑

25

Soon after Ardeshir's arrival father took ill. He hardly came out of his room, ate little and basically kept himself busy, praying. That was one activity he never ignored. Besides the large collection of our scripture books that we hid in the mountains surrounding Mehrigard, father always had his daily prayer book close by. And his bond with his faith grew even stronger, thanks to the presence of a Fire Temple in Herat. The Arabs naturally knew of the temple but turned a blind eye. Father made it a point to visit it as often as he could. After the barren years at Mehrigard, he was starving to finally sit and pray in the house of our God. Our own sacred fire that we had carried across the salt deserts was given the pride of place in our home, as we continued keeping it alive day and night.

A few years after we settled down at Herat father had set his mind to further my progress in our religious studies. He started tutoring me for my *Nozud* ceremony and, in due course of time, with the help of other priests the long ceremony was conducted. Now I, also, was authorised to conduct a few of our rites. He had wanted to do same for Farehdun at Mehrigard, but could find no other priest to assist him. Now it was too late for Farehdun.

A couple of years later, father went a step further. He organised for me a ceremony that was most sacred and of the highest order, the *Martab* ceremony…something father himself couldn't complete due to circumstances beyond his control. Now I was a full-fledged priest, capable of conducting any and all of our sacred ceremonies. I did perform at the fire temple a couple of times, but much to my father's dismay, it was not my calling, and I slackened in my duties.

It was early evening when I rushed back home from a short trip to Herat. The family was at the dining table for supper.

"Yaser has the permission he sought," I gushed out breathlessly. "The Caliph has given him the permission to burn down our fire temple in the town."

The news was greeted with hushed silence and supper was forgotten. It was as though someone from within the family had passed away. Fire temples tended to do just that…become part of the family.

"But it will take a few days for Yaser to get his hands on it," I continued. "The governor is outraged that such an order was proclaimed undermining his own sentiments. Worse, the execution of same has been conferred upon an outsider. He has ordered his guards to protect the fire temple till he decides on its fate."

I could see father was devastated by the news.

"There's nothing we can do about it," opined Ardeshir, speaking aloud my fears. In spite of his painful experiences I expected the situation to help change Ardeshir. If not bring out his sword and run out to defend the last semblance of our religion, like he had done by joining Zahl, I hoped he'd at least show some concern. But obviously here was a man with a cruel memory that he was not going to shed too easily. But somehow, I still held hope for him.

"We have to save it." The gentle yet determined voice reassured me that we could still boast of being Zahl's family. Father pushed his dinner plate aside and stepped out of the house.

Ten minutes later he returned. "I'm off to meet Esadvaster. Will return late."

Esadvaster was the high priest at the fire temple at Herat. He was regarded in great esteem amongst the Zoroastrians, and even some of the Arabs. His knowledge and understanding of our religion and its tenets was so complete and inspiring that nothing happened in our community without his consent. He lived his life simple and totally dedicated to his duties. He was such a spiritually evolved person that the Islamic clergy were very apprehensive of him. Many a time, he had locked horns against them, but they could do little against him as the local governor admired this bold yet holy man.

"Esadvaster?" asked Farehdun sceptically. "How can he help the situation? He is too pure a person."

"And what is wrong with that?" I wanted to know.

"Such people are more dangerous than useful."

I didn't want to hear any more of my brother's lopsided logic. "I'm coming with you," I said, stalling my father. I looked around for support but none seemed likely to come. "Ardeshir, joining us?"

It was not just a question. It was almost an appeal from me. Deep inside I knew there was more to this man than the weak peevishness he was currently harbouring.

He looked about, confused. He stood up hesitatingly, but returned to his seat the next moment. "I…I…don't know. In any case, what can we do?"

"You can go and find out," snapped Mahafrid, visibly upset at the new Ardeshir.

Reluctantly, he joined us.

When we reached Esadvaster's house, which was quite close to the fire temple, we were met with a small group of animated men. There were shouts of, "Let's fight!" and "We have to resist!"

"There are only five guards posted there," one of the men pointed out. "We can easily overpower them."

"And then what?" asked Esadvaster. "Their entire army will pounce upon us. Will you be able to overpower them too? In any case those guards are there to protect the temple, not destroy it."

He saw us and beckoned father to him. We may be comparatively new to this region, but father with his quiet authority, was already a man people respected.

"What can we do, Peshotan?" asked the aged Esadvaster. "Any day they will bring it down."

"There is only one thing to do."

Silence followed the quiet statement. The three of us had driven into the town in our closed carriage and all along father had not spoken a word. He must have been setting a plan.

Fifteen minutes later a small boy approached the fire temple with a bowl of black tea. It was cold out in the streets and was getting late, so there was hardly anyone moving about.

"The officer told me to give you this," he told the guard at the entrance, pouring the liquid in a cup.

The guard, shivering in the cold, smiled as he reached for the cup. "And I thought nobody cared about us, even as we do our duty through the night. Now go inside and also give it to my colleagues. And if any is still left, leave it for me."

The boy went in and gave the tea to the other guards, waited till they had finished, and collected the cups. Outside he gave more tea to the guard.

An hour later we walked in. The streets were now totally deserted, so without much fuss fifteen of us entered the garden outside the fire temple. As expected, and as planned, the five guards were all heavily drugged and fast asleep.

"Hope Esadvaster's wife didn't get carried away and put in more sleeping powder in the tea, than recommended," I whispered to Ardeshir as we circled past the snoring guards. "Doesn't look like they're getting up for another twenty four hours at least."

There were two Zoroastrian priests attending to the sacred fire and the premises. They came running out, anxiety writ large on their faces. They saw Esadvaster and relaxed.

Into the temple we went and stood in front of the sacred fire. It was placed in a dark room that was the sanctum santorum for our people. No one was allowed to enter it, but for the priests maintaining it. The urn that held the fire was very large. The stand stood about four feet tall and the urn had a circumference of about eight feet. From its intricate design we knew it was ancient and special. No fire rose from it but the glowing embers that were evenly spread at the top emitted a warm flush around the chamber.

"Let's waste no further time," Esadvaster said, entering the room. Father and I followed him, along with the two resident priests. No one but a priest was ever allowed in. The rest waited outside, unsure of their next move. "You might as well come in too, as it will take many strong hands to lift this urn."

Not only were they asked to enter the sacred chamber, but the men would actually touch and lift the revered urn. An action that could have almost excommunicated them under other circumstances.

The men removed their footwear and hesitatingly stepped in. It still had not sunk into them that what they were about to do would be the most honoured task ever to be bestowed upon a Zarthoshty…save their sacred fire from destruction, and worse.

A while later six men carried the urn out of the temple. They were all bent low, holding the urn just a foot above the ground, so that its gravity remained low and didn't topple over.

Three closed carts, including ours, had already drawn into the garden. We dismantled the seats of the largest one and carefully lowered the urn into it. One of the priests who had opted to come with us, the other preferring to get to his home fast, volunteered to ride with the urn and nurture it during our covert journey. The rest of us crammed into the other two carriages, and we were on our way...to where, I had no idea.

All our actions till now had been performed in extreme silence and stealth. What we were daring to accomplish was something unheard of.

Nobody talked as the three carriages steadily weaved their way through the dark city roads. And just when we thought we were safe a sharp voice rang out.

"STOP!"

Too scared to peep out I knew a patrol had caught us. Ours was the leading carriage so the officer of the patrol strolled over to us. "Where do you think you lot are going at this time of the night?"

There were seven of them and I felt assured we could overwhelm them if the need came. The mission we were on was too important to be abandoned now. I got my little dagger that I lately carried under my robe ready.

The officer wrenched open our door. "Step outside!"

Esadvaster, who was riding with us, slowly stepped out. The attitude of the officer instantly changed. He was apologetic and well-mannered as he recognised the sombre figure in a white robe. Down the years Esadvaster had made many a friend in the city, including the governor.

The officer peeped into the carriage, saw our grim faces and quickly withdrew. He turned back to Esadvaster. "What…I mean where…are you going, Sir?" He knew the elderly man in front of him ranked way above him.

Esadvaster looked skywards and stood in stoic silence. Unnerved, the officer shifted his gaze to the second carriage…the one harbouring the sacred fire. Still undecided, he casually strolled towards it.

"Step outside," he repeated his order. As no one came out he moved forward and peeped inside. In a flash he took several steps backwards. Bewildered beyond words he looked towards Esadvaster for explanations. But once again he was met with silence.

Everyone in Herat knew of the order to destroy the fire temple, and everyone was not in favour of it. The officer put two and two together and knew he was facing a dilemma. Do what his commander would have expected him to do, or do what his conscious dictated. A moment's deliberation and his decision was reached.

"Its okay, let them pass," he called out to his men.

It was only when our cavalcade reached outside the town limits that we started breathing again. The second part of our daring operation was over. We were either plain lucky…or well protected by unseen forces.

❑

The journey beyond the town was slower as the road was rough. As we rattled over stones and gutters I felt like I would soon develop the shaking disease. The road we were using led northwards, towards Margiana. I had never used this route before and noticed the sudden increase of mountainous terrain. *Where were we headed for?*

An hour's ride and Esadvaster called for a halt. I noticed we were exactly in the middle of nowhere. But he obviously knew where we were.

"We shall proceed on foot, hereon."

I got off thankfully and moved about, settling my rattled bones. All around us were dark, high mountains with just the narrow road we were on breaking the monotony. There was absolutely no sign of any inhabitation for miles in any direction, and hopefully no wild life either. What our high priest had in mind I still had no idea.

"We shall first conceal the carriages behind those rocks, before we continue," he suggested.

Continue where? Up those mountains?

After the carriages were out of sight of any chance-traveller using this road, six of us lifted the urn and followed the high priest with the rest. A relay system was planned for carrying the urn. The stand was not a problem. I noticed Ardeshir was not averse to help with the lifting.

Esadvaster climbed the rocks and the narrow passage leading up, like a young man. Father, in fact, found it hard and laborious to keep up with the older man. But where was our senior priest leading us to? He seemed to know his way about and later we learnt that he often came to these parts to be alone, to think and to pray.

After the initial rocky area the climb comparatively eased, though the six of us lifting the heavy urn found it impossible to maintain the pace. Every hundred feet or so we needed to stop and change the team, and were worried about the distance our leader had in mind. When the next team took over the pace increased, but only for a short while. It was a continuous struggle with the climb and the loose rocks. We stumbled and slipped a dozen times, but held on dearly to the urn with its precious load. Luckily, the skies were clear and we did benefit from some heavenly light. When all of us were totally spent and knew we couldn't last long, we came across a natural path cut through the mountain side. The progress hereon was easier and faster.

We must have been a sight for the man on the moon. He would have seen a huge dark and inhospitable region, and in the middle of it a small group of men stealthily carrying a glowing vessel, as though it was the most valuable, most central object in the world.

But to us, Zarthoshties, indeed, it was.

Thirty minutes after we had started, Esadvaster took yet another sharp turn in the mountain and called for a halt. Our tongues half hanging out in exhaustion, we immediately hit the ground, not even caring to admire the strategically beautiful location we had finally come to.

Ten feet above where we stood was a small cave, we now noticed, overlooking the entire valley below us. Esadvaster had climbed the ten feet and stood majestically at the edge.

"And that is the east," he proudly said, pointing ahead. East was where the sun rose, and was considered the most auspicious direction for us.

Lifting the urn up the ten feet was the hardest part of the mission. But with every hand straining its every muscle, we finally did it. The urn was placed facing the mouth of the cave, a good thirty feet within. The cave entrance was small, but within it we could have gathered over a hundred people.

We placed a large quantity of wood in the urn and ignited it. Suddenly, as though to reward our efforts, a huge burst of flame happily sprang out, and relishing in its new home, it covered the entire cave with a crimson glow. As all our faces blissfully glowed in its light, I knew this had to be the happiest moment of my life. I looked around and was convinced that it was the happiest day of all my colleagues, too.

"Now let the Arabs try and destroy it," challenged Esadvaster.

❑

In time the Arabs learnt of the secret cave, but in the beginning didn't bother to do anything about it. Temporarily, everyone seemed happy about the situation. Yaser was happy he destroyed the fire temple, which he did with zeal, bringing down the entire ancient structure. Soon we knew a mosque will come up at the same site, as they had appeared at many other sites where the fire temples were destroyed in the country. The governor was happy that his will prevailed and the sacred fire was saved. And the Zarthoshties were happy that they still could pray in front of one of their most precious Avatar.

A week later we faced reality. We learnt of a move by the Muslim clergy. They found the presence of the holy fire within a cave, intolerable. A group was formed to supervise its destruction. But we had half-anticipated it and had made contingency arrangements. With a few strategically placed rocks and shrubs, we completely sealed the entrance from sight. The Arabs knew the approximate sight of the cave but never the exact location. When they failed to locate the cave, we thought we had beaten them. But then came rumours that now they had found the exact spot and yet another large group was organised to destroy the large *Urn* and the holy fire.

That very night some of us returned to the cave and carried it away to another safe place, a mile away. This time when the Arabs came they did locate the cave, but found it empty. They returned a few days later, but still found it empty. We now had found the temporary hideout convenient and had decided to continue using it till we were sure the Arabs would leave it alone.

A couple of months later the Arabs gave up on finding the holy fire, and soon we returned the *Urn* to the cave.

To safe-guard it further, the resident priests agreed to stay back in turns and attend to the fire. On our part, we agreed to return regularly with relevant supplies, and build a temporary shed for them, close by. In another month's time a small house was built with basic amenities.

Word got out about the special grotto and Zoroastrian residents of Herat made regular journeys to the blessed cave and their own sacred fire. Soon, people from faraway places started making the difficult journey to pay their respects. All devotees felt special, first making the pilgrimage, and then standing in front of the holy fire in that rugged and dark cave.

The tradition carried on for centuries thereafter.

❑❑❑

26

Since that day the general feelings within the family was on the up. In spite of losing our fire temple, our rescue act of the sacred fire was seen by many as sanctimonious and special. It did wonders to our spirits as the incident exemplified the belief that one can destroy a body, but never its spirit.

Though, after that event father's participation in the field lessened significantly as now he devoted his time to two new occupations. He would come out with us every morning, and make sure the days work was well distributed. Then he would either visit the cave and pray, or go to the town's library and read. The small library at Herat provided him with sufficient reading material. After the rout of the fire temple, we wondered how long before the next target in the city will be the library.

"I fear our days for remaining in our country is limited," he confided in me soon after that eventful day. "You already know where we hid our second most important legacy, the sacred books. It's time for you to learn of our third most important legacy, the secret place where my uncle hid our material treasures near Pasargadae." With that he fished out a rolled up scroll from a bag. "I have made out a map showing the exact location where that treasure is located. It is far greater than you can ever imagine so be not impatient to excavate it, as the responsibility for safeguarding it thereafter will be enormous. It is safe where it is, and will be so for generations. *So go after it only if and when required."*

I thought it a great burden to have the map around. So for many days I spent time to completely memorise the location as given by my father. Once I had acclimatised myself with every aspect of the map, I destroyed it.

Now I carried two maps of utmost importance in my head. ❑

One evening, after work, father and I were seated at the porch when I asked him about the book he was reading.

"It is by a Greek writer and the name of the book is, 'The Life of Zarathushtra'. It is less of the scriptures and more of history."

I wanted to learn more of our history, but hesitated to ask father. He would probably have advised me to read about it for myself. But whenever books were mentioned, my mind invariably went back to the cave near Mehrigard, where we had hidden our sacred books years ago. I often wondered about its safety and the duration they will have to remain within that dark and dry cave. When will they see the light of day and when will they once again be read copied and circulated.

"When do you think we'll get the chance of retrieving our books from the cave?" I suddenly asked.

"Doesn't look like it is going to happen soon," said father sadly. "But remember to pass on details of the exact location of that cave to your children, and they to their children, until our time comes. The teachings of Zarathushtra cannot be allowed to fade into oblivion."

"Who was Jathutra?" The poignant question was put up by Khushrav, the five year old son of Farehdun. He was trouble with a capital 'T'. He must have overheard the last part of our discussion, but it was enough for him to catch us for a lengthy discourse. He hopped on to his grandfather's lap and instantly settled down to a comfortable position. They say the only bad quality in him was inherited from me…the habit of asking incessant questions. Sometimes I imagined that even his body shape with his big head tilting forward and his thin frame, when viewed from a certain angle, resembled a question mark. The best method of escaping his clasp, I learnt from experience, was to answer what he wanted to know quickly, and get on with your life. But he was my favourite and my constant shadow.

"Zarathushtra!" father corrected him sternly. "The Greeks called him Zoroaster. The story of His life is long so I'll tell you all about it some other day."

"You do not know the story."

"Of course, I know," said father, a bit louder than his usual quiet voice.

"So why don't you tell me?"

Father hrmphed and groaned and looked about for an escape route. But with his tormentor right on his lap, he had little chance. So he took a deep breath, hoping to get over it quickly and said, "Zarathushtra is our prophet. He was born about two thousand years ago and was the son of a horse breeder, Pourushaspa. His mother's name was Dughdhova, the same name as your grandmother's."

"Grandmother is Jathutra's mother?"

"No, no, no." It was still the beginning of the interrogation so father displayed complete patience. "We honour our ancestors by taking on their names."

"Where was Jathutra born?"

I knew it was going to be a long evening so I settled myself more comfortably. I could do with some brushing up of our past, too.

"Nobody knows for sure. It was so long ago. Some say he was born at Rae, an ancient city close to where we are. Many say he was born on the plains of Central Asia that is much North of us. When He was about thirty years old, and was roaming the vast mountains, Lord Ahura Mazda spoke to Him. He explained to Him the meaning of life, and how to live it."

"Who's Ahura Mazda?"

I could feel father's patience running thin, but he continued stoutly.

"He is the Divinity that created the universe. He is what you call, God."

Khushrav nodded several times as though now he understood it all. "So how did God want us to live?" he picked up the thread.

"By being righteous and truthful, always. *Ashoi!* That is the core philosophy of our religion."

"I thought, Good Thoughts, Good Words and Good Deeds was the core philosophy," I chipped in. Though I had officially become a full-fledged priest, and knew my prayers well, my knowledge of our religion's philosophy and history was still slight.

Father looked at me exasperatedly. Was he destined to be trapped between two of the biggest questioners in history? He took time before he tried to clarify my doubts.

"You may call the three principles you mentioned the very pillars of our faith. It is these pillars that support the foundation, which is the core philosophy...*righteousness and truth.*" I had already learnt the importance of truth in the mountains between the salt deserts, during our journey from Mehrigard.

Poor Khushrav looked at us blankly and then turned to me angrily, "Why did you disturb grandfather's story? Let him continue."

The reprimand clear, father thanked him and continued. "When Jathutra…I mean Zarathushtra, tried to impart Ahura Mazda's message to the people, nobody believed Him. So He travelled to different lands trying to explain what Ahura Mazda had revealed to Him. Only His cousin, Mediyomah believed in Him and followed Him wherever he went. Until finally, He came to the land of Bactria, where its king, King Vistasp, believed in Him and became His disciple."

"Why did he believe Jathutra?" Considering the irritating followers He had today, I, too, wondered.

"Because He performed a miracle right in front of the king."

Khushrav's eyes instantly brightened. "You mean like magic?"

"Er…yes, like magic."

"What did he do?"

Peshotan coughed lightly and looked around for a place of escape. None appeared, so he continued after a long sigh. "The king's favourite horse, Asp-i-Siyan, was very sick as all his legs were drawn into his belly. The king asked Zarathushtra if He could cure the black steed. And Zarathushtra cured him, as one by one the legs were released and he could stand."

Khushrav sat dumbstruck. Actually, so did I. I wanted to know more about the miracle but father didn't look ready for further interruption.

"Only one magic?" asked Khushrav, hoping, like me, for an encore.

"In front of King Vistasp, only one. But he is said to have performed many more miracles in his lifetime. Thereafter," he continued, "many people started believing in Zarathushtra and His followers increased. They, as we, are called Zarthoshties."

"Did He have children?"

"Yes, but enough for today." Peshotan knew what would follow if he took the bait so he lifted Khushrav off his lap, placed him on the ground and gently smacked his bottom.

The spiritual class for the day was effectively over.

❑

Later that year, father passed away.

There was no serious ailment that struck him. It was just that he was not a happy man. He brooded for too long. Losing his father after the brief reunion hit him the most. The loss of five families from Mehrigard was another painful memory for him. He held himself responsible for both the tragic events. And then the conditions at Khorasan.

When we came over to Khorasan, he thought it was the end of all persecutions and we would be leading a free life. That was not to be. The region was comparatively lenient, but that was all. We were still considered *'najis'* (impure) here and *'ajam'* was a frequently uttered insult that we bore. It was not so bad when we first came to the region, but each year we noticed the domination of the Arabs increase. New laws were put in place to put us, Zarthoshties, in place too.

In every walk of life, we were constantly reminded that we were unwanted. And father couldn't live with that. At Mehrigard we went through much greater hardships, but we were left alone. Except for the few minutes every month when the tax collector came.

The family was broken apart as its main pillar departed. Mother tried to maintain some cheer amongst us, but it was in vain. Finally, she took to be alone and tried to deal with life in her way. Her only respite being her routine duties, and her grandchildren. Farehdun, Ardeshir and I kept ourselves busy in the fields all day, had our dinner and retired for the night.

27

A month went by settling down to our duties and adjusting to the new life without father.

"Why don't we skip our field work today, and go to the town," I suggested to Ardeshir one day, trying to break the cheerless lives we had settled down to. "There are a few supplies we need for the house."

It was a busy day and Herat bazaar was streaming with people. I liked that. The thought of so many people, each living a totally different life from any other, yet rubbing shoulders with one another, daily, fascinated me to no end. Each face, a front for a set of unique problems and joys, all of its own. Each face harbouring a hundred dreams, a hundred nightmares. Each mind constantly coping with thoughts of hopes, guilt and fears. Each emotion handled as per individual psychology. All these facets rolled into one being, never to be duplicated by anyone else, any other time. And yet destined to share their lives and space with others. And we term that as *life.*

But today I was in no mood for philosophy. Today I wanted to enjoy my day. So plucking up my spirits I tried to infuse same into Ardeshir.

"Let's go to that old tavern and have a good drink," I suggested.

"You know I've stopped drinking," replied Ardeshir, sternly. "But I don't mind accompanying you. I'll stick to a glass of milk."

Into the tavern we went and soon the grief of the last few weeks vanished. The wine here was said to be the best in Persia, and I whole-heartedly agreed.

"Just have a sip," I tried coaxing Ardeshir as he sat beside me, holding a glass of milk and looking about gloomily.

"Only a sip," he warned and tasted it. "It's good," he accepted, and took a larger gulp. Soon he called for his own bottle.

Two hours later when we returned to the streets outside, life once again looked good. A *kabab* stall was doing brisk business close by, so we stopped and had our lunch there.

Totally contented with life we went about purchasing some essentials that we needed at home. Midway in our work I became aware of being stared at. A derelict old man was looking hard at me. He would look at my face and then would shift his scrutiny to my chest. And then back to my face. He did that a few times and I noticed his mood changing. From showing interest in me he was getting visibly agitated.

Uncomfortable, I urged Ardeshir to move on to the next shop.

"Seems like a mad man," I deduced.

The old man followed us. As I was in the process of buying something he stepped forward and peered directly into my eyes in an insolent manner. And then his focus went back to my chest. I had enough of this so I faced him directly.

"What is it?" I asked, more in irritation than anger. "What is it you want?"

For an answer he reached out towards my chest and grabbed the *Asho Farohar* I was wearing. It was the one my grandfather had given me. When he had given it to me it used to dangle at the level of my stomach. Now it hung high on my chest. Generally I wore it under my robe, but it must have slipped out at the tavern and was now in view to all.

"Sorry, I can't give you that," I told the man and tried to remove his hand from it.

Suddenly he jerked at it, trying to break the chain that held it. It held on.

"Stop it," I said aloud. "What are you, a thief?"

But he just kept staring at me and pulled harder at the *Asho Farohar*. The move almost unbalanced me as I staggered a few steps in front. Luckily the chain had not snapped. But I didn't expect it to as I knew it was made of a very stout metal.

"It's him!" the old man said slowly and gave the chain another violent pull. The back of my neck got scratched, but the chain held on. I was about to apprehend the old man when he went berserk.

"*It's him, I tell you!* IT'S HIM!! *CATCH HIM, SOMEBODY CATCH HIM!!*"

People around us stopped to stare. Most didn't want to interfere seeing a mad man was involved and proceeded on their way. The old man looked about wildly, as though seeking help. Children playing nearby gathered around us… thrilled at the prospect of witnessing a madman during one of his bouts. They shouted and jeered him, encouraging him to continue with the show.

"Help me! Somebody help me..." he screamed, now holding on to my robe so that I won't escape his clutches. I tried to force his hands away from me but it only made matters worse. He suddenly lunged on me and held me by my waist, and dropped to his knees.

I felt trapped and humiliated. I saw Ardeshir scrutinise the old man and immediately come to my rescue. With his more powerful arms he wrenched open the old man's grip and set me free.

Just then a man in cleric clothes ran up to the scene.

"Father, what happened? Why are you shouting?" He looked at me sternly for causing harm to the old man, but returned his attention to the old man.

"*Quick,* let's get away from here," said Ardeshir, urgently pulling me away from the scene. As we set off at a brisk pace we could hear the old man suddenly cough and splutter. We turned around to see him clutch his heart and stumble down. The cleric man was holding him and trying to soothe him.

"Wh…What happened?" I asked as we hurried on. "Who was that man?"

"Yaser!" said Ardeshir through his teeth, "and he's recognised you. And the cleric was his son. We must get out of the town fast! *Run!"*

Meanwhile Mohammad had lifted the old man from the street and carried him to a shelter. He loosened his clothes as the old man gasped for breath.

"It was him…I know it was him" the old man mumbled.

"Shhh…quiet father. We'll talk later."

"NO! He'll get away! Catch him *now!"*

"Catch who, father?" Mohammad asked concernedly. He could see his father was in bad condition and was livid at the people who caused it.

"*The Mahrespandan boy! I know it was him. You must get him!"*

"How do you know it was the Mahrespandan boy? It's been so many years since…" Mohammad was certain it was another case of a mistaken identity.

"*I know*…that emblem he was wearing…it was the same one." Yaser continued, fighting for each breath. "He was wearing it in that village. I recognised it instantly…it's one of its kind. The same crude design…very old…and the chain unbreakable. I had tried…to break it…in his village… but, it was unbreakable then…and it was unbreakable…today."

Mohammad whirled around to try and spot the two men he had seen getting away when he arrived. But they were not in sight.

"I have seen them, father. But they didn't look like…"

"*It was him! I am absolutely certain! I saw his eyes...same as Zahl's... devilish!* You will get him, son…him, and his entire family."

Yaser's body convulsed and Mohammad got worried. His father was in a very serious condition. He tried to appease his agitated state of mind. "I'll try to get him, father…now please…"

"No trying!!" Yaser hissed through clenched teeth. He gasped for air as he took his son's hand and pulled it to his chest. *"Swear to me, son…swear that you'll get that family…and wipe them off the face of this…world. SWEAR TO ME!!"*

Mohammad was mesmerised by the sheer commitment of his father. If this was his beloved father's death wish, *then he'll do it!* He held his father with both hands as he whispered, "I swear father! I swear I'll hunt down that family, and destroy them!"

Upon hearing the words Yaser rolled his eyes upwards and dropped his head, for the last time in his life.

❑

By the time we reached home we were gasping for breath and were soaked with sweat. We had half jogged all the way from the town.

"Run away?" Mother asked, exasperated. "What do you mean? How can we run away from home, *again?*"

"Mother, you've got to understand," I pleaded. "Yaser recognised me, and his son has seen us. It's only a matter of time before they come looking for us. And you know what that man is capable of."

A heavy gloom had set in within the entire family. Nobody even wanted to think of undergoing another long journey.

"Why don't we go away some place else for a few days, and return when things cool down," suggested Farehdun.

"*A few days?* You think Yaser will forget us in a few days? He's been hounding us for nearly a dozen years, and he has given no signs of ever giving up."

"But you said you saw Yaser falling down, probably with a heart attack," reminded Mahafrid.

"Yes, but we do not know if he's dead. And then his son is there. He saw us, too."

Dughdhova paced the floor, like her husband used to, deep in thought. Without him, the onus of decision-making had fallen on her. *Wish Peshotan was here*, she thought. He'd immediately assess the problem and give the right solution. But now she was in charge, and she must make a decision.

"I think we must not take an immediate decision," she finally opined. "Let's see how the situation transpires at the town, find out if Yaser is alive. And if not, find out what his son intends doing. May be they too are tired of this hunt and wish to abandon it."

"And if they are at our door tomorrow morning? That would be the end of the Mahrespandan family…*and you know that!*"

"We'll take that chance," Farehdun sided his mother. "In any case, even if they decide to hunt you down, it'll take them days to locate you. They won't know where you live."

There was no point in trying any further to convince this lot, so I just shook my head and retired to my room. I was infuriated beyond words, but neither could I contradict mother, nor could I force them into action. How could I? I understood what must be going through their minds. Here we were finally well settled and I was urging them to abandon it all and hit the road once again…that treacherous and unforgiving road. It was many a year that had passed by, but the memories of that journey, the ordeal and the heartbreaks, were still fresh in our minds.

So we waited. Two days later we got the confirmation. Yaser was dead, and his son was looking for us.

❑

Seeing his father die in his arms changed Mohammad forever. Holding him close to his chest he made a silent vow. He will continue where his father left off…he will bring down every member of that accursed family called Mahrespandan. Over ten years he had already sacrificed enough trying to track them down. But his heart was not in his duty. He had merely gone through the motions just to satisfy his father.

But now it will be different. Now he'll devote every minute of his life, expend every ounce of his energy and not leave these shores, till his duty was done.

And now he knew what the face of the enemy looked like. There were two of them, but it was only the younger one that father remembered. He'll remember it as well, *and it will be etched in his mind till that face lies lifeless at his feet.*

Immediately after burying his father, Mohammad set about the task. He first contacted the senior-most Muslim cleric in the region. He already had met him before and had earned his respect. With him Mohammad visited the

Governor. Soon he walked out with a warrant in his hands that allowed him to enter every house in Herat, search the premises, question the residents and arrest whoever he suspected of knowing the Mahrespandan family. Along with the warrant, he was also put in charge of a small unit of a dozen soldiers.

And so began a chapter in the history of Herat and Khorasan, when every non-Muslim resident was treated as a suspect, harassed beyond endurance and subjected to humiliation not seen in those parts, ever before.

The reputation of Khorasan being a safe haven for non-Muslims became extinct. From that day onwards the residents learnt the true nature of the Arabs, their selfish motives and stubborn religious fanatism.

For the Zoroastrians, the first seed of thought for moving on to a safer place was planted.

❑❑❑

28

"They are searching every house in the district," informed an alarmed Farehdun, after his short reconnoitre trip to Herat. "They're emptying out complete houses, checking every inch of it, and destroying any structure that looks suspicious. House after house, road after road, they're covering the whole town. It's only a matter of days before they'll be looking in this area too."

The worried faces all around spoke of the intense anxiety the family nurtured. What they dreaded most these last few days, was now a reality.

"Not that it's going to help anyone now, but why don't you throw away that Asho Farohar?" asked Ardeshir, a little testily. "It's just a piece of junk and has caused us all a great deal of trouble."

I looked at him aghast. This cannot be the same man who fought alongside my grandfather. I wanted to tell him a hundred reasons why I thought his suggestion was despicable, but preferred to reply with silence. He didn't deserve a reply. But I still gave it.

"This is mine, and will remain so." I said mildly, not wishing to escalate the situation. "And in any case, it's no reason to harass other people, the way they have,"

"*No reason?*" he countered angrily. "You have been the cause of his father's death, *and you find no reason?* That is the problem with the Zoroastrians of today. They complain of persecutions at any given time, and ignore the pain they give to the Arabs."

I could hold back no longer. *"Pain??* You talk of their pain? *Have you forgotten the pain they've caused us?* Have you forgotten that man has personally killed my grandfather? Have you forgotten he has slaughtered my family in Pars? And how could you forget that because of him, our village was demolished, its old residents along with five other families butchered and the rest of us forced to make an impossible journey? *Pain to them??* You pitiful excuse of the man you once were…*you…you…Judas!*"

I was known to never get angry, but I couldn't help myself that day. I was ready to continue my onslaught but Mahafrid recognised the consequences and quickly intervened and changed the topic.

"But with the force the governor has under him they could easily search the entire town in two days," she said loud enough to quieten us. "Why are they taking so long?"

"Only Mohammad has seen their faces, and only he can identify them," Farehdun chipped in, eager to put an end to the family flare-up. "He alone is conducting this search, along with a dozen soldiers under his command. But they're still moving fast as there is no resistance. Some children also saw you, but they were of no help to the search party."

I was glad of the diversion as I immediately realised I had said too much. But Ardeshir's attitude was boiling within me for some time now, and it needed just a spark for me to explode. I was even more perplexed as I thought that the divine experience we all had, after rescuing the town's holy fire and seeing it ablaze at the cave, would have changed Ardeshir too. It had changed me completely, and I cannot overstress of how proud I was of all of us that day, after that unique experience.

"Luckily no one in the city knows us as Mahrespandan," said I, half to myself.

"Maybe, but I fear the owner of the grocery stores we buy from," continued my brother. "According to you, your scuffle took place right in front of his shop. And he knows us, not as Mahrespandan, but as Athavian. Today, when I was snooping around, I saw him staring at me directly. But he didn't say anything. I only hope he didn't see you, as he certainly knows where we live."

"The grocer is a good man," Mother opined. "We have dealt with him for many years and he's been a good friend. Even if he recognised you, I'm sure he won't inform them."

"He's an Arab," reminded Farehdun.

"So *what* if he is an Arab," countered Ardeshir angrily. "You think they are all thugs and killers? You refuse to have confidence even in a friend, just because he's an Arab?" He turned to me with a sneer. "There is your holier-than-thou brother-Zoroastrian speaking. *It makes me sick!*"

That was it! I didn't want to hear more. Turning to the rest, I asked, "So, what's it going to be? Wait for them to come and identify us, or do something about it?"

The uncomfortable question floated over every head like a rain-sodden cloud…full of potential dangers.

"Why don't the two of you go away some place for some time," suggested Mahafrid, "and return after a month or so, when the search will be over?"

"They have already thought of that," Farehdun said, shaking his head. "The search for the two will be conducted every month, Mohammad has threatened, till the two have been apprehended. He is convincing the people that it would be better for them to point out the renegades, or face the unpleasant harassment of a search every month."

Some more brooding.

Eventually I got up and tried putting the situation in the right perspective. "Can't you see there is no other way? We'll have to leave this place for good."

"Not me." Mother's voice was soft but it had all the finality in it to discourage any arguments. "I will not leave this house…not without your father. Herat has been his final resting place…so will it be mine."

I swallowed this news with a broken heart. Leave without mother? How will she cope alone?

"Me too," I heard Farehdun say. "I will stay back with my family. They will probably not harm us if they do not find you here. They will not know that we are the Mahrespandan family and connected with you."

I was totally devastated. Was I destined to live the rest of my life away from my family…my home? Was Yaser's curse so effective against us?

"I don't want to leave either." I decided to take a stubborn stance too. "We ran away from Mehrigard. We ran away from other towns of Khorassan. Why should I run away again?"

"Because you're *not* running away!" My mother's quiet voice rose above all else. "You're leaving us because by doing that you're giving us what we desire most."

"What?"

"*Hope!* If you're away from this predicament, there will remain a hope in our hearts that you may finally succeed where we have all failed...survive and somehow save our religion."

Words my father had said to me, too. *But how on earth do they expect anyone to save a religion by running away?*

I looked around for support but both, Farehdun and Ardeshir were busy studying their toes.

"Okay, so I'll leave on my own." I was getting tired of the indecisions.

So easily father had convinced fifty people to join him under similar circumstances. Quickly Khushrav came beside me and stared at me with disbelieving eyes. He grabbed my leg as though he will never leave me I knew it will be difficult leaving him.

"But you're too young to be on your own," mother once again came to my rescue. "You've never been alone before."

"I'll be quite all right," I stated with confidence. In fact, I thought it would be great to be my own master, finally.

"You must take Ardeshir along."

"*Why me?*" asked an exasperated Ardeshir. "I was not wearing that tell-tale *Asho Farohar*?"

"Because they've seen you too. And because you are part of the family," said my mother firmly. "And in this family we all take care of each other."

Finally, much to my dismay, it was decided that Ardeshir and I should leave the district immediately, and indefinitely. Ardeshir refused to let Mahafrid and their child accompany us. And I was not exhilarated at the prospect of spending months, and maybe, even years, with Ardeshir alone.

"So where should we go?" I asked, searching their faces. "Hyrcania, in the North? They say it is still the best place for Zoroastrians."

"*Not Hyrcania,*" said Ardeshir, with finality. "I'll never go back there."

Good, I wanted to say. I'll go there alone, and you go wherever you want to. But that's not the way families work out problems, I was just reminded. If nobody wanted to agree with me on anything today, I decided I'll give up making suggestions, and simply follow orders.

"I believe Hormuz is another comparatively safe place for us," informed Faredun wisely.

"And where may that be?" Geography was never my forte…amongst other subjects.

"South, it's a port on the Arabian Sea, leading to all the other major ports of the world."

"You mean all the way down there? It would be as long a journey again as the one from Mehrigard?" I was hoping for just a couple of days trek.

"Longer," came the sombre correction.

I looked towards Ardeshir for his reaction.

"I don't like it, but we have little choice," he finally said. "Though we don't need to go that far immediately. We can find a safe place somewhere in south Khorasan itself, and pray for a positive change here. I refuse to leave my family forever for a…a…" Thankfully he didn't complete the sentence. He was blaming me entirely for the situation we were in.

But his suggestion sounded good enough for me, so at least the first step was taken. Just when I thought of going and packing my little belongings, mother gently informed us, "And, of course, you'll be taking the *Urn* with you."

"What?"

"We cannot risk the holy fire to remain here. If unfortunately they do discover that we are the Mahrespandan family, they will leave nothing standing in this house. *They will destroy the Urn, and our precious fire!* As it is the most important member of our family, its safety must be our priority at all times."

I loved our sacred fire with all my heart, but I knew the difficulties of carrying it around.

"But Mother, you know how hard it will be for us to move around with it. It will be more difficult for us to protect it, with more dangers to threaten it, than if it remained here."

"We did it once, we can do it again. It will be safer with you as there are two young men to protect it. Here we only have Farehdun. With us womenfolk and the children to take care of, he has more than enough on his hands. I thought you'll be glad to take charge of it?"

She always had the nicest way to force things on to me.

When our things were packed and it was time to say goodbye, I suddenly melted. The momentum of the events had helped camouflage my feelings till this moment. But standing in front of Mother and bidding her goodbye broke all my inhibitions as my Adam's Apple started bobbing up and down, and tears started welling to the brim of my eyes. Khushrav clung on to my leg as though it belonged to him. Controlling whatever emotions I could, I quickly pushed him aside and came out on to the road, to darkness and some salvage of pride, as the tears spilled over. I noticed Ardeshir was experiencing a similar situation.

We hit the road leading southwards almost immediately. I knew the entire family was out, waving us goodbye. Khushrav was screaming and crying aloud. But I didn't look back once. They say it is bad luck to look back.

We had with us one mule, recommended, and strapped, by Farehdun. On one side of it he had placed our beautiful *Urn*, in exactly the same fashion as when we had carried it from Mehrigard. There again was no fire ablaze as the embers had been limited to the bare minimum. We just needed to add little fuel regularly to keep it alive. I often wondered why we had to safeguard such an innocent and beautiful element of nature. It was unfortunate that after centuries of being honoured and revered by one and all, the Arabs found it guilty of mischief and trouble-causing, and had convicted it.

On the other side of the mule were some provisions. A portion of Father's ever-beneficial gold reserves was packed too, to see us through the initial hard times. I took charge of it.

Ardeshir seemed to know his way so I let him lead the way, as I followed him with the mule. He walked on as though mountains separated us and he was alone. He tried his best to maintain as big a distance between us, as he could. Every now and then I saw him brush his face with his sleeve and felt sorry for him. Had I insulted him too harshly? But that couldn't be the only reason for his sorrow. After a volatile period of a few years he had finally settled down to a secured life, and suddenly everything has gone hay-wire. He was once again alone, once again vulnerable to circumstances and once again without a roof over his head.

But so was I, *and I was not making such a big fuss about it.*

My thoughts went back to home and I wondered when I could get back and be with Mother again. After Father had gone, I was drawn closer to her than ever before. Like at Mehrigard we would sit on the porch outside our house, almost every night after supper. She would talk endlessly about her life before she met Peshotan, and of her days after she came to Mehrigard. She was most proud of the way Peshotan had looked after that entire village for so many years, as though they all were part of his family. "Never a thought for himself," she said. She used to talk of the fame and wealth Peshotan's family at Pars was renowned for. And she talked of Zahl's exploits as she had heard, especially when he was a young and dashing commander, details of which I could never tire of.

Happy memories were all she kept. That's what gave her the strength to live on with her life. And that was a secret, I learnt later, that can keep everyone happy, too.

Manashni, she was blessed with.

Gavashni she consciously practised.

Khunashni was what she strived for.

❑❑❑

29

We travelled for a week before we hit upon a small settlement of four houses. It was not even on the main road and was inhabited by four Zoroastrian families, all quite elderly. Just what we needed.

At first they were wary of us. But after spending a few days with them they found us harmless enough. An elderly couple who lived alone needed some odd jobs to be done, and we obliged. Soon all the repairs and maintenance work in the settlement was passed on to us. Temporarily, we were allotted a stable for putting up. It was winter and terribly cold, but we managed. The ever beneficial *Urn* gave us some of the warmth we wanted.

Ardeshir maintained his distance from me, and spoke only when required to do so. But I didn't mind. His attitude towards the Arabs had disturbed me for long, and then when he spoke of his distaste towards Zoroastrians I thought it best to avoid him. Here we were driven out of our home by the Arabs, sheltered in the house of a Zoroastrian, and yet this attitude? It was beyond me.

A month passed by and it was freezing. One of the families allowed us to sleep in their kitchen and finally we could spend our nights more comfortably.

"I'm leaving back for Herat tomorrow morning," Ardeshir announced one night as I lay awake thinking of Mother and the others. I wanted to join him, but he had stressed on '*I'm*'. So I didn't say anything. "I'll survey the situation there and call for you if all is well. Else, I'll return."

That was the longest speech I heard from him since we had left home. The plan was okay by me, as now, I will have time to myself.

He left as planned and took the mule along to carry him. It was a happy and carefree month for me. I started making plans about changes on our farm.

I wanted to bring back the family together, to be as close-knit as we were at Mehrigard. I wanted to bring more happiness in mother's life and help her be more comfortable.

But when Ardeshir returned, it brought the end of my youth, end of my innocence…the end of *everything* I cared about.

As he got off heavily from the mule I could sense something was wrong…something terribly wrong. He wouldn't look up as I approached him, but when he did, I saw the saddest, the most depressed and devastated man I had ever seen. He couldn't have slept for days, and his face and hair were totally dishevelled and dirty.

He looked at me with red and pitiful eyes as he blurted out in a low voice, "They've killed them all."

A knife went through my heart, as I tried to figure out what he could be meaning. I searched his face for some clarification. What was he talking about?

Mother! Farehdun, his wife! Mahafrid! The children! Their images suddenly flashed past in my mind. Surely he was talking about someone else. Before I could ask him I saw him lean towards me.

"Our entire family!" he whispered and fell into my arms, unconsciousness.

❑

Later, when Ardeshir came back to his senses, he found me sitting close to him. We searched each others eyes for the right words to say. But none came. Finally, when he could bear the tension no longer he burst into tears.

"They…they didn't spare even the children," he sobbed aloud. "Those… those *animals*…those…"

"Mother? Khushrav?" I still held on to a desperate hope.

He didn't answer. Just kept his head down, shaking it over and over again.

After a long and eerie silence I asked with a hoarse voice, "Their remains?"

"Esadvaster did the rituals. When the town's people came to know of the massacre of the family of the last hero of Persia, yes, everyone now knows you belong to Zahl's family, they say hundreds gathered outside our burning house for the last rites. That night when they returned to Herat, there was a small riot."

Didn't help anyone, did it? I wanted to ask. When men become mice, *they have no right to justice*. If the same people had shown some pluck down the years, if they had resisted the domination by hitting back once in a way, the Arabs wouldn't have dared to do what they did.

"How did you find out the details?"

"My friends…yes, my Arab friends in the city, told me all." Then his eyes turned mean as he continued, "They also told me that it was the grocer who pointed us out."

I felt terrible…and sad, at the prospect of living the rest of my life without my family. How could such a thing happen? And me, a hundred miles away! *Might as well have been a million miles away,* for all the good I did! But what was most hurtful was the deceit of the grocer. So many hardships we had suffered to reach Khorasan, so many hopes and aspirations were preserved for the future, and all shattered to pieces…because of one treacherous man. *A friend*, mother had said! The actions of Yaser's son I could understand, as there was bad blood between our families. But the grocer, whom we had never harmed in any way? My fingers curled into a tight fist as I looked up in exasperation.

"You needn't worry about him," Ardeshir said softly. "I killed him that very night."

Why did no joy come to my wounded heart on hearing of the grocer's death? I doubt if I'll ever rejoice over the death of any man again.

"I wanted to go after Yaser's son too, but my friends hurried me out of the town. The day after the riot, the Arabs retaliated," Ardeshir continued, "They say they went into a frenzied spree as they murdered scores of Zoroastrians, out in the open streets and within the safety of their homes. They pulled out families and killed them with no regard to the law and reputation of the district. They said the likes of this had never been witnessed before in these parts. The situation has got so bad that hundreds of families are leaving Khorasan, and like us, migrating to Hormuz. I passed quite a few families on my way here."

I got up and left the stable. Not a tear had appeared in my eyes since I heard the news. They just wouldn't come out. Me, the biggest cry-booby of the family…after Mahafrid? But tears come when one gets emotional. I had got cold.

Revenge? The thought didn't enter my mind. How does one take revenge on a collective belief? Mohammad was not my enemy. It was their conviction that all non-Muslims must die, that was what we were up against. I wondered where such a belief would take them in future.

Just one thought ran through my head all of that day. So many people had suffered so much, *and all because of my Asho Farohar!* How could that be true, I desperately tried to reason, when on the contrary, it was supposed to protect us? And since it has failed to fulfil its duty, then Ardeshir was probably right. I should throw away this ancient emblem of my family. In a moment of madness I circled my fingers round it and unconvincingly tugged at it. After a second weak attempt I just slumped forward in grief and held it tight in my fist.

What had happened, I convinced myself, was not due to this piece of engraving. It happened because man had lost its sense of reasoning. Maybe, man did not want to reason. Maybe, they knew that reasoning would have stopped the madness that had ensued...*and man didn't want that!* Civilisation was just a word we used to satisfy our depraved minds. *Our basic nature was still that of a beast!*

All I knew was that now I was truly alone. Not a single blood relative of my own. It made me feel uncomfortably hollow, as though all my insides had emptied out. It left my head weightless, my thoughts rudderless. And an unnatural sense of darkness and silence engulfed me from all sides.

Not a single Mahrespandan left, but me?

Me and our sacred fire! I stared at it as a child would at its mother when lonely and frightened. I got the urge to hug it close to my body. I suddenly remembered how Mother had insisted that the *Afaghan* must go with us. Did she have a premonition of what was going to happen?

Did she know they really had no chance, and the holy fire had to be saved?

❑

Mohammad stood in front of the angry governor of Khorasan. A palatial house in Herat was where the governor resided, surrounded by beautiful gardens, lakes and open spaces. This was the stately home all dignitaries, local and foreign, often visited as the governor promoted peaceful trade, tolerance and prosperity. Generally the meetings held here were known to be cordial and friendly and the visitors left satisfied with a fruitful dialogue. Today's meeting was different.

"*Twenty years work gone up in smoke,*" the governor fumed, "And all thanks to you and your father."

"Would you rather see the prestige of Islam be grounded to dust?"

Mohammad countered, not one bit cowed down by the man in front of him who held great respect in many faraway lands. "Can't you see that the presence of anyone from that family is a direct threat to our people, a slap on the face of our religion, our fallen soldiers?"

"No, I didn't see them as such. They were a peaceful family, minding their own business, slaving for their existence. And now you have gone and massacred them all."

"*They deserved it!* They killed my brother and they were responsible for the death of my father."

The governor was not impressed. "It's your personal feud. Why did you have to bring it at my doorstep? Do you have any idea the damage you have caused this province? *A riot! In my province!* A month ago it would have been unthinkable. Today, hardly a month since your attack and what has followed? Hundreds of wealthy families have already left our city and many more preparing to leave for a safer place. Traders from other countries are scared to continue doing business here. The reputation we held for so long *has been irreparably dented.*"

"Why are you so regretful now? You gave me the authority and the men to carry out my duty."

"I expected you to capture them and bring them to justice, not obliterate them all! And then after their small riot, the retaliation from our people! Why did so many more have to die?"

"That was justice, and no fault of mine. My interest lies only in the Mahrespandan family. In any case, I didn't kill the entire family. Two managed to escape…the one wearing the emblem, and his brother-in-law. I will now go after them, wherever they are."

"*Not with my men and not in my territory!* As of now, you are alone. And get out of my province if you intend continuing with your hunt."

Mohammad walked briskly as he left the governor's house and headed for the town.

"Give up the hunt?" he asked himself angrily. "*Never!* If he'll spare me no men, I'll do it alone. Let him try and stop me."

❑

Two days later we left the small settlement and headed south towards Hormuz. We now had no home and no family to go back to, and moving ahead was our only option. I wished a terrible natural disaster would suddenly appear and *all* of us, the victor and the vanquished, would perish. When God forsakes you, neighbours betray you and the word 'hope' becomes extinct, why should the world go on rotating? Its very existence has clearly been outlived.

The route to Hormuz was once again a subject of great debate. I had casually inquired amongst the residents of the settlement we were putting up at, if there was a route. I was under the impression that I'll probably have to return to the route we had taken ten years ago, between the two salt deserts, go up to Bafq, and then swerve southwards towards the Arabian Sea.

"Yes, there is a route, though a difficult one," had explained the senior-most resident of the settlement. "One should move directly southwards, past the eastern-most part of Dasht-E-Lut. After the desert you'll encounter a chain of mountains. Keeping them to the right too, keep moving southward. There is no road as such, but caravans occasionally travel by it. Why, do you intend going there?"

"No, no. Not at all." I didn't want anyone to know where we were headed in case our pursuers reached this settlement too. We had decided not to share our sorrowful tale with them either. "We will be visiting some relatives at Quhistan, and then return to Herat."

"Half-way to Hormuz you'll pass Lake Hamun," continued the elderly resident kindly, ignoring my clarification. "Make sure you pay respects to the pilgrimage place. Continue southwards as you'll pass the city of Dowsdab. From there you can seek fresh directions."

Somehow, they seemed to know of our tragedy. Some of the men obligingly travelled with us for a couple of miles before returning to their families. Soon we were once again alone, the two of us, our raw memories, and the long and lonely route.

I neither had any idea of the distances involved, nor any inclination to find out. I tried pushing my memories behind me by walking purposefully and planning the future. But though I walked on boldly, it was a blind walk. Though I looked like a man with a mission, my mind was blank. Though it seemed I was after some quest, my heart was empty.

During the journey we passed a number of families who had abandoned their homes at Khorasan and were now seeking a new refuge…a place to live in peacefully, and be allowed to follow their religion without interference. It made me sick with remorse to think that it was I who was really responsible for such a course in history; for causing so much hardship and sorrow to so many. But a small voice within me reassured me that it couldn't be because of me. Deep down the mood of the Arabs in Herat was already primed and just needed a spark to explode. And I unwittingly provided that spark.

It was winter and intensely cold, but the weather failed to neutralise us. Our numb minds simply didn't acknowledge the frigid conditions as we went on our way.

We just walked, and walked and walked…from morning till dusk. No one bothered us just as we didn't bother the people we passed by. We ate once a day, hardly exchanged a word between us and pretended to sleep all night. We had just a single-minded purpose…reach Hormuz. What we were going to do after reaching it, we had no idea.

I remembered twelve years ago we had a similar objective…reach Khorasan. But what a journey that was; exciting, bonding with each other, sharing every bit of love and understanding...and most of all, dreaming of a new life.

❑❑❑

30

About a month later our listless trek came to a temporary halt. We were moving steadily southward when Ardeshir stopped a traveller coming from the other side and exchanged some words.

"Lake Hamun is to our left," Ardeshir informed me taking over the lead.

He saw my blank face and clarified, "that is where the old man at the settlement advised us to visit."

More blank faces and he impatiently elaborated further. "The pilgrimage place."

I instantly remembered, but had no idea we were on a sight-seeing tour. Grudgingly I followed him. I had little or no choice. He was the last and only symbol left of my past life. Our cold fight had evaporated, but there was no warmth to take its place either. We had each other to share the trek, and that was all. Oh, how I missed my family.

It had been a painful month with images of each of my family members constantly flashing past my eyes. How I wished I had stayed back and perished with them. It is a mean and ugly world out there, as it is. To live in it without anyone to call your own, it is a cold and extremely lonely place.

It was also a month of trying to make sense of what had happened. *Why didn't God take care of them when they needed him most?* It's a question I knew I'd be asking myself for the rest of my life. Weren't they Zarthoshty enough? Weren't their prayers, their commitments to Him, pure enough? Which almost made me wonder the wisdom of my continuing to wear my *Sedra* and *Kushti?* It didn't seem to make sense.

And like earlier, I once again found the *Asho Farohar* round my neck heavy and uncomfortable. Twice I had angrily removed it and almost flung it away into the wilderness. After all, what good had it brought to me, but trouble? *In fact, it was the very reason for the massacre of my family!* It was just a piece of crude metal, but I mistakenly thought it had the powers to protect me.

Yet it was my grandfather's only gift, and I valued that. So I let it go on hanging from my faithless neck.

But my conviction in my religion was really shaken. No longer had I the smug feeling of being born under the greatest religion. Blind faith was now replaced with ugly questions. Wasn't the combined power of Ahura Mazda and Zarathushtra strong enough to protect my family? *Why didn't they help them?* I had always been taught that in times of difficulty just the *Ahu Nozud* and *Ashem Vohu* prayers would ward off any and all dangers. I was sure my mother and Farehdun must have said those prayers a thousand times over when Yaser's son led the attack against them.

So why weren't they safe?

It could only mean that theirs, the Arab's, religion was stronger than ours!

When they had defeated our army half a century ago and conquered Persia with a much smaller army; that, too, had shown that in aggression, Islamism was stronger than Zoroastrianism. Now in defence, it was obvious to me, that we were once again,the weaker ones.

During that month I also thought a lot about the wise old man in the mountains at Mehrigard. 'Leave this country,' he had advised. 'Go where they would allow you to follow your religion'. Now I was seriously considering this proposal. But follow what? *A weak and an uninspiring religion?* Was it worth it?

I did want to get away from here, my country…from the pain and humiliation and horrid memories. But to where? I had little or no choice. West of our country the land was totally Arab. North was again partly Arab but mostly China. I heard our last king's son, Pirooz, had settled down there, and was doing well for himself. But it just didn't appeal to me. Immediate East of Persia was unknown and unsafe territory. Further East was Hind, but again, too far. South of us was the never-ending sea. So, I should have asked the old man, where can one go, if one has to leave ones own land?

Nowhere! And even if you do, it will never become your country, or your home.

Soon we were guided to Lake Hamun. It was a combination of three very large lakes, and though each had a separate name, together they were more commonly known as Lake Hamun, and even Lake Kansaoya. But the place was a far cry from being a sight-seers delight. The water was shallow and the surrounding area, marshy and muddy.

I was surprised to find the place well inhabited. Obviously the pilgrimage place held more respect than just another shrine to bow down to. But I wondered of its spiritual value. Another tale to make us believe in Him, I was sure.

"It's not even beautiful," I sceptically remarked to a local who was guiding us. "And what is so holy about it?"

He looked at me as though I had insulted him. "Don't you know? I thought you said you were a Zarthoshty."

"I am, I am," I confirmed patiently. "But I'm new around here, so please tell me of the myth behind the belief."

"*Myth?* You think this is a *myth*?" He sounded annoyed and I realised I should have used another word. *"You think Lord Zarthushtra was a myth?"*

I gulped. Now he was getting positively hostile. I quickly apologised for my choice of word and repeated my question. He looked at me distastefully and considered if I was worthy of the knowledge he was about to impart. All along Ardeshir stood aside, seemingly uninterested in the proceedings. But as the man began his explanation, Ardeshir moved in closer to us.

"It is said," my guide continued, "that this holy lake is the keeper of Lord Zarthushtra's seed. It is said that when the world faces complete turmoil, three virgins will enter the lake. And they will be miraculously impregnated by Zarthushtra's seed. Each will bear a child who will grow up to be a great *Saoshyant,* and the ultimate saviours of our world."

I liked the thought behind the belief. If only it was true.

"Our country today is going through a period of complete turmoil," I reflected aloud. "So why don't the *Saoshyants* come and help us out of it?"

"*Do you now doubt the great prediction?"* The man stared at me with total contempt.

"The *Saoshyants* will appear when Lord Zarthushtra decides it is time," said Ardeshir calmly. "Times are bad now, but much worse will follow at some other time. It always does. When the disorder peaks, and the final renovation imminent, the *Saoshyants will be there*."

I was taken aback at this intrusion. I was sure Ardeshir would be least interested in such predictions. And the manner in which he spoke, it was obvious he knew of the myth, and believed in it, too. Considering his recent ranting against Zoroastrians, this was a welcome change of heart.

"There you are!" my guide gushed. "Your friend here knows more of this lake than you do."

I didn't mind the admonishment one little bit. I was just happy to see the change in Ardeshir. The month-long silent march we had indulged in must have helped him doing some serious introspecting and soul-searching.

What was ironic is that the event that was shaking the very roots of my faith was the same event that was giving him strength and rekindling his faith.

❑

Ardeshir was more than impressed with the pilgrimage place so we extended our stay there by a month; at the end of which, my sceptic views towards my religion reduced marginally, and Ardeshir's confidence in it grew back many-fold.

We continued our journey southwards and reached the city of Dowsdab in early spring. A lazy city with little trade or industry, we decided to put up there for some time.

Two days later Ardeshir found a job suitable to him, but I found it difficult to accept one. There were plenty of hard labour jobs available and Ardeshir didn't mind one. I preferred less strenuous work. So that left me basically with one option only…a government job, a job I didn't want. The Arabs were no good in the running of the government establishments and invariably depended on the services of converted Zoroastrians. But I was not a convert, so thankfully, I was not even considered. Another option for me was that of a priest in a fire temple. But the three temples that had thrived in this city not too long ago had been razed to the ground, and mosques constructed where they once stood. So I remained without an occupation, for almost three months.

"Why do you carry such a lofted opinion of yourself?" asked Ardeshir one day, as we shared our lunch. "Work is work, and your father used to say that one must take pride in whatever one does as a profession. So what is wrong in being a labourer? As a Zarthoshty you are supposed to be humble, remember? Or is it too inconvenient a decree?"

Ever since the Lake Hamun episode, Ardeshir had taken upon himself to discipline me, particularly in my religious views. Suddenly he was my elder brother, my best friend and my mother, all rolled into one. Instructions, advice and concern poured out of him at every turn. My sudden indifference to my faith was a point of concern to him and my poor work ethics were met with disapproval. I really didn't mind working, on anything, anywhere. But I just couldn't bring myself to being *a labourer to an Arab*. The people who have ruined my country and my family, the people who have decimated my people and my religion, *how could I work for them and contribute to their prosperity? I was the grandson of the great Zahl!* I'd never give the Arabs that pleasure.

Money was not yet an acute issue, as father's 'inheritance' was still seeing us through. But I knew very soon we'll be using the last of the gold coins, and then I'll have to find work.

"But why do you work for them, when we don't even need their money?" I countered. "These are the very people who have killed your family too, remember?"

"Because work is food for our body. It is said that it nourishes our body and keeps it healthy. And when our body is strong, our minds become strong, too. I don't think of the Arabs when I'm working, I think of myself, my well-being."

I was in no mood to argue so I excused myself and went for a walk in the market area. It was afternoon and few people were around. I made my way to a tavern selling cheap wine, and got myself comfortable in it. Of late, I was taking a lot of refuge in the comfort that the divine liquid provided. It made me not romantic as the poets would have us believe. It didn't even lift my spirits as its reputation boasted. It just helped me get through a few hours of boredom, helped me forget that I was a refugee in my own country, hounded by the authorities for having a name they despised. And something else that I was sure I'll never fathom…being abhorred by my fellow human beings for my religion.

Yes, the warm red nectar certainly did help me forget. Though it was not always, I remember, that we drank to forget. I remembered the small make-shift distillery we had at Mehrigard. The wine we made there was from a mixture of over-ripe fruits and vegetables, but my father boasted it was the best he had ever had. Of the fruit wine, my favourite was the pomegranate wine. The distillery was active just once a year, before our New Year on 21st March. But enough of it was made to see us through most of rest of the year.

I had found a secluded table in the dark corner of the room where I nursed the ravaged ego of my people. My thoughts were suddenly interrupted by the sound of a scuffle at a table across the room.

"Who gave you permission to drink here?" A swarthy young Arab stood threateningly over a table where two middle-aged men were drinking. Alongside the young man stood four more Arabs, all looking in a menacing mood. They were completely drunk and could barely stand on their feet.

The middle-aged men recognised the situation and quickly got up to leave. "Where do you think you're going?" asked one of the bullies. "You may have paid for your wine, but now you've got to pay your taxes for it to us."

"Taxes?" asked one of middle-aged man. "There are no taxes for wine."

"Of course there is," said the young man, gripping the middle-aged man by the front of his tunic. "For you Zarthoshties, there has to be taxes for everything. *Now pay up!"*

Zarthoshties! Not too long ago there were quite many of us in these parts too, but now the numbers had come down drastically. The Arabs had decimated the original population by constant harassment of the *Jizyah* tax and conversions. As in other cities, the usual practice was to hang a placard round the neck of a Zoroastrian with the amount of *Jizyah* he owes written on it. He was to put on the placard wherever he went. But he could reduce his tax liability, if he attended the mosque regularly. The reduction was done when he stepped out of the mosque. The more mosques he attended, the lesser the tax he had to pay. The Zoroastrians felt so degraded with such constant humiliation and the tax burden that they eventually converted to Islam.

I got ready for trouble. If these men were bullied any further, I decided to side with them.

"But...but...we are converts. Now we are as much Muslims as you are."

Converts! I had no sympathy for them. Let them fend for themselves.

Suddenly one of the bullies slapped the converted Zarthoshty. "*How dare you!* How dare you compare yourself with us?" A rain of blows fell on the man as the other bullies joined in. When the man almost collapsed from the onslaught, the Arabs turned their wrath on the other convert. Two hard blows and he too went down on his knees.

What happened next I'll never forget. I saw one of the Arabs grab a knife from their table and threateningly approach the fallen men. I half got up to help the Zarthoshties when one of them suddenly leapt up and pulled out a large dagger from within his clothes. Before anyone could react, he plunged it into the midriff of the Arab. He obviously had reached his boiling point, and could take no more.

In the chaos that ensued, the two converts ran away. I too took the opportunity to get away from the tavern and found a safe place in a Zarthoshty's house across the street. Shouts and screams emerged and soon we learnt that the young Arab was dead. What followed was mayhem of the ugliest kind.

The young drunks provoked the sensibilities of the Arab population in the city and within a short space of time, a riot ensued. They started by beating up any Zarthoshty on the streets. They next looted Zarthoshty places of business and even their homes. By evening over a dozen Zarthoshty houses were on fire. A crowd had also gathered in front of the house I was taking shelter in. Stones rocketed in, the main door was almost shattered and their shrieks almost deafened us.

"Give us those two men, and we'll stop!"

Those were the words they screamed across the city. Nobody gave themselves up and by midnight more than ten Zarthoshties had paid the price with their lives. More houses were burnt down as hundreds of Arabs took to the streets with burning torches.

Finally the two converted men gave themselves up.

Within minutes they were clubbed to death, stripped and hung upside down in the middle of the bazaar.

❑❑❑

31

Next morning my few belongings, including our sacred fire, were packed and loaded on the mule. Overnight my love for my religion had returned and escalated in intensity, manifold. I realised it was such a simple and beautiful religion and demanded nothing extra-ordinary from its followers, and nothing from its antagonists. It was like a pretty flower in the wilderness. You can pick it up if you wish and enjoy its fragrance, or you can ignore it and walk on. No ill-feelings.

I only prayed nobody would find the *Urn's* presence too conspicuous, and demanded an explanation. If ever it got out that it was an offspring of the Atash Behram at Yazd, which in turn was consecrated with the Great Fire of Adur Burzen-Mihr, its very existence would be in jeopardy. And without it, I'm sure, I'd stop breathing.

I suddenly hugged the *Urn* fondly and made a solemn promise. "I'll die if I have to, to save you and your honour."

"Just one incident and you want to run away." Ardeshir had been after me from the moment I had announced that I was leaving Dowzdab for Hormuz, immediately. "We have a roof over our heads now and no one is bothering us. So why keep shifting like vagabonds?"

Yes, we did have a roof over our heads, thanks to Ardeshir's contacts. But really, was it good enough to live with those heads down, our dignity and pride in shreds, our beliefs ridiculed? From what I had witnessed yesterday I was convinced that under no circumstances would I be able to live a day longer in this hateful city. They had conquered us and had the right to rule the land the way they wanted. *But why must religion come into play?* Why must that be the sole difference between the conqueror and the conquered?

Ardeshir and I seemed to be riding a perpetual see-saw. Just as my mood was once again swinging towards my religion, Ardeshir's was once again tilting towards the Arabs. I had no objection for him to stay back, but if he couldn't understand why I had to leave, I didn't consider it worth while to explain what was in my heart. I just nodded and left.

"You know, you've always been running away," goaded Ardeshir, is voice trailing behind me. "Like you said, you and your family ran away from Mehrigard, you ran away from Herat and now you're running away from Dowzub. Can't you for once show some guts and overcome the situation *without running away from it?"*

It hurt me immensely to hear him say this. In a way he was right, I knew. But each time there was a reason why I was running away. I could have explained the reasons, but I didn't feel he deserved an explanation. And my standard excuse of keeping alive 'hope' was too weak under the circumstances.

What the chain of events, of these last few months, did confirm to me was that I was not the man my predecessors were known for. Neither did I possess the courage and strength of my grandfather, nor did I have the wisdom and unbound faith of my father. Neither could I ever inspire an army, nor could an entire village ever depend on my leadership. I wondered, if I had children, what would they see in me? An immature weakling who ran away from all realities? *A nobody, going nowhere!*

I tried brushing away my self-criticism, but deep down I knew it was not going to be easy. I had to learn to be tough, and the best way to go about it was to try and make it on my own. My weakness, I surmised, was a weakness of the mind. If you allow the mind to rule you, it could become the proverbial 'devil's workshop'. If you have control over your mind, it could become a 'temple of constructive production'.

It will be my mind, I resolved, that I will seek to harness henceforth.

As I made my way out of the city I inquired of the route I should be taking to reach Hormuz. There was one that took me to Yazd first and then to Hormuz. I didn't want that so I took the second route and headed directly south. It was a straight-forward route that made me go all the way south to the sea, and then I was to veer off westwards.

I had an empty feeling as I left the city behind me. Ardeshir and I were the only people left from our village of Mehrigard. And now I was moving away even from him. But I knew a time comes in everyone's life, when the lines get drawn and finally one has to do what is the deepest in one's heart.

Next day, late in the evening, I saw somebody behind me, walking fast. It was Ardeshir.

"I thought of it," he said, panting hard as he levelled with me. "And I agree with you. That was not a place to live in."

I was taken aback but was glad he saw sense in my move. "Have you, also, now come to appreciate our religion?"

"*Religion!* I wish there was no such thing as religion! It has done nothing but separated people. It has brought in hatred where none existed. I think the best way is to lead your life the way *you* see it, do what *you* think is the best, and live the way *you* feel right. I think *that* is the best religion!"

I wanted to remind him that all religions did not breed hatred, and that they had, in fact, brought different people together through the ages. But I was sure, these were lessons one is supposed to learn for oneself, *and not be taught.*

The important thing was that we were together again, and together we could tackle any problem.

On the way later he told me that one of the five drunkards in the tavern, he had found out, was one of his new-found friends.

❑

Two months later we tiredly trudged into the port city of Hormuz... penniless, hungry and very, very weary. It was an extremely busy place with people from different countries trying to do business with the locals. At Herat we already were exposed to the presence of foreigners, but here at Hormuz, their numbers were much larger. Ships from across the world found this city a convenient mid-way port. Some came from Hind and farther east, looking for trade with countries to our west. Similarly, ships from west always made a stop here en route to their destinations in the east. As a result, the bazaar area was full of these foreigners driving hard bargains.

We learnt that the Zoroastrian community had shifted mostly to the Island of Hormuz, a stone's throw away from the mainland. Next day we crossed over to the island.

I took to this island from day one. It was quiet, not as busy, and most of all, very cosmopolitan. A number of Zoroastrians from Khorasan were pouring in regularly here, yet there was room for more.

Ardeshir immediately found work at the docks and our money problem was solved. This time I too was ready to work, even as a labourer, as our masters wouldn't necessarily be Arabs.

But I didn't have to do that. I found a job at the local fire temple. *Yes! The fire temple on this island was yet left untouched.* When I told them of my background and my *Martab* ceremony, they allowed me to be a junior priest within the premises. It wasn't as if I was dying to be a priest, and even the wages was meagre, but it was an honourable profession and I put my heart into it. They gave me accommodation within the premises, and I shared it with Ardeshir.

Within a month we were well settled in.

❑

It was another year of fruitless search for Mohammad.

A total of twelve years of his life wasted!

And on what? *Chasing shadows; hunting invisible people!* And while his life had stalled in this foreign land, his wife was left unsupported in his own country, barely making ends meet. If the final outcome of these years of pain and suffering was success, it may have been worth it. But neither was his mission fulfilled, nor had he made any fortune or fame. In fact, he was totally dependent upon his father's wealth, and his name had sunk in mud! If this was not pure madness, he asked, *what was?*

He used to think his father wasted his life targeting a family. But what had he done? *And why?* His father had led a very successful and fulfilling life till he set about this accursed mission. But he, Mohammad, had just started his life when he got caught in the same snare. The only success he had seen was bringing down that Mahrespandan family outside Herat. But that too was partially successful. The young man who caused his father's death was still free, and he could do nothing about it.

Not that he hadn't tried. Immediately after the governor of Khorasan had warned him, his search had begun. The warning had not discouraged Mohammad one bit. He had a sacred duty to perform. A few angry words were nothing. Within hours of that meeting, he was once again on the trail of the young Mahrespandan. He had learnt of his new name...*Jamshid Athavian!*

Ha! The spineless devils had changed their family name to survive. No Arab would have done that. But that won't help him any longer as now he, Mohammad, son of Sayyid Abul Yaser, knew what the fugitive looked like. He will not escape his clutches next time, he had sworn.

Mohammad had clandestinely searched for him, first in Herat, then out of the city limits, and then all over Khorasan.

Nothing!

Like the earlier times, the ground seemed to have swallowed Jamshid and his brother-in-law. They must be some evil magicians, he was convinced. Then Mohammad heard of the exodus to Hormuz, and a couple of months later he was there. He scoured the town and kept a constant watch on a section of it where Zoroastrians had colonised in a group.

Nothing!

He searched every corner of the dockyards as though he was looking for an ant. He visited every fire temple a number of times and even tried to persuade a few Zoroastrians for information. He had crossed over to the island and checked out on the community's movements.

Nothing!

Weeks went by and then he gave up. The men he was looking for did not live in this town or island, he was convinced. He was on the point of going crazy when he got a message from Arabia. His wife was seriously ill.

So after thirteen long years on foreign land, he returned home, a despondent and failed man. His life was cursed, he was sure, and he blamed the 'magicians', the Mahrespandan family. Soon after he returned, his wife passed away. Now, he, too, was truly alone in this world.

He tried to return to his old profession as a clergyman. He put his heart and soul into it until he was recognised all over as a senior Imam.

Ten years went by and Mohammad seemed to have forgotten his Persian ordeal.

❑

My progress as a priest in the fire temple was slow but steady, and soon it was no longer work but a passion for me. Before dawn I would begin my duties by first washing and cleaning the entire premises. Prayers and special ceremonies would take up the rest of the day and finally it was my responsibility to lock up before retiring. My dedication was recognised and I was made a full-fledged priest.

What I valued the most during my initial period in this town, and in my new occupation, was the peace of mind and solitude I enjoyed. Here, in the calm and quiet abode of my religion, I was able to sort out many quagmires of my mind.

I now understood that my mixed feelings of my faith were unreasonable and immature. I now understood that I had no reason to lose faith in Ahura Mazda and Zarathushtra, and condemn my religion as weak. I now understood that there was but one God, one Supreme Being, known by different names. That God chose and sent enlightened souls as His Prophets, at different periods of time, to preach righteousness and goodness to the people, as He revealed to them. That it is *how* these revelations and translations are interpreted by the people, *that* makes the difference. I learnt to accept Islam and Christianity and other faiths as good religions, as well, but never again to question the Faith I was born under.

In time I got married and was soon the father of a boy and a girl. As they grew of age, I performed their *Sedra-Pushun* ceremony. It was a proud and happy moment for me when I placed Zahl's *Asho Farohar* round my son's neck. I prayed it would prove to be more beneficial to him, than it had been to me.

Time went by at a leisurely pace on the Island of Hormuz. The migration of Zoroastrians from Khorasan and other regions had continued down the years and now it was the only place in Persia where we could live honourably. We heard of atrocities and persecutions in different regions of our country and were pained that conditions had not improved or changed.

But with the excessive presence of our community on the island came the unnecessary attention of the Arab administration. New laws started to appear and stricter vigilance took over the earlier lackadaisical surveillance.

As intolerance increased, Hormuz even became a victim of hatred and persecution. Travellers were harassed and residents made to go through unnecessary travails. Anyone disobeying was dealt with severely. Persecution became the norm and conversions the order of the day.

I took it upon myself to help the new-comers to our island, wherever I could. These small gestures of support increased and soon any Zarthoshty coming into Hormuz first approached me for instructions on how best to settle down. My secondary activities came to the authority's notice and I was censured time and again to check myself. So I restricted myself only to the extent of helping my community after dark and in secret locations. Twice the authorities tried to implicate me in acts of violence and conspiracy. Both times I managed to wriggle out without imprisonment. I knew it was just a matter of time before they got me behind bars.

Besides these confrontations, I was now a contented man…but not a happy one. No one, anywhere, could be happy if he could not lift his head, say what he wanted to, and do what he liked to. A physical prison is a difficult place to live in. A mental prison is more unbearable, more painful. But a prison that chains your very spirit, is but *hell on earth*.

❑❑❑

32

In Arabia, Mohammad was similarly contented with life, but not happy. How can he be happy, he argued, if his most sacred duty was left unfinished?

So one day he suddenly made an announcement.

"Tomorrow, I return to Persia. God will not allow me to die, with my mission incomplete."

On the very first day of his arrival in Persia, he continued his hunt for the Mahrespandan boy. He changed his strategy this time. He decided to search places that the family was known to have lived in earlier years. He began his hunt at Pars, the original home of the family. He found that even the name, Mahrespandan, was almost forgotten in that district. His father had done a great job obliterating that family in this province. Nobody knew of the escape of the boy, Peshotan. They had heard of Zahl, but that was all.

Mohammad next went to Mehrigard, but it was a ghost town. After the handiwork of his father, nobody dared to occupy that village again. He searched the slopes of Zagros, where Zahl was known to have put up that last resistance, but there were no rebels left, no Zahl, and certainly there was no Jamshid.

He thought of taking a break and decided to put up with an old friend at Yazd. One evening, chatting with a group of travellers who had just come from Hormuz, he heard one man boasting of the achievements of Islam.

"Yes, we have these Zarthoshties crawling in their own country. Our stamp of authority is now everywhere."

"Not quite," his fellow traveller reminded him. "The Island of Hormuz is still comparatively free. They are not aggressive like the lot from beyond the Albruz, but they are continuing with their lives without any heed to our laws. The fire temple there and others at the port city still functions as they have been for centuries. And even a priest at the fire temple is proving to be a thorn in our flesh. He's actually defying us by running a help centre for the Zarthoshties. What was his name?"

"Jamshid," said the first traveller, with a sneer. "But that will not last long. From what I hear all fire temples at Hormuz too will be brought down soon. That will put a complete stop to all their hopes."

Mohammad heard the name but didn't show the pain it brought to him. "What was this priest's full name," he asked softly.

"Jamshid Athavian, I think. But he will..."

Mohammad did not hear the rest. He had already left the house.

❑

Ardeshir looked as excited as he felt. It had been a month-long session of planning and organising. Now everything was finalised, and the date was fixed.

Tonight!

"Jamshid you must come along with your family," he implored, for the hundredth time. "You know our days are indeed numbered in our motherland. If you want to live freely, if you want to pray openly, you must join us."

Working at the docks Ardeshir had learnt of a secret plot by a group of Zoroastrians. They intended sailing away to a safer country where they would not be persecuted and where they'll be able to follow their faith without prejudices.

"But who will have us? Maybe the next country is worse than ours." I was never a pessimist but this mission they were embarking upon was full of strife and uncertainty. I couldn't risk my family's well-being to such foolhardiness.

"I've told you earlier, we'll be sailing east, to Hind. Many ships from that country have come here for years, and we have come to understand that it is a very free country, with no restrictions on the religion you wish to follow. We know of a rich shipping merchant. The Arabs are threatening to confiscate all his ships so he has to leave these shores, soon as possible. He doesn't have enough sea-men at hand to help him escape. And he doesn't have the guts to do it alone. That's where we come in. Some of our men have good sea experience and the will to pull this through. The merchant has agreed to use three of his dhows to carry as many Zarthoshties as the boats can hold. We already have confirmations of over three hundred of our people."

Three hundred? I was aghast. I was sure, just a handful would fall for such an expedition and the planning of it was more of wishful thinking, than a certainty. *Tonight it seemed they were actually going to embark on this voyage.*

"Who has arranged this... this incredible voyage?"

"There is a strong group of Zarthosties from Sanzan in South-West Khorasan. Their leader is Dastur Naryosang and they're trying their best to save our religion. Others too who have come from different parts of Persia, have agreed to join the exodus."

"How will so many families get into the boats without being spotted by the guards?"

"They won't be trying to get in together. We've told them to come in stages, all through today. Many families have already boarded and are hiding in the boats. Three of the boats will be sailing from Hormuz, and two more will join us as we pass Makran in the east."

"And when you try to leave in the night? The guards at the docks will be there."

"We've taken care of that as well. Heavy bribes have been paid to the few guards who keep a watch at night. Come on, Jamshid. This is the chance we have all been waiting for."

I hated myself for the decision I had taken. Ardeshir was now more close to me than anyone else, ever. We shared a house, shared the joys of a close-knit family and shared each other's happiness as well as sorrows. To see him go would mean the loss of a part of me, but I had to do what I had to do.

"I can't Ardeshir," I said regrettably. I knew I should be with them, but I was concerned about my new responsibilities. "You know I have to help our people here. I cannot let them down. I'm the only one who knows the ropes here and I would be betraying our people if I left. Yes, I would love to live a free life, too. I would like to see my family safe, and like mother used to say, give them hope in their hearts where only misery resides. But my priorities tell me to complete my work here. Maybe, some day in the future..."

"It is risky staying back here. Waste no further time, Jamshid, say you'll come with us."

"No, I cannot come. I wish you and the others good luck. May Ahura Mazda guide you to a safe haven."

And that was it. We parted our ways, me and my only friend.

That was in the morning and the rest of my day dragged on with my mind and heart on no work. *God,* finally some of my brethren will be free, and there will now be hopes of saving our religion. But first they must escape the clutches of the local authorities as the Arabs guarded the docks well. How will so many people get on to the boats without being detected? All it will take is one guard giving the alarm, and the plot falls through.

After a light dinner I stepped out of the house for a stroll. I wanted to be alone. I knew I wouldn't be able to sleep that night. I glanced southwards, towards the sea, and imagined the tense scenario that must be playing out at the docks. Should I go there just to see how things went for them? I decided against it, as I may prove to be in their way.

Having walked on for some time I heard a footstep behind me. I turned around but couldn't see anyone. It was dark outside and only shadows abounded. The moon was at half-strength but the faded light was enough to see a few yards. I started walking towards the bazaar hoping to see some activity to divert my tense mind. But nobody was around. The streets were deserted and everyone was where they should be…in the safety of their homes.

Again, I heard the shuffle of a footstep and whirled around. I spotted a figure quickly dart into the shadows again. This was not good. Have they set someone to spy on me? That wouldn't be beyond the Arab authorities, I knew. Maybe, I hoped, it was a Zarthoshty newcomer to Hormuz, and just wanted to chat with me. Or, maybe, he's a thug, after my money?

By now I had walked far away enough so I turned around to walk back home. I kept my eyes wide open to spot my stalker. Within a few minutes I came upon him.

He stood legs apart, in the middle of the road. He didn't even try to move away when I got close to him. He was glaring at me insolently and dared me to get him out of my way. I was a little apprehensive now. This couldn't be a thug, or a Zarthoshty.

"Jamshid Atthavian," the man murmured softly, as though the words were choking him. "Also known as Jamshid *Mahrespandan*."

Now I felt cold.

❑

The man blocking my path was Mohammad, son of Yaser, I easily surmised. I didn't recognize him as such, but his aggressive stance and his speaking out my real name, left me in no doubt that I was facing the nemesis of my family.

"What do you want?" I asked, praying that my voice would quiver less.

"*You!*" he said simply. "*You*, the killer of my father. *You*, the grandson of Zahl, the killer of my brother." His face suddenly contorted to a mask of revulsion. "Tonight, one of us has to die, and it won't be me."

Who had to die, I was left in no doubt. As if on a cue, two shadows disengaged themselves from the wall of darkness around us and stepped out in view. They were dressed as local guards. They were armed with spears and now stood on either side of Mohammad.

"Three verses one, even your God will not wager on your chances," mocked Mohammad.

"Three verses two," said a steely voice from behind them. Ardeshir walked past them confidently and stood defiantly next to me. He pulled out a short sword and smiled at me.

After the initial shock, Mohammad smirked. "Good, you're here too. Now I won't have to hunt for you."

I frantically looked towards Ardeshir and hissed under my breath, "*What are you doing here?* You should be away, in the boat!"

"There is still time, so I came back for you. Your wife told me you walked in this direction," he whispered back.

"But why did you come back? I told you I won't forego my duty!"

"Because soon you won't have any duty left. A guard at the docks informed us that *tomorrow they intend burning down the fire temple at the island,*" he explained slowly and softly.

I reeled in shock upon hearing this news. Was that last symbol of our faith going to be brought down, like the others?

"That is why I've returned. *You must flee with us!*"

"*Enough!!*" The sharp command from Mohammad brought us back to our current predicament. "*No more talking!*" He turned to his men. "You take care of the other man. Leave the priest to me. He has to die by my hands only."

Saying that he crouched low and menacingly advanced towards me. The two guards singled out Ardeshir and readied to attack him with their spears.

I knew there was no escape from these men and their intentions, so I too got ready for the onslaught. I heard Mohammad curse under his breath as he lunged at me. I swiftly stepped back and felt the swish of his swinging arm. We faced each other in the stance of wrestlers, circling round, looking for the right moment to attack. From the corner of my eye I could see a more sinister fight between Ardeshir and the guards as their weapons clanged angrily.

It was a bizarre sight. There we were, two men of God, in a dirty, deserted street, under the dim light of an embarrassed moon, seeking to kill each other with our bare hands. Nearby were professional fighters busy with the tools of their trade.

Suddenly, Mohammad charged and took me down with his weight. For a brief moment we struggled on the ground, each trying to get an upper hand. He succeeded, as he got on top of me, both his hands around my throat. His intentions were clear; he was going to choke the life out of me.

I couldn't remember the last time I was in a fight. Probably twenty years ago, as a small boy. But as his grip tightened, I almost stopped breathing. I thrashed about wildly trying to shake him off me. But it proved to be in vain. He still held on to my throat and now his entire body weight was behind him as he got on his knees and kept pushing me down. Shrugging off his hands was getting to be impossible. I could feel my senses swinging and I knew my end was near.

But that's when the natural instinct to survive, probably the strongest instinct of all, took over. Without realising my right hand managed to get a grip on the little finger of his left hand. Whatever little strength I had left, I used it. I pushed that finger outward till it snapped with a loud crack. He yelped and relaxed his hold for a moment. But it was all I needed. I brushed away his hands and at the same time pushed him off me.

I took a quick glance at the other combat. Ardeshir had one guard down and was exchanging blow for blow with the other.

Moments later Mohammad and I were once again circling each other. I prayed somebody would chance by and stop this outlandish combat. But no such saviour appeared.

Mohammad's face was a mask of rage and excitement as he suddenly brought out a curved dagger from within his robes. "There will be no escape for you today, *pig!* After I kill you, I'll go for your family," he said with an evil grin. "Yes, I know where you live. I'll do unto them, what I did to your family at Herat. *Obliterate them!*"

The reminder brought blood to my head. I felt weak as images sprang to my mind and the world started swinging.

When I saw the glint of the dagger my knees went weak. I had never faced such a deadly situation before. I had no weapons of my own to fight back with. I knew there were a lot of loose stones nearby, but how was I to get to them? This fanatic man was hell-bent that I do not live long enough to see another stone in my life.

I saw Ardeshir in difficulty with the second guard as both were fighting hard at close quarters. Suddenly both drove their weapons forward…*and both found their target.* A scream and a deep growl and that fight was over. Both were on the ground, unmoving.

Mohammad's right hand swung in an arc even as I hopped back. The tip of the dagger tore through my clothing and slashed across my stomach. I clutched at it in pain and took a few quick steps backward. He charged straight at me with a wild cry. As I tried evading him a small root of a tree caught my heel and I was caught off-balance. Even as I started falling backward his dagger plunged into my shoulder. Involuntarily I cried out in pain and my hand gripped his robe for support. As he too was lunging forward for his next strike, my pull was enough for him to lose his balance, and we both crashed to the ground, him once again on top of me. Instantly he straddled me and raised his dagger. I saw the gleam in his eyes as the moment of truth for him arrived. In his extreme excitement he didn't see my fingers curl round a stone next to us. Before his armed hand could come down, I crashed the stone into his face with all my might.

I heard him grunt in pain as he fell over. My next strike was on his head and he lay still. I thought I might have killed him and pushed him away from me. As he lay still I quickly unarmed him and tied his hands behind his back with a piece of cloth.

I ran to where Ardeshir lay. He was still breathing, but the long spear protruding from his stomach said another story. Tears rolled down my face uncontrollably. He suddenly pulled me closer and with a broken voice said, "Go to…pier number three…call for…Dastur Naryosang…tell him…tell him…."

But he couldn't complete. Ardeshir died in my arms.

There he lay, my blood-brother, my hero, my very conscious, never to look into my eyes again. He came back to inform me of the burning down of the fire temples…*he had risked his life to tell me that!*

Distressed beyond words I was at a complete loss as to my next move. What was I to do now? After this combat they'll be after me with their full might. Leave Hormuz? And go where? There was no longer any safe place in Persia. Take Ardeshir's advice and catch the boat? But to leave Persia without Ardeshir was unthinkable! *And I didn't want to leave Persia.* Even if they burn down the fire temple, I still had a role to play in this country.

A noise interrupted my thoughts. Mohammad was recovering his senses. He was just momentarily dazed, as I saw him blink rapidly and look about. He quickly regained his composure and tried to get up. But he found his hands tied and looked around for me.

I slowly walked forward and stood above him. *What was I to do with him?* I bent down and placed his dagger on his neck, an ugly intent on my mind. I only had to slide the weapon across his throat and my worries were over...for the day. He understood his precarious position and looked at me inquiringly.

As we both breathed heavily I looked into his eyes for the first time, and he stared into mine. He wasn't as handsome as I remembered his father to be, though his high forehead and proud nose did give him a distinguished look. But his eyes betrayed him. They lacked the character and intensity of Yasser.

I wasn't feeling very steady as I had lost some blood from my wounds. But I wasn't worried about them. They were really minor wounds and just needed dressing.

"Kill me, Zarthoshty," he said quietly, feeling the sharp point of the dagger on his throat.

Did I have a choice? I knew he'd come after me and my family the minute he could. The thought made blood rush up to my head again. I tightened my grip on the dagger.

"Go on, Zarthoshty," he goaded even as blood dripped down his face from the gash I had given him. "Or do you, like your ancestors, lack the guts?"

He had guts, I had to give him that. He faced death with arrogance. But I couldn't kill him. I wanted to as the faces of my mother, my brother and my sister floated in front of me. I remembered the children, and I almost gave in to my wild instinct. And now Ardeshir lay just feet away, a wasted hero. Even the dagger seemed eager to get on with its utility as its point involuntarily scratched his skin and a drop of blood oozed out. But I held on. Then in sheer disgust I got off him and started walking away.

"*Come back, Zarthoshty!*" he screamed. "Kill me, when you can."

I walked on, throwing a last glance towards my dear friend.

"*The minute I get free, I'll come after you,*" he threatened.

I walked on. I started walking faster, trying to get away from this sinister spot, soon as I could.

"I'll kill you first, and then I'll kill your wife and your children!"

I stopped. I breathed heavily as a thousand thoughts ran through me. Suddenly I made up my mind. I turned around and walked briskly back towards him.

I saw his bravado yield for a moment. I picked up a large stone and brought it down heavily on his head. Without a sound he slid down and remained unconscious. I felt his pulse. He was still alive.

I tore part of my robe and stuffed a large piece into his mouth and tied it up. Next I dragged him and then the others, away from the road till they couldn't be spotted. Finally I tied Mohammad against a tree. If not till morning, I knew he would be no problem to me for the next few hours at the least.

Then I rushed home. I had to hurry, or it'll be too late I feared.

❑❑❑

33

A half hour later I had my family in a cart, along with a few essentials. The *Urn* certainly accompanied us and I instructed my little son to make sure it doesn't topple over. I took the reins and we were off. I wanted the horse to gallop away, but that would have drawn the attention of one and all. With one eye constantly checking my back for Mohammad, we rode through the town at a steady pace. All along I was praying softly that the boats had not left already.

If the boats have left, it would be the end of me and my family.

My wife had given me the required first-aid and I was feeling all right. I had lost blood and was feeling a bit weak. My stomach wound was negligible but the shoulder injury was deep and it was quite an effort to finally control the blood flow.

I guided the horse to the gate at the docks, and stopped. I once again took a quick glance backwards. *Did Mohammad recover, and was now catching up on us?* That was my paramount fear, as I knew his loud threats were real and his taunts will live with me forever.

Leaving the rest outside I sneaked into the docks. Everything seemed quiet and eerie. There were no people around and absolutely no activity of any sort.

Have they already left?

My heart beat faster and louder than the drums of Africa. I frantically looked about for the guards, but couldn't spot any. I moved on towards pier number three. I strained my eyes at the number of boats bobbing up and down. And then I recognised the boat Ardeshir had talked about. The large sail was fluttering in the wind, impatient to begin its historical voyage. But then my heart sank.

The boat was about to pull out! The anchor was being hoisted up. Two boats were already sailing and this one, also, was about to pull out. It must have been waiting for Ardeshir.

"*Dastur Naryosang! Dasrur Naryosang!*" I called out desperately, not caring that I could be heard even by the authorities.

Suddenly an old priest appeared at the bow and looked down inquiringly at me.

"We're coming with you!" I cried, excitedly. "I am Ardeshir's friend, Jamshid! My family is with me!"

"Where's Ardeshir," he asked, his eyes searching the quay.

"He...he...won't be coming. He...he..." I couldn't finish.

The priest waited for a moment. Then I saw him talk excitedly with the captain of the boat. There was an argument as the captain was not happy about waiting any longer. A few minutes later, a plank was placed between the boat and the quay.

"Quick! Climb aboard! We set sail immediately!" the old priest instructed urgently.

I ran back to the gate and guided the cart to the boat. As my family clambered up the plank, I boarded last, carrying our urn with the holy fire.

"Stop!" cried out Dastur Naryosang. "What is that?"

"Our holy fire."

"You can't bring in that," he said incredulously. "You know it is strictly forbidden in our scriptures. No holy fires can cross the seas."

I was stumped. Of course, I knew of this stricture but I didn't think for a moment that it would apply even at this crucial juncture.

"But...it is part of the fire from the Atash Behram at Yazd."

"All the more reason not to carry it over the waters. Now please stop wasting time and let us be on our way."

I felt devastated. I looked around desperately for some support, but got none. Some of the passengers looked on anxiously, hoping to see a quick end of this dead-lock.

"I...I... cannot leave it behind. I will not..."

"*Stop being stubborn*," the old priest hissed. "Think of your family."

"*This is part of my family*," I reminded him hotlly. "If it cannot sail with us, I will not come. You can take the rest of my family."

The next moment my wife and children trooped down the plank and stood beside me. Their decision needed no clarification. I threw a nervous glance towards the gate for any sign of Mohammad and his men.

"Let's get out of here!" the captain of the boat urged. "Or we'll never get out."

Dastur Naryosang looked down at the hapless family with exasperation. He wanted to help them but how could he, a senior priest, disregard an established law?

"Bring the fire with you," he said in a low voice, lest the Almighty hear his words. "But let the responsibility of the breach of law be on your head."

We needed no further prodding as we rushed up the plank. The urn was taken to the safety of the hold below, where it warmed and comforted the families hiding there.

A quiet order from the captain, and we set sail.

Awhile later I returned to the deck. I stood there, controlling my emotions, watching the coastline disappear slowly into the darkness, into history...*for eternity.*

An old woman stood alongside with the same emotions. "Don't be sad, young man," she said bravely. "I'm sure one day we'll be back and the glory of ancient Persia will once again rule supreme."

Somehow, I didn't feel convinced. Something inside me told me that a long and colourful story had just concluded, and a new one will have to be written afresh...somewhere else.

Was my heart heavy?

No, I had left it behind.

Was my mind still undecided?

No, it was fully occupied with the painful sight of Ardeshir with a spear sticking out of his chest.

Was my spirit free?

Yes! That it was!

I looked up at the stars and thought I saw the smiling eyes of the old man in the mountains of Mehrigard, looking down at me with approval. I looked down at the dark sea and in the reflections of the stars I saw the faces of my family and Ardeshir bouncing merrily on the bobbing waves, as though wishing me goodbye. And much as I tried to avoid, tears finally found me.

The land that was my ancestors for thousands of years, the land they built into a powerful empire, the land they protected and expanded for centuries, *and the land that was lost by a single generation*...was now but a thin line on the horizon.

And was I once again running away from it all?

NO!

This time I was sailing towards *hope.* ***—The End***

❑❑❑

Epilogue

Our journey to Hind was smooth and swift. On the way we had lost two days waiting at mid-sea for our colleagues from Makran to join us. Their two boats had managed to slip out without much fuss too.

In less than three weeks we spotted land and knew we had reached our destination. We learnt from the few natives who came out to see us that this was indeed Hind, and we were on one of its provincial islands, *Diu.*

We learnt we were not on the mainland, but on one of the poorer and backward province. Our progress here was slow but still we persisted; certain that things would change as we were in the land of the rich, the ancients and the peace-loving.

But things didn't change and after nineteen years, we decided to move more inwards, into the mainland. We readied our old boats once again and set sail further eastwards. On this short journey we were hit by a violent storm. As the storm raged on for hours and our boats tossed about on the wild waves, we feared the worst. It seemed impossible that we'd come out of this storm in one piece. The ferocious winds penetrated the stout holds and even threatened to extinguish our sacred *Urn* for good, or sink it with us.

That's when our priests, some forty of us, including me, got together and prayed to our most powerful spirit, Varharan, or Behramyazd. We appealed to Him to save our boats and rescue us from this calamity. We promised to build an *Atash Behram* at the place we land, in His honour.

Soon the waves subsided and we knew we had survived the storm. When our boats finally reached land, we got off, knelt and kissed the land, and thanked the lord for delivering us.

The year was 716 C.E.

❑

Upon landing many natives came out to greet us. They stood there smiling and asking a hundred questions we couldn't understand. Finally word was sent to the local chieftain. His name was Jadi Rana. He sent a messenger to our leader with a full bowl of fresh milk. Dastur Naryosang called for some sugar, and pouring it into the milk, returned it to the messenger.

"Tell your king that we'll be like the sugar in the milk. We'll mix easily with the people, and at the same time, sweeten your land."

The king appreciated the gesture and allowed us to stay back. Soon he granted us a beautiful piece of land. We aptly named it Sanjan, after the city of Sanzan in Khorasan. The natives called us 'Parsi', which literally meant 'a resident of Parsa'.

We cultivated the land at Sanjan, traded with natives of nearby kingdoms of Hind, and even ventured out to other countries in our trusted boats.

Soon a small group of priests was sent back to Sanzan in Persia. In due course of time they returned by land with the embers of a holy fire from an *Atash Behram*. That was the greatest piece of achievement for the future of our community.

We built a small house and called it our *Atash Behram*. We consecrated a sacred fire and called it *Iranshah,* in memory of the Kings of Persia.

The fire for an *Atash Behram* is made up of sixteen different fires, including lightening. Each of these fires are purified individually, and then purified together. Thirty six priests are needed for the ceremony that can stretch up to a year.

It was the proudest day for me when they used our salvaged fire as part of the consecration ceremony. It could not be used in the making of *Iranshah* as it was considered 'defiled', but it was there to bless the proceedings.

When all was completed, we knew we were finally home.

Alas there was one aspect that left us incomplete. None of us had carried the complete texts of our sacred books. Very few were available in Persia, but here we had none. We did carry a few essential texts, and we knew more will be added to the collection as more of us travel to this land. But a complete set? That was left a dream. I then realised just how important was the collection we had left behind within the mountains of Mehrigard. I made a detailed map on a soft piece of leather of the location as I remembered, and strongly impressed on my son of the need to preserve it, and when time and circumstances permitted, to return to Persia and rescue the books. If not in his time, I prayed, somebody from our family would one day bring back those books and complete the scriptures of our faith. I also made and passed on the map showing where our material treasure lay buried within the barren mountains near Pasargadae, as explained by my father. The two maps and our sacred fire was all I could pass on to the next generation.

❑

Forty years later, as I sat watching the green fields stretching for miles in front of me, my heart swelled with pride. Our people had almost doubled and finally followed the faith we strived for.

I reflected on the many lessons we learnt on the ways of our new country and its people. We learnt of their tolerant religion and their rich culture. We learnt of their non-violent ways and their vegetarian diets. We learnt of their industrious and hard work mentality. And we appreciated and respected their ways.

I reflected on the many things that had helped us on the long journey from Mehrigard, to Hind. It took a lot of courage and patience, a lot of suffering, but most of all it took a lot of belief and faith.

I remembered my original family and wished they were with us…to share my moment of joy and pride. I remembered Ardeshir, as I did almost every day, and wanted to pass on one thought to him...that I'll never run away from this place...*ever.*

But most of all I remembered my mother's words about our religion being akin to the great Huma bird. This was the third time we were almost obliterated, but yet, here we were, on the threshold to another lease of life.

As my emotions grew, I saw my little grandson walk up to me and ask, "Why are you crying?"

I knew next year would be his *Sedra-Pushun,* and his neck will adorn the great *Asho Farohar* of our family.

"I'm not crying," I said brushing off the tell-tale tear. "I'm just happy."

For now we were *free!*

And yes, now we had what my mother and father had prayed for...*HOPE.*

And then like my grandfather had expressed grief to Ahura Mazda long ago on the mountains at Mehrigard, I, too, stood up and raised my hands, but in gratitude, and cried,

"*Ya Ahura Mazda!* What a beautiful land you have bequeathed us, which we now call home."

Bibliograph

In Search of my God

Outlines of Parsi History, Zoroastrian Religion and Ancient Iranian Art. *By, Dastur Dr.Hormazdyar Kayoji Mirza.*

Zoroastrainism. *By, Khojesta P. Mistree*

What Parsi should know. *By Ervand Jal Rustomjee Vimadalal*

History of the Parsees. *By Dosabhai Framjee Karaka*

From the Iranian Plateau to the shores of Gujarat. *By Mani Kamekar; Soonu Dhanjishah*

Qissa-i Sanjan. *By Baman Kaikobad Hamjiar Sanjana.*